STUCK IN TWINDLE

S.B. DUNN

Stuck in Twindle
Copyright © 2024 by S. B. Dunn.

This publication contains the opinions and ideas of its author. It is intended to provide helpful and informative material on the subjects addressed in the publication. The author and publisher specifically disclaim all responsibility for any liability, loss, or risk, personal or otherwise, which is incurred as a consequence, directly or indirectly, of the use and application of any of the contents of this book.

MILTON & HUGO L.L.C.
4407 Park Ave., Suite 5
Union City, NJ 07087, USA

Website: *www. miltonandhugo.com*
Hotline: *1- 888-778-0033*
Email: *info@miltonandhugo.com*

Ordering Information:
Quantity sales. Special discounts are available on quantity purchases by corporations, associations, and others. For details, contact the publisher at the address above.

Library of Congress Control Number: 2024910092
ISBN-13:   979-8-89285-104-6   [Paperback Edition]
                  979-8-89285-103-9   [Digital Edition]

Rev. date: 04/25/2024

This book is dedicated to my supportive family
for being by my side during this journey.

Chapter One

I replaced the plant stem on the microscope lens as Emily continued to babble about the weekend drama. Her *differences* weren't noticeable to me right away. She stayed outside my apartment door so I assumed she was one of the neighbors, always filling me in on all the school's gossip. I first moved here three months ago and after saying goodbye to my only friend back home, I had to start fresh.

Emily was my only friend that I made, not for lack of trying. Although, I wasn't sure if Emily would choose our friendship if her situation was different, but it's not. So she was my school guide, telling me who slept with whose boyfriend and what clicks to avoid if I want to have a social life. I glanced over to look at her, letting her know I was still paying attention to her. She sat crossed legged on the lab table, continuing her gossip.

When school first started, she was trying to give me fashion tips. She let me know that the gray hoodie and legging combo wasn't going to turn any heads when I walked through the school halls. Little did she know, I wasn't really looking to stand out. Twindle was such a small town, way smaller than Springfield. I was able to blend into the walls no matter what I wore at Springfield High. I knew that wasn't going to be the case with only 80 kids per class. Not to mention, most of the Twindle girls were blonde or brunettes.

My cherry red was illuminated by the harsh school lights. Most students turned to check me out, if only for the hair. I had a group of girls come up to me the first day of school to ask if it was natural. It was, of course, but the one with the bad attitude wouldn't believe me. I loathed the girls who had been like her, but it seemed to be the norm here.

"Just tell me who does it," she pushed.

"I promise it's natural," I said, holding my hands up before moving on from them.

Her pumpkin orange hair was definitely not natural. Then some brown had crept through her roots. I didn't see Pumpkin Head after that day though so I assumed she fixed the bad dye job. I was just glad she didn't continue to bother me, but no one really did.

My mother and I had to move to this small town after she divorced my father. They were still working through the divorce when we were first settling in. I could hear their phone calls through our thin apartment walls. My father developed a gambling addiction when the economy started to tank. When he lost his job, he used what money they had saved for my college to try and support us through the addiction. His scheme lasted about a month before my mother caught on.

I think they tried to keep their marriage going for a few more months after his lies started. Sadly, what goes up must eventually come down, and down it came for my father. He went to rehab for his gambling, but only learned how to better hide it before coming back home. When he got out, he looked brand new and shiny for my mother.

She stupidly fell for his act, but I couldn't blame her. He was her high school sweetheart, and I thought he was changing too. He told us he had a new job and would be better for us. Little did we know that new job was stealing what things he could here and there. My mother was oblivious of anything happening, until the red and blue lights shone through her classroom windows.

She was working at our middle school when my father thought it would be a genius idea to try and hijack a deputy's new hot ride. Of course, my father didn't realize he stole a deputy's car when he did it. He quickly realized when he had been pulled for a traffic stop. He somehow thought running to my mother was his best option, but really it was the moment that ruined her life in Springfield.

The divorce papers came before his court date and mom had the house sold before they could set his bail. She moved us to Twindle because it was the small town her grandparents grew up in. Sadly, both of them passed away about five years ago. So now we don't know anyone in the town, but every so often when we are out shopping or getting gas, someone will ask if she's Julie's granddaughter.

"So yeah, Billy was caught macking lips with Erin," Emily said, bringing me out of my thoughts so I could refocus on the class assignment. I vaguely looked in her direction to let her know I was in fact paying attention to her. She had one of her long curls wrapped around her finger. I didn't really remember who Billy was, minus the fact that he was a football player, but Erin was in my morning class.

We had only started school about a month ago, but I knew everyone's name. It wasn't hard to memorize our small class but that didn't mean I had class with everyone, so I really didn't know what most people actually looked like. Emily was always talking about someone so I knew the names better than the faces.

"And I'm judging that Rachel caught them," I whispered to Emily. I didn't want Mr. Blackford taking extra notice while working through the microscope assignment. I leaned into the scope looking at the different layers of the stem.

"Of course she did!" Emily exclaimed, "It was happening at her house, so of course she was bound to catch them."

"That explains why Erin's eyes were puffy in English." I muttered, shrugging at the drama. I didn't really care what was going on at the school but Emily loved to indulge me in it and she was my only friend so I listened to it.

"Well, I'm sure Rachel kicked her to the curb. I mean she broke the girl code," Emily scolded.

"Billy is just as much to blame," I gave her the side eye.

"This is why you should never trust those football boys," Emily laughed, "They already play the field, so you should just expect it, honestly." I made a sort of scoff laugh at her comment, which drew a few eyes to the back of the lab.

"Class, if you could start packing up soon, the bell is going to ring," Mr. Blackford's voice boomed, while opening the cabinets where the microscopes go.

"See, that's a man a girl wants," Emily practically purred in my ear, peering at the back of Mr. Blackford's head. I rolled my eyes at her and gagged.

"He's like thirty-five," I whispered, disgustedly.

Mr. Blackford wasn't old compared to some of the other dinosaurs that roamed the halls, but I still couldn't believe Emily would look at a teacher like that. Maybe because my mom is a teacher, but I hated the high school student/teacher trope. Springfield had a different scandal every week it felt like. I was tired of seeing the headlines.

"Look around. There isn't much to look at with the boys here," Emily replied, rolling her eyes when she said *boys*.

I couldn't really argue with her. There were two types of guys at the school, farmer or rich boy. The farmers only care about their crops and sports and the rich boys only care about their money and sports. Not things I really cared about. Emily needed someone who could listen to her talk but also provide commentary so I get why she would think an older guy could fulfill that, but still an actual adult? Gross.

Mr. Blackford reminded me of every generic teacher. His wardrobe seemed like he shopped at the teacher outlet store. I didn't see him without a long button down and khakis. Always khakis, because the teachers got the option to wear jeans on Fridays, but he never did. Even with the hotter months, he never wore short sleeves. I thought it was weird, but the longer I had been in the biology room the more it made sense. Mr. Blackford kept the room freezing pretty much all the time.

I removed the plate from the microscope, so I could pack up my backpack. Emily hopped off the table top, mentally running through her list of weekend drama to make sure I was up to speed. I knew there was a Labor day party going on at Rachel's but I couldn't imagine too much could happen over one weekend.

"Well, I know Kayla got super drunk and puked in Rachel's parent's hot tub," Emily shared, practically jumping up when she remembered. "I remember hearing Rachel complain about her parent's grounding her and making her clean it at her locker today."

"You really shouldn't be eavesdropping on people's conversation," I scoffed, giving her a clear look of disapproval.

"Oh, who cares. Plus who's going to know I was listening?" She questioned "They don't know I even exist and I only tell you." She shrugged and readjusted her curls.

"I mean I guess you're right, but I still think it's wrong."

"Plus if I'm not eavesdropping, how would you know all the ins and outs of the school?" Emily asked. "It's not like you ever get it." She teased more about my lack of social life. I couldn't really argue with her, but it was hard to break into the groups that have been formed since first grade.

"I can't help it," I whispered, going to my desk.

"Class, please remember to do your reading assignment tonight," Mr. Blackford's voice boomed, interrupting our conversation about drama. I put my biology book back into my backpack and quickly jotted down the chapters and pages listed on the white board.

Mr. Blackford's body almost covered the whole board. He was a bigger man, but he wasn't fat. He was built like one of the high school linebackers. His broad shoulders filled any space he was in. I had to peer around him to make sure all the assignment information was correct. I assume I wasn't the only one, as I watched Mr. Blackford tilt to the side. The sound of vigorous pencils confirmed my assumption.

Emily continued chatting next to me. I knew she didn't care to get the assignment stuff written down. Even though I enjoy listening to Emily give me the rundown like she's some tabloid, my mom would kill me if my grades started to slip. Plus, she got all of my class' syllabus so if I tell her I don't have homework when I do, she'll correct me.

That is the con of having a teacher mother. Luckily she doesn't teach at the high school, but the middle that she teaches at is attached to the high school. Actually in Twindle, all the schools are attached, which gives her the opportunity to check up on me during her free period. This is probably why Emily is my only friend. No one wants to be friends with the teacher's pets.

The other kids whose parents taught were usually very studious. They typically stayed in their own clique because they're parent's had been coworkers since they were babies. A lot of times they stayed after school together, while their parents graded papers and tests. I didn't enjoy hanging around them, so I often walked home when mom had to work late. Emily helped keep me company if that happened too.

The bell finally rang, releasing the students into the hallway. The day was half over and many students were heading to lunch. The smell of pizza traveled through the air, filling the nostrils of the hungry students. The pizza always smells delicious but honestly, the cheese is cardboard and I think they use stale pepperoni. The cafeteria food looked and smelled better than it actually tasted, which is why I brought my lunch.

There were only three hallways in the high school so it didn't take me long to get to my locker. Emily leaned against the locker next to mine as I fiddled with my lock. I couldn't ever remember which way to rotate the combination numbers. I kept pulling down trying to get it to unlock.

"13-27-41," Emily said.

"What?" I asked in frustration.

"Your locker combo, it's 13-27-41," Emily replied, nodding at the locked lock in my hand. *And sometimes I forget my combination number.* I sighed and twisted the code into the lock. *Click!* The lock came undone. Finally, I was able to access my lunch. I slung my morning books into the locker and reached for the plaid lunch box.

"I really think you're going to have to tattoo the combo on you," Emily said.

"I'm still learning, give me a break," I said, rolling my eyes at her.

"You started the school year with everyone else, so don't try to use the new girl BS with me."

"The school year only started like three weeks ago."

"You haven't been able to memorize three numbers?" She raised her brows at me.

"I just forgot it for a second, but I know it," I said, shutting the locker. "Come on, it's time for lunch."

"What did your mother dearest pack for us today?" she asked, peaking over my shoulder.

"You know you can't eat my lunch," I laughed at her and moved away from her peering eyes.

"You can't answer a question with a question. What's in the box?"

"Umm I'm not sure but probably grapes and a wrap or something," I said, lifting the lunch box and giving a little shake. It rattled in response.

"Do you think maybe a bag of chips?" She asked, raising her eyebrow again. I shrugged.

"Yeah maybe."

Emily walked slightly ahead of me with a bounce in her step. She reached the opening to the cafeteria and waited for me to catch up. The skirt she was wearing ruffled around her when she twirled back to look at me. The scent of pizza surrounded her as I got closer.

"They've got pizza, tacos, and chicken salads," she said, putting her hands on her hips and gleaming at me.

"That's nice but I've got mom's cooking," I countered, shaking the box at her again. "Do you want to meet up in the courtyard?" I asked. Her eyes were following two girls whispering to each other. She looked back at me and nodded in approval. She was on a mission to see what new drama she can scoop up. We headed our separate ways.

The courtyard was just a small square in the middle of the school, but the school tried to spruce it up a bit more. They planted a few trees for shade and added spots to sit and eat. I headed to the back area and picked a spot under one of the trees. I placed one headphone in and set my phone next to me. Opening the box, I realized our guess earlier was pretty accurate. Mom packed a ham and turkey sandwich, a bag of grapes, and my favorite bag of barbeque chips.

It wasn't too hard to guess what was in there because mom had been packing similar lunches for me since middle school. It's always a bag of fruit and some sort of meat and bread. On holidays and special occasions, it would be different. I didn't much mind what lunch was because dinner was usually great.

I leaned my back up against the cool brick, letting the feeling give some escape from the summer heat. It wasn't awful outside, but the black leggings were attracting more heat than I had anticipated. I threw a few grapes into my mouth, their sweet juices escaping with each bite. The courtyard was slowly starting to fill with more and more students.

"Oh my god, this school is a bunch of a-holes," Emily whined slamming her hands down on the pavement next to me.

"Yeah, why is that?" I asked, shoving my sandwich in my mouth.

"Barbeque chips," she shouted, snapping and pointing at my lunch, "I knew there would be chips in there. Momma Weber never fails." I rolled my eyes at her. I knew she was avoiding my questions because those so-called a-holes were probably making comments about me.

"Go on with the a-holes," I reminded her.

"Well Adam and his jockey friends were just saying how they didn't think there was anything good under your hood," she did little air quotes around good, "and then of course Robbie had to pop up and talk about how you don't talk to anyone. Well obviously besides me," she finished smiling and batting her eyes at me.

"Oh well, who really cares what they think," I said, grabbing at the grapes again, "Plus they probably peaked already so let them talk."

"Exactly, come back in five years and see who's talking about who," Emily said, adjusting herself for a better shit talking position. I prepared myself for whatever gossip she was getting ready to dish out.

"So obviously now that the start of the school/labor day party has happened, the planning for the Halloween party has begun," she said, like I should know that each holiday meant some sort of party.

"Okay so Rachel is throwing a Halloween party?" I asked.

"No, silly. She threw the labor day one." Emily grabbed her stomach laughing.

"So then who's putting on the party?" I asked, getting annoyed at her. I barely knew Rachel so how was I supposed to know that she wasn't the only party thrower in town.

"Girlie, the kids with the big backyards put on the parties. Rachel had the pool, hence why she did Labor Day. Jessica Johnson is in charge of the Halloween one," Emily said a little softer as if she realized her bullying was getting to me.

"I thought she was a farm girl," I said confused.

I will never understand how any part of this school works. Rachel came from the rich kids and Emily said her party was invite only, super hard to get into. I can't imagine Jessica could be so mean. She had a locker a few down from mine and helped me to my homeroom the first day of school.

We had one class together and we had just finished it. I hadn't really spoken to Jessica a lot besides the first day of school, but we were in the same icebreaker group on the first day. Her fact was that she lived on a farm so she helped with the birth of livestock. I thought it was pretty cool to hear about but a lot of the other girls gagged at the thought of handling that.

"That's why she's the one hosting it, she has a corn field so it's perfect for Halloween," Emily explained, waving her arms to get my attention.

"Oh I guess that makes sense," I said.

"You know if you wanted to go," Emily paused, giving me a mischievous grin, "I think you could talk to Jessica."

"I don't know about that, like Robbie said, I don't talk to anyone."

"Yeah, but Jessica is super sweet. Just ask her about her horse and she'll be like pudding in your hands."

"I'm not sure if I'm ready for a party yet," I started to argue, "Plus I don't even have a costume idea in mind."

"Well good thing it's September and Halloween is my favorite holiday," Emily squealed, clearly not ready to give up on this. I hesitated a second too long for her.

"Charlie, I'll help you find a costume, pretty please just go," Emily crawled to her knees and pushed her lip out as far as she could. She transformed her normal sparkle sky eyes into giant doe eyes, pleading with me.

"Fine, I'll go talk to her," I finally said, sighing, which released the breath I didn't realize I was holding.

"Plus I can't have you pouting too long, you know what my grandpa always said, birds will poop on your lip if you stick it out like that" I finished as I pushed myself up.

"Very funny," she said "Where are you going?"

"I'm going to go find Jessica," I said scanning the courtyard, "She normally eats outside and I won't see her again until tomorrow's bio class."

"You can't just go ask for an invite," Emily waved her hands in front of me.

"I wasn't planning on it, crazy," I answered, still scanning the courtyard.

I spotted the back of Jessica's head. Her brown waves looked similar to Emily's curls, but not so defined. She was sitting with two other girls. One I recognized as Mallory Watson, but I didn't know the other one. I pushed myself forward, forcing myself to follow through with my plan. I knew Jessica had been struggling with the class material. I took a quick inhale before I reached the group of girls, who could decide my popularity at this school.

"Hey Jessica," I said, giving a little wave from my hip, "Hey Mallory."

"Oh hey Charlie," Jessica said, putting down her pizza and actually getting up to give me a hug. Mallory just gave a little nod of her head but continued to pick around at her salad.

"Have you met Britney?" Jessica asked, moving aside so I could get a full view of the third girl. Britney had jet black hair, which was a sharp contrast from Mallory's straw-like blond hair and Jessica's brown wavy hair. It had been cut short in an asymmetrical style.

"Um, no, I don't think I have," I replied, reaching my arm out towards her.

"She's a junior so it makes sense," Jessica said, while Britney stared at my hand, "She used to date my brother Jacob but once she got her common sense back she picked the better Johnson." Jessica gleamed at me, trying to outshine the cloud that Britney was casting over us.

"Oh, yeah that makes sense," I said, turning back to Jessica, since she was the target of my goal.

"So have you been understanding the lessons in Biology?" Jessica changed the subject.

"I never understand any of the words coming out of Mr. B's mouth," Mallory finally piped up.

"Well, we all know you don't understand, Mal. You're better at lit anyway," Jessica said.

"Um, yeah I think I am understanding the class," I mumbled, trying to grab control of the conversation again. "I just forgot to get the chapter readings for tonight," I lied.

"Oh that's not good," Jessica said with a smile on her face, "I have them written here." She looked through her backpack, grabbing a planner covered in horses.

"Oh, thank you," I smiled, lifting my sleeve. I wrote the page numbers on my arm to make it look like I really did need them.

"So I have been hearing about the party that happened this past weekend," I started to say.

"Oh yeah, I wasn't actually invited to that," Jessica interjected.

"Ha, I was," Britney boasted, examining her manicure, but not looking in our direction.

"I wasn't invited either," I admitted, trying to make Jessica feel better.

"Why would you?" Mallory asked, "You're new and Rachel is a snob."

"Please ignore both of them," Jessica said. "You're new and everyone here has grown up together." She glared down at Mallory's grimacing face. I got the feeling Mallory didn't understand why she was being scolded.

"I'm not trying to be mean," Mallory said, throwing up her hands in defense, "Rachel would never let anyone outside her clique go to her exclusive party." Mallory did a "better than you" type of shimmy when saying "exclusive" party. "I'm just saying, a new girl doesn't make anyone's cut."

"Yeah, I get that," I chimed in, not realizing I had planned too. Jessica looked a little surprised that I spoke up. "I'm working on coming out of my shell."

"Well I'll happily help you," Jessica jumped in ready to stop the awkward tension that was growing. "If you're understanding the bio material, could you help me study for the next test?"

"Yeah, of course." I leaped at the opportunity.

"Great. Mallory and I are going to the library this weekend," Jessica said, "Would you want to join?"

"Yeah, I'd love to."

"Super, you know where it is right?"

"Yeah, actually, I went once or twice when I first moved.

"I guess I could use the studying," Mallory said as the lunch bell echoed through the courtyard.

"Great. Meet there at noon Saturday," Jessica hollered over the commotion of students as she followed Mallory.

"Sounds good," I said, heading back to my area, "I should go clean up my area."

"Okay, I'll see you in class tomorrow," Jessica said walking through the courtyard doors, waving as she left my view.

I walked back to Emily. I didn't need to tell her what happened. I saw her peering at me the entire time I was talking to the girls. I simply gave her a thumbs up as I got closer. She threw her fists in the air in triumph. I gathered my things, knowing the gloat session she was getting ready to have.

"I told you!" she practically yelled, jumping up and down with joy. "She's nice unlike that bitch Britney she hangs out with."

"Yeah she didn't give the warmest vibes when I was over there," I admitted. I didn't like dissing people with Emily, but some of the girls here could be really mean. I headed to the trash near the door back into the school. Emily followed behind me while discussing some issue she had with Britney. I had distracted her gloating with disgust. Her favorite emotion.

We walked back to my locker so I could throw the lunch box back in there. Kids hurried through us as we went. The second lunch kids were more hungry than us with less food options so they pushed past the ones going back to class, ready to devour something other than the course material in their class.

The students that had to go back to class moved at a sloth's speed. Their stomachs filled to the brim with pizza and breadsticks. They're ready to crawl into a big comfy bed and sleep. Not go back into brightly lit classrooms, where teachers will yell at them to keep their heads up and stop doodling in their notes.

Emily and I reached my locker, I was able to put the combo numbers in on my first try. That was partially because I could hear Emily's voice in my head saying I really think you're going to have to tattoo the combo on you. The other part was because I could feel Emily watching me, waiting for me to screw the combo up so she could say she was right.

"Are you ready for the afternoon classes?" Emily asked, pushing herself off the locker so she stood more into the hallway.

"Not really," I said being honest, "I think I would rather just go home."

A group of rowdy boys pushed through the hall. They probably each had to stay after in their class to get a stern talk from their teacher only to go out into the halls, acting like animals again. They ran right through Emily. Her body disappears for a split second, as they continue down the hall to the cafeteria. She shimmered as her form started to take place again.

"I don't think I will ever get used to that happening," I expressed, still a little stunned after watching her presence form again, pushing the locker shut.

Oh yeah did I forget to mention, Emily is a ghost.

CHAPTER TWO

It took me a few weeks to realize Emily was a ghost when I met her. I remember the first time I noticed her. It was a few days after mom and I moved into the building. I was carrying up a box of my stuff from the car. We still needed to make trips to the storage unit to get the last of the stuff.

I grabbed the last box and mom headed straight back to the unit. She wanted to try to finish using it before the month, so she didn't need to rent it for another full month. I had rounded the corner, going up the stairwell, when she was there. She had been staring from the opposite corner. Her eyes were filled with so much wonder, I didn't realize they had lacked life. I had nearly jumped out of my skin, losing grip of the box. One side slid down causing me to readjust. She didn't move.

"Jesus," I screamed, "You scared the shit out of me."

"I'm sorry," she said, puzzled, "I didn't realize you'd be able to see me." That statement should have clued me in but I wasn't expecting the thing that just scared me to actually be something people fear. Blood had slowly rushed back to my body, allowing the comment to slip through unnoticed.

Emily walked down the stairs in the opposite direction, instead of vanishing right in front of me, so I used that as my excuse to not see she was a ghost right away. About a week after our stairwell encounter, I learned her name. She had been playing with a small orange cat that lived outside. Most of the apartment people helped take care of the cat and I had heard that the office workers often let the cat inside to stay warm during the winter.

I was coming back from an early morning run, when I rounded the building to get to our stairs. Emily was hunched over the cat, its little green eyes like saucers tracking her movement. I still had my headphones in as I walked towards the two.

"My name's Emily," she said, catching me off guard as I pulled the headphones out. The cat had seemed intrigued by her as she wiggled her fingers at it. It batted trying to catch them, but just barely missing each time.

"Charlotte," I puffed, "but I go by Charlie."

"Charlie," she thought on it for a second, "I like that."

"Thanks," I said, pulling the door open, "You staying out or coming in?"

"I'll stay out a little while longer," she grinned at the cat.

"Be careful with the little thing," I called, "It had got me good a few days ago."

I looked down at the scab that was forming. Emily's laugh echoed through the lobby as it slithered through the closing door. It sent an uneasy chill through my spine. I had tried brushing it off as I bolted to our floor. Mom had commented that it looked like I saw a ghost. I tried ignoring the comment, still wanting to hide behind the signs in my face.

I finally realized she was a ghost one afternoon shortly after our cat encounter. Mom had gone into school early that morning so she could set her class room to her liking. I had decided to sleep in, but some neighbor kids had different plans. There were loud giggles and thumping through the hallway. They sounded like a herd of elephants running through my bedroom. I wanted to go out there and ask where their parents were. Or ask if they were raised by animals.

When I was first woken up by their explosive behavior, heat flashed through my body, but by the time I was able to throw a sweatshirt and shorts on to yell at them, I had calmed down enough. I swung my front door open to see the chaos, when I noticed her standing on the other side in the hallway. She was admiring them playing and having a good time, leaning up against the wall.

"Any of them your siblings?" I asked her pointing at the rowdy kids. I am an only child so I didn't know what it was like to have a sibling. People normally responded with some sort of comment about how lucky I was, but a few would express how they couldn't live without their siblings.

"Lady, who are you talking to?" one of the kids asked. I looked at them and noticed that they were staring at me. Most of them looked confused, but one or two looked scared. I pointed back and turned to realize no one was really there.

Thinking I imagined seeing Emily standing there, I said "no one," and went back into my apartment. I rested my head on the door, hearing the kids go back to their rowdy behaviors. I tried to rationalize that my mind was just playing tricks on me since I had just woken up. *Yeah, that was it,* I thought again.

"You just woke up," I told myself, "Your brain is playing tricks."

My head was still pressed against the door, so my voice came back in a tiny echo. It reassured me that nothing was in the hallway. The little apartment ghost girl wasn't real. I was starting to believe my lies, until I turned around. She was sitting at the kitchen island, her icy blue eyes piercing me the moment they met mine. I didn't know if it was her stare or the shock that froze me in place, but I didn't dare move. Silence fell over the apartment, the sound of the rowdy children gone, or maybe the fear in me had been drowning out all noises.

How the hell did she get in? I thought to myself. I must have left the apartment door open, and she slipped past me. I was trying to come up with justifications for what I was seeing. None of them really helped calm any nerves I had been feeling.

"Who are you," I stuttered, freaking out, "Or what are you?" I narrowed my eyes at her and walked towards the knives.

"Those won't do you any good," she chuckled. She must have realized where my mind was. I stopped in my tracks and turned to fully face her.

"And why not?" I asked. I tried to make my voice strong and calm but I could feel the tremble as the words came out.

I didn't know when mom would be back and I wasn't sure what her intentions were. Maybe she was just a crazy neighborhood kid, or maybe she was a secret stalker killer. Pieces of my life began playing in my head as I let all the rationale go.

"Because I'm a ghost, silly," she had said so nonchalantly, as if everyone knew that. All of our previous encounters were starting to make more sense. The shock that I was able to see her in the stairwell. The fact that she had laughed at me when I told her to be careful with the apartment cat, so he wouldn't accidentally scratch her. Mom told me there wouldn't be kids my age in our section. All the pieces fell into place and I could see the picture for what it really was.

"But the kids can't see you," I said pointing back to the hallway where the giggles had returned.

"You're the only one who has been able to see me," she said looking down at her hands.

"Wait, what? Why can I see you?"

"I don't know."

"How long have you been here?"

"Honestly, I don't know."

"Well then why are you here?"

"That's another thing I do not know." She finally cracked a smile, "but I do know it feels like home when I am here, so I stay."

This was how the first few days went after I realized Emily was a ghost. I would ask her questions about her past life and she would answer with "I don't know" or "I can't remember." I wasn't sure if she was being honest with me or if she was just protecting herself until she felt she could trust me more.

"Where did you live?" I probed when she appeared one afternoon. I was unpacking a box of desk things. I had walked back to the box to grab more and when I had turned around she was sitting in my chair, trying to get it to rock.

"I'm not sure," she replied, tapping her chin.

"You don't think it was here?" I wondered.

"No, silly," she giggled, "I don't think I lived in your room. Or died here, is what I'm assuming you meant."

Her giggles were filled with an airy light to them, but her voice went cold, harsh, as she finished the sentence. I realized I was pointing down, but I meant the apartment complex.

"No, no, no," I stuttered, throwing my hands in defense, "I just meant did you live in one of the apartment buildings."

She shrugged. "Don't remember."

As we got closer throughout the rest of the summer, I realized that she really didn't remember a good portion of her past life. She knew she had a mother and a father, but was pretty sure she had a younger sibling. Sometimes she would say it was a brother but other times it was a sister. I think one time she said her sibling's name was something unisex like Logan or Skyler and that's why she couldn't remember.

She definitely didn't remember how she died and didn't like discussing it. The first time I brought it up she immediately shot me down and said she didn't like how the discussion of death made her feel. Closer to school starting I had tried again, but it had ended worse than the first time.

"So you really can't remember anything about it?" I pried again.

"No, I don't," she had snapped, "And when I try to think about it my throat gets tight."

"Does that mean you were strangled or something?" the words ran out of my mouth before I could realize what I had really asked her. As my words processed in her mind, her normal inviting eyes turned into icy daggers. She stared so intently, I swore her eyes flashed red with anger.

"Do not ever ask about my death again," she hissed, gritting through her teeth. Her jaw barely moved; she was holding it so tightly.

"And never imply I was murdered, do you understand."

I knew I had screwed up big time because I could barely get my apologies out before she had vanished from my living room. She didn't come around for weeks afterwards and I had started the school year without her. I stumbled through the halls, nearly tripping over students. I felt like I was stuck in the middle of a swarm of ants. They knew the routine, and where they needed to be, able to move almost uniformly through the halls. I was the annoying tree branch that fell into their path, causing disruption wherever I went.

I desperately wanted to talk to someone from back home about Emily. David would have probably laughed me off, but I think I could have convinced him of her. It didn't take much to convince him of anything, which was what made our relationship so great, until I moved. I didn't even mention it to mom, trying to play her off as some weird summer long fever dream.

Emily randomly appeared in the empty seat in my home room class after my first day. I had been so excited to see her again that I forgot others couldn't see her. I jumped with excitement when the brown curls registered in my head. You would have thought I was reconnecting with a lifelong friend by the beaming smile I wore.

The other students who had been in the room to hear me ask a desk where it had been gave me looks and moved away from me. This is what started the new girl as a freak rumor. It didn't help that the first week of school, I had asked people about any recent dead girls. I assumed with a town as small as this that the people would remember how she died. Most of the kids I asked, would look at me like I was coming after their dog and in a pointy hat. Some kids gave a few accidents that had happened over the years but none of those involved a girl named Emily.

I had decided to go to the library to see if there were any local papers written about her. If she was accidentally killed the paper should have her obituary and if she was murdered then they should have definitely covered it. I didn't know much about ghosts, but all the TV shows made it seem like they only stayed if they had unfinished business. Maybe I was supposed to help Emily cross over to the other side. I really didn't know how I was going to accomplish that, but I assumed knowing about her death would give me a start in the right direction.

I walked in, finding an older woman sitting behind the librarian desk. Her silver hair had been pulled tightly into a bun, reminding me of the ballerinas at the Nutcracker. She looked up from the novel she was reading and stared at me through her coke bottle glasses.

"Well what can I help you with, miss?" she had asked, looking me over. I could tell she was trying to place who I was, seeing if I belonged to the Smiths from church or maybe I was a granddaughter of someone in her book club.

"Hi, I just moved here with my mom," I said to stop her racing mind. "I was just doing some research for a school project and needed to read some old local papers."

"Oh welcome honey," she said, "All local newspapers will be in the back left side. You can read anything back there but unfortunately we do not allow you to check those out, just the books."

"I understand," I nodded, gripping my shoulder strap tight, ready to book it to the back corner. "I didn't think I was going to need to check anything out today anyway."

"Well if you change your mind, just come back up to the front and I will get you set up with a library card.

I sat in that library for what felt like hours. I read through every article that talked about missing or murdered girls in this town. Luckily I didn't have too much to read, but unluckily it didn't help my search for answers. There were seven missing Emily's, but no murders. I wasn't sure which Emily was the ghost in my apartment.

The dates of the girls' disappearances ranged from 1976 to 2005. I knew the 2005 missing Emily couldn't be mine, because she had only been eight when she disappeared. Of the seven girls, four of them fell in the age range I thought Emily was. I was pretty sure she was around 16 or 17 but I wasn't sure because Emily hadn't actually confirmed. She probably couldn't remember herself.

Sadly, the library trip didn't provide me with any extra information. The Emily's that I was left with had been runaways before or came from troubled homes. Maybe Emily left on her own and wasn't able to survive as well as she thought. Maybe she was kidnapped but no one cared to look further than a runaway. I was never going to get my answer and I didn't want to lose the only friend I have made here trying to figure it out.

I tried not to ask too much about her past anymore. Knowing the pain it brought Emily when she thought of her life, I avoided it. She remembers that she did performances in high school. One time she explained how happy she felt on stage singing, but the smile she had on her face while retelling the stories was washed away when she realized she would never feel that joy again.

It makes her happy to discuss the high school drama, the life she wants to have. She has been pushing me to get out more so that she can relive some of her life, but talking to myself instead of my other classmates turned me into a pariah. Most of them didn't want to be associated with the new girl who was obsessed with death.

Hopefully, the Halloween party will help get me on the better side with my peers so I can start actually fulfilling Emily's dreams for me. She clung to me for life, but I was almost as invisible as she was. She really got screwed over with me being the person to see her. I knew she wished it was someone like Jessica. A person with a social life already, someone to enjoy the gossip sessions with her. If she had her way, she would throw out my entire wardrobe and set me up with jeans and girly shirts to show off my assets, as she likes to say. She would revamp me into a movie star in her eyes.

CHAPTER THREE

The rest of the day had been a blur. After lunch, my brain felt the same food fog that the other students were feeling. My monotone teacher didn't help the drowsiness that I felt creep through my body. My head had jolted up when the last bell echoed through the homeroom. I tried hustling through the crowd, ready to get my things and leave. I watched Emily follow a group of guys, as they jostled each other down the hall. She would reappear when the gossip had run out.

Mom was already waiting at the car by the time I finally got to the parking lot. Her hair had been pinned up, unlike the loose curls she had it in this morning. The sun caught the few gray hairs that peppered through her brown strands. Her glasses pinched the bridge of her nose as she looked at me. She didn't normally wear her glasses while teaching, she must have been grading assignments when she realized she needed to get us home.

A box filled with folders and binders sat in the back seat. Looks like she was going to have more homework than me tonight. I grinned at the thought of that. She had been on me since we both started, trying to make sure that my academics didn't suffer because of the divorce. Now, she was the one drowning in work.

"What's in the box?" I asked, feeling a little guilty if she was actually struggling because she was too focused on me.

"Oh, just a few book review essays," she said, turning back to look in the van.

"Gonna need any help with grading?"

"No, no, I should be fine. These are the kids who turned in their assignments early." So she wasn't struggling, but actually working ahead.

Way to go, mom. I should have known she wasn't going to give herself a spare minute to think so she was going to stay in overdrive mode.

"So when are the essays due then?"

"Next Monday." I looked into the box that had to have at least 30 or more essays in it.

"Why are your middle schoolers so productive?" I huffed.

"There not," she said laughing, "Now get in the car, let's go home. You getting hungry?"

"Not really at the moment. What are we having tonight?"

"I was thinking spaghetti?"

"Oh can we have meatballs?" Mom started the car, then sat back in her seat thinking.

"Do we have meatballs?" she finally asked. I nodded my head vigorously. I remembered putting the bag in the fridge after our Saturday grocery trip.

"Then spaghetti and meatballs it is." she hollered. We pulled out of the lot and headed towards home. The apartment complex we moved to was only about 10 minutes away from the school, so our car rides were short. Mom would ask about my plans for school in the morning on the way there and on the way home would ask how each other's classes went. She tried to get as much detail out of me, but I tried turning things back onto her.

"Did you get a lot done homework wise in your home room?" she asked. The middle and high schoolers got a free period at the end of the day for homework. It was really so we didn't get out before the elementary school kids. The school didn't or probably couldn't pay the bus drivers to pick two schools up and then come back for the third.

"Yeah, a good chunk is done. What did you do during homeroom?" I asked, turning back to see Emily sitting next to the box. I jumped not expecting her. I saw mom's eyes flash in worry towards me. She had noticed that I was more jumpy recently.

"You good?" she asked.

"Yeah I just caught part of a car in the corner of my eye and it looked like he was going to hit us." I lied. Emily snickered in the back. I gave her the evil eye through the rear view mirror. She often enjoyed just appearing out of nowhere.

"How are classes going?" Mom asked.

"Not too bad," I said, peering at my books, "Few tests coming up."

"Don't forget to study," she said.

"Oh that reminds me." I practically jumped again. "I am meeting a few friends to study, can you take me to the library this weekend?"

"What friends?" she peered over at me, the concern filling her eyes.

"Jessica and Mallory from Biology," I said with a nonchalant tone.

"Well, have I met Jessica and Mallory from Biology?"

"Oh come on mom," I pleaded, "Don't be like this."

"Be like what?" she pressed her hand to her chest. "I just want to make sure my daughter isn't hanging with the wrong crowd. You know, selling drugs."

My eyes instinctively rolled as laughter bubbled through my throat. I knew she was joking but her overbearing protection was a killjoy sometimes. She feared the world, constantly complaining about the changes. She didn't want my world ruined by the reality of society.

"I'm not going to the library to sell drugs," I said.

"I know you're not," she teased, "I will take you, but I do want to meet these girls."

Mom pulled into the apartment complex. The pretty welcome center faced the entrance. We lived in the back part, so mom stopped and turned onto the streets until our villa numbers were visible. Of course none of the front parking was available. All the stay at home moms beat us back from the school pick up. We drove past our building numbers towards the turnaround area.

There were always spots by the dumpster so mom headed that way without looking for anything else. Of course she was able to pull straight into a spot and parked the car. Emily popped out first and pretended to open my door. I felt my lips pull into a smirk as I looked down at her. She bowed as if she was my servant.

"Do you want me to start making the spaghetti right away?" mom asked, grabbing the box in the back seat.

"That's up to you," I said. I pointed at the pile that drowned her small figure. "When do you plan on tackling that?"

"Maybe during TV time," she answered, hoisting the box onto her hip.

"Sure then. Let's make dinner, eat with TV and then you can grade after we're done." I said holding the front door open for her. She started walking up the stairs, she wouldn't even look in the direction of the elevator. She has been afraid of them her whole life. I naturally followed, even though our creaky one doesn't scare me as much.

Once inside, mom ran the box to her room before dropping anything else off. I slung my bag on the living room table, my body doing the same on the couch. I planned on doing homework while mom graded so I didn't see the need to throw it down the hall into my bedroom. Mom came back already out of work attire and in her comfy lounge wear.

She had thrown her hair into a messy bun and put her glasses back on. She never looked messy though. Even now in sweats and a basic tee, she still looked like she could take the world if she wanted to. That's one of the things I praise her about. No matter how tough things are getting, she will always have a strong front.

"I'm gonna get dinner started," she said, rummaging through the cabinets to find the pots and pans she needed. "Did you want Texas toast with it?"

"Mom," I halted, staring directly at her from the back of the couch, "You cannot have spaghetti night without Texas toast."

"Texas toast it is," I heard her mumble under her breath.

I turned back to get the TV started, ready to let my mind melt away. A loud crash from the kitchen distracted me from my objective though. Placing the remote down next to my bag, I glanced back to make sure mom didn't need any help. Our smaller kitchen didn't fit all the pans mom had brought, so sometimes it was a fight to get what we needed.

"So when are we going to talk about Halloween costumes?" Emily asked, plopping down onto the couch next to me. She had propped her feet on the table. I wanted to tell her to take them off, but the last time I did that she responded with "Why? I'm dead. It's not like I'm going to get it dirty."

"Hey mom, do you care if I call Ashley out on the balcony," I cringed at her name.

"Sure sweetie, tell her I said hi, would you?" mom said not knowing. Ashley had been my closest friend back at Springfield, but she destroyed our friendship shortly after I moved away. I didn't tell my mom that because I could pretend to call her and talk to Emily instead.

I went outside on the balcony. The wind had picked up a little bit more and the sun was low in the sky. I was glad I had been dressing in hoodies and sweatshirts. I pulled my Sony out of my back pocket and slid it open. No missed calls and no messages. That didn't surprise me, but my heart ached nonetheless.

"I don't know why you keep lying to your mom," Emily said.

"Well, I thought, hey mom I want to talk to the ghost that haunts our apartment, doesn't sound too good."

"Well at least you don't have to worry about a ghost sleeping with your boyfriend."

"They didn't have sex," I said sharply and coldly. I narrowed my eyes, wishing to shoot daggers out of them, but it wouldn't really work on a dead person.

I wasn't really sure what all happened between them, but I didn't want to think about it. It only took about two weeks for Ashley to sink her claws into David. I knew she had a crush on him since middle school but he was always interested in me. *Or so I thought.* We had been together for almost a year when the news about the move came. I saw their texts for the dinner of our anniversary.

I knew the relationship was in shambles before then, but I was trying to convince myself it was just the move and nothing else. He had practice late so that's why he forgot to text, was my excuse for him a lot until I read the truth.

"Relax, all I'm saying is I think you could get away with saying it's a kid from school."

"Oh yeah and what happens when she wants to meet said friend?" I asked, sitting on the patio furniture outside. Emily followed.

"You know, I guess you've got a good point," she said "But that isn't why we're out here, so let's get down to business."

"I've never been to a Halloween party and I don't even remember the last time I dressed up," I confessed.

"Well there's always the basics," she started, "You could be a sexy black cat, a witch, or a nurse." As she listed off each idea she manifested a little prop to go with it. Her black ears turned into a pointy hat that shifted to a nurse hat.

"My mom will not let me out of the house as a sexy anything, so maybe not those."

"Is your mom going to even let you go, miss goodie-goodie?" I had to sit for a long second and think about it.

"I mean she never did let me go to the ones back home, but that's a bigger area."

"So maybe since it's at the local farm, she won't have a problem with it?" Emily raised her eyebrow.

"I don't know, honestly."

"Well you have to at least ask her."

"I know I do but if I say something now she'll have all this month and next to think of reasons why I shouldn't be able to go.' I slumped in my chair, I could definitely wait until it was closer but Emily didn't like waiting, and I could tell by how fast her leg was shaking that she was antsy to get costumes picked out.

"At least bring it up to her tonight," Emily said, clasping her hands together and pouting. Her eyes became like saucers as she tried to guilt me.

"I haven't secured my invite, yet" I stammered.

"Fine, then back to costumes," she said, settling back in "Do you think we should go as something together?"

"Yeah right, because everyone will be able to see my other half." I laughed at her.

"You know what they say, Halloween is the night where the veil between the worlds is lifted. Maybe they will be able to see me." She lifted her hands up like a creepy ghost in a bad horror film would do.

"That would be just great," I said "Everyone would think I was more of a freak if they could see the dead girl following me around."

"Oh you know you couldn't live without this dead girl," she said, attempting to push me. Her hand went straight through my shoulder, sending cold tingly through my arm. I gave a small shudder and she quickly pulled her hand out. I wasn't used to the feeling of her "touch" but I tried not to react to it.

"I'm sorry," she whispered.

"No, no, it's fine," I started, throwing my hands up in defense. "It's cold outside and I just didn't expect it." Her eyes darted behind me to the glass door. I turned to see what had startled her. It was my mom walking towards us. I could see the bowls sitting on the table, meaning she was coming to grab me. I quickly turned back to Emily as she just as quickly vanished.

"Yeah, yeah it was good talking to you, too," I said as I heard the click of the door. "Talk to you soon, Ashley."

"Charlotte, it's time for dinner." I slide the phone closed.

"Perfect, Ash and I just wrapped up our recaps of the school year." I replied, walking towards her. The smell of spaghetti had followed her out and my stomach responded in pain. The oven began dinging, probably letting mom know that the Texas toast was finished.

"Oh, anything fun?" Mom asked, holding the door for me.

"At Springfield?" I asked, "No, not really, but here. Here, there was a weekend party." I got settled on the couch, turning the TV on.

"And why was that fun?" mom asked, bringing me a piece of toast.

"I guess not really anything fun, but juicy gossip," I started "What are you thinking we watch for dinner?"

"Um, well it's Tuesday so Suspicious Acts is on tonight. What was the juicy gossip?"

I flipped through the guide until I could find the show, Shawn Mather's character was interrogating a potential suspect.

"Oh, um, the host's best friend and boyfriend got way too drunk and started making out in the pool," I said all in the rush, never looking over, just staring at the screen and my spaghetti.

"That's a trashy move," mom said, blowing on her first bite, "What awful friend would do something like that?"

"Yeah, what kind of an awful friend." My heart had dropped a little bit, thinking of how close to home it hit. I didn't tell my mom why David and I broke up, just that we started getting distance after the move. I guess that wasn't entirely wrong.

After the pang in my heart, I didn't feel like continuing a conversation. Mom stayed so engaged in the show and then into her essays that she didn't really seem to notice. I finished what little homework I had and then went to bed early. Emily didn't make an appearance again either, allowing me to easily drift out of this world.

Chapter Four

I stared back at my eyes, but they were attached to a face I hardly recognized anymore. The chocolate color was masked by the long lashes. Everyone confused them for black, but mom would correct them, telling them they are a rich mahogany just like her mother's. But they didn't have a familiar feeling anymore, I could tell the coppery shine was starting to dull.

Hiding myself under the layer of baggy clothes was starting to warp my sense of reality, warping the feeling of who I was. I let myself get lost in the protection of those bags and now I feared coming out of them. My nerves had been shaky all week, but now that it was finally the day, my legs could barely hold me up. I didn't understand the fear I was having. I was just going to study with people from school.

I gripped the sides of the sink, trying to steady the wobble. I repeated, you are just studying with friends. That word, friends, lingered on the back of my tongue. Was Jessica really someone I could consider a friend? She had invited me to help them study, but if I didn't understand the material would she? The only real friendship I had before coming to Twindle was Ashley.

I wasn't as awkward in Springfield, but I have always struggled with making friends. Ashley had been the extrovert that helped bring me out of my shell. I wasn't sure I really knew how to be outside of it without her. Emily sadly wasn't going to be able to bring me out even though she so desperately wanted to. Her desperation was actually part of the reason I was still so hidden.

I looked back to the mirror, trying to feel comfortable in the t-shirt Emily picked from my closet. I knew she was still in there matching the shoes and limited accessories I had in my room. I was the little doll she finally got to dress up for a tea party with the other dolls. Disappointingly though, no matter how she dressed this doll, my freak status wasn't changing anytime soon. I thought back to yesterday as school was ending.

"Charlie!" a girl cried from the hallway.

I wasn't used to the kids at school knowing me, so I kept walking. Also, when you go by Charlie you eventually assume people are hollering for Charles and not Charlotte. I was trying to drown out the background of high school with my music, so I couldn't be sure where the voice was coming from. I pushed through a group of kids to get to my locker.

I spun the little combination, finally getting the hang of it. A hand grabbed my shoulder, making me nearly jump out of my skin. I heard a small yelp leave my body as I turned to face the owner of the hand. I knew it wasn't Emily because her hand would have gone through me.

"Didn't you hear me calling for you?" Jessica said, a small look of worry taking over her face.

"No, sorry," I said in a rush, my breath finally coming back to me. Who would have thought that having a dead best friend would make you afraid of the living. "I had my music in." I held up the cord since my jump forced the buds out of my ear, my face heating.

"Oh well no biggie," Jessica said, shrugging it off, "I wanted to confirm you're still going to the library tomorrow?"

"Oh yeah I'll be there," I said reassuring her.

"Great. Mallory will be there, too."

"Sounds good, noon still right?"

"My mom can drop us off around lunch," she nodded in agreement.

"Oh okay, I will let my mom know."

"Mallory will most likely stay with me tonight, so I will make sure she's up early."

Jessica bounced away to her locker. Probably trying to gather her stuff before the buses left for the day. I stood there watching her effortlessly get in to grab her bag. It looked kind of like a saddle would for a horse. Images of Jessica racing through the woods on a horse played through my mind. After a moment or two, I realized I was still staring at Jessica.

Shaking myself back to reality, I forced my head into the locker, looking for something. Realistically, I was looking for my dignity because I'm sure the kids who were peering around their lockers to look at me probably thought I was a stalker. I continued rummaging through my locker until the voices around me had died down. I could feel my face was still hot, so I was hoping most of the kids would need to catch the bus and leave, taking their gossip with them.

"Are you almost ready to go?" mom hollered from the hallway, bringing me to the present moment. I took a deep inhale, watching my chest rise in the mirror.

"Yeah, I'm coming," I hollered back to her.

Throwing the bathroom door open, I tried throwing away my freak girl fears, but they were staring back at me. The sky hidden behind them as she blinked at me. She knew mom would hear us talking, well me anyway. Her eyes moved rapidly, almost like she was trying to use the blinks as some sort of Morse code.

Shrugging my shoulders, I let out an exasperated sigh as I pushed past her. I didn't know what she wanted and now wasn't really the time, but I didn't want her trying to continue the spy talk during study time. I walked through my bedroom door, knowing she would be behind me.

"Mom, I'm grabbing my books then we can head out," I called, before getting too far in.

"Okay honey," I could hear her faintly call.

"You have a minute," I shot back towards Emily. "What was that?"

"I wanted to know why you were in the bathroom for so long," she tapped her foot impatiently, arms crossed.

"What do you mean?" I didn't think I had really been in there that long.

"You were in there forever and I couldn't match the rest of the outfit because it walked away," she started, first the arms went in the air, then the pacing around the room began. "If you didn't like the outfit you could have told me, I can handle that, you know." I watched her continue her little circle, almost expecting her to actually cut through the floor.

"You know, you didn't need to hide in there." Her rant went on as she pointed to the bathroom. Her words were finally starting to hit my ears, or my brain was starting to understand what she was saying.

"Do you think I was in there because of you?" I finally asked. It stopped her in her tracks.

"Well what were you in there for, then?" she questioned, confusion starting to take over the worry.

"I haven't really gotten close to anyone, but you," I started.

"So it was because of me," she cut me off.

"Well I guess in a sense, yes. But not for the reasons you think," I tried to reassure her. "I haven't really had an easy time making friends and I am just worried today will go wrong."

"Because of me?" The confusion was slowly vanishing.

"No, no," I threw my hands up defensively, "I'm afraid it will go wrong because of me." I confessed.

"Because of you?"

"Well yeah," I sheepishly said, "I haven't really talked to anyone but you and I can't really use you as a crutch today."

"I guess that is a scary thought to have." She cracked a smile.

"A terrifying thought," I chuckled in agreement.

"Charlotte," mom hollered, "What's taking so long?"

"Sorry," I hollered back, quickly grabbing the book bag.

I rushed through the hall trying to get to her. I didn't expect the conversation was taking that long but I knew mom wasn't going to understand sorry mom my ghost friend and I were having a disagreement. I, instead, decided to lie and tell her I couldn't find the text book that I needed for biology.

"Somehow it was hidden under a pile of dirty clothes," I scoffed as we made our way down the stairs, "I really have no idea how it got there."

"Well that just means you need to work on cleaning that room when you get home later tonight," she said a step ahead of me. Great, I just added chores to my to-do list. I mentally added blame Emily to that imaginary list.

There wasn't much talking that took place during the drive to the library. I mainly kept my head on the window, slowly learning the routes in the town. It was a small enough town that there was almost a trail to get anywhere. I just needed to learn which place would take me where. Mom listened to her teacher's station. I didn't think it was actually a station for just teachers, but the morning hosts were retired teachers that provided advice or told horror stories provided by listeners.

We had pulled into the library lot right as the two women were telling a story of a first time teacher's first day with an over populated class. Listening to them, I never wanted to become a teacher. Not that it was really something I had thought about before them.

"So are the other two girls here?" mom asked, putting the car into park.

"I'm not sure," I said, peering my head around to look at the lot. I didn't think either of the girls could drive and even if they could, I wouldn't know what car to look for. Plus Jessica did say her mom would just drop them off.

"And remind me what their names are," she said, keeping the door locked.

"Jessica and Mallory," I answered, reaching for my bag, "I think we just need to go in and look."

"Alright, let's go," she said, grabbing the keys out of the ignition before following me to the doors.

I didn't think mom actually wanted to meet the girls, but I knew she was going to make sure I wasn't having a random Internet hook up. She had been spending more nights watching true crime shows about the dangers of the Internet. She lectured me about making sure I knew who I was talking to. Little did she know, I hardly talked to anyone outside of Emily. But today, today that's going to change.

As we reached the front door, mom pulled the handle releasing a squeak as she escorted me inside. I did a mini bow as I walked through and she returned the gesture. As soon as we walked through, mom stared up to the second floor. The lobby of the library led up to silent rooms on the second floor. I assumed that was where Jessica and Mallory would be so I headed up the stairs, using the rail to pull my body up each step.

The second floor had one long hallway right after the stairs, and then circled around the other side of the steps. Still holding onto the railing, I peered over the ledge to see the next people walking into the library. It was an elderly couple carrying a few books. I continued following the railing around the oval-like structure upstairs.

All the rooms were empty though; doors closed and lights off. After walking the full oval and peering into each room, I made my way down the hallway to see the same fate. All the doors closed with their lights off. I could feel mom behind me, probably wondering the same thing I was.

"Is this where they told you to meet?" she finally asked after I confirmed the last door.

"They said library," I started, turning back to face her, "They didn't technically say upstairs, but I assumed the silent rooms would be where they'd want to study."

I threw my hands up in frustration, feeling my heart begin to race. I knew this was going to be some joke. They probably never planned on showing up here, I thought to myself. Make fun of the new girl because she's an easy target.

I shrugged and headed towards the stairs, ready to accept defeat. Maybe Jessica wasn't as nice as Emily had thought. It stopped me in my tracks. *Emily!* I bet she had already been searching the library to find the two. If they weren't here, she would know it. I could see brown curls as I got closer to the stairs, and I hoped they were going to belong to Emily. I was just too far away to see her face.

"Where are we going now?" mom asked from behind me.

"Uh...downstairs," I said, working my way closer to the stairs.

At the sound of my voice, I watched the curls turn towards the stairs. We were both heading in the same direction. I could see Emily's face as she made her way up the stairs. Clearly by her expression, going to the silent rooms was the wrong move. She held her hands up to indicate her confusion.

"Why are you upstairs?" she asked, finally getting close enough for me to whisper.

"Isn't that where the silent rooms are?" I answered her question with a question.

"How do you know about the silent rooms?" I guess we weren't going to answer each other. "I didn't think you'd been to the library before."

I could see she was eying me suspiciously but I wasn't going to let her know my reasoning for my previous visits. I wasn't ready to start a fight, and especially not in front of mom. I just kept looking down at the steps, pretending I was just watching for caution and not just to ignore her.

When I made it to the bottom step, I turned and waited for mom. Emily didn't. She moved off the last step and stood directly in front of me. She was so close, I could feel her coldness on my face. I fought to keep from stuttering.

"Well if you aren't going to answer me, then I guess I won't tell you where they're at," she said. I could see her arms cross over her chest as she said that.

Now, I resisted the urge to whip my head around to look at her. I knew she had scooped out the place already. I hadn't watched her walk in with us, but I knew she never went anywhere without surveillance of the area first.

"Well where to?" mom asked, walking towards the library's entrance.

"That part I'm not sure about," I said, tapping my chin. "If only they had trackers." Mom laughed at the little joke, but Emily got what I meant.

"There's a teens section," Emily said, "follow me." She waved me through the check-out area and I urged mom to follow me.

"I think there might be an area where the teens study," I told mom looking back at her.

The three of us bobbed and weaved between rows of books. I started worrying that Emily didn't actually know where the teen section was. Maybe it wasn't the same section she remembered. I darted my head in between aisles as we continued to the back, hoping to spot the girls.

"There." Emily finally pointed, as she stopped in her tracks. I stopped too, but mom walked through Emily, sending her into a million little particles. I watched as mom gave a small shiver afterwards. She felt it too.

"I think this room is the teen section," I told mom pointing to the all windowed room. It wasn't much bigger than the conference rooms upstairs, but it was split into two sections. I could see one side that was filled with computers, while the other only had tables. In the middle sat a middle aged woman, probably the library supervisor.

"They have a room for just the teens?" mom asked.

"Guess so," I said, "I know towards the front is the kids section, but I didn't see what all was in there."

I hadn't actually seen the kids' area when we walked in, but I remembered seeing it the first time I came to the library. I had to pass it to get to the newspaper section. It was similar to this room but I could tell there was a giant area in the front for them to play. It had windows to the outside, so people could easily see the jungle tree set that was in the middle. I think it was a big factor for parents.

The two of us stood, staring at the room. I tried glancing through the windows to see the girls, but it was hard to make out the faces of anyone in there. I started heading towards the door, hoping mom would just leave me there. A kid not much younger than me, probably a middle schooler, burst through the door, allowing the chaotic noise of that room to escape into the silent library. He pushed past us, heading back towards the bathrooms.

"Well I guess this is where I leave you?" mom asked, her eyes following the boy running through the books.

"Yeah I can see kids studying so I am hoping one of the tables has Jessica," I said trying to get a better view now that I was closer to the door.

"What time should I pick you up?"

"How bout 2pm?"

"2pm, it is," mom agreed, giving me a gentle peck on the forehead. I leaned my head forward to make it easier for her.

She bobbed and weaved back through the path. Luckily the library had a lot of large windows, so I easily watched her get into the car and pull out of the lot. I let out a sigh of relief after realizing that Jessica, and more importantly Mallory didn't watch my mommy walk me in. I turned back to face the glass doors that held my fate. Inhaling deeply, I pulled the door open, bracing for the loud noise.

I didn't brace myself for the pungent stench that engulfed me. It took everything in me not to gag. I could practically feel myself turning green the longer I stood there. Middle school eyes gawked at me, their fast fingers ceasing to a halt once they caught a glimpse of me.

I had put in a little more work then I normally would have, but I assumed they were staring more because they hadn't seen a girl in real life before. It was only boys that had been crowding around the computers. I hadn't noticed that when I was on the other side of the glass. They had to be the cause of the awful smells that were probably embedding themselves into my clothes right now.

"Over here," a girl hollered behind me.

Mortified at my thoughts, I quickly turned to look at who was calling. I prayed it would be Jessica and not some girl giving me an out. I easily spotted Jessica's smiling face. Her arm was still in the air, inviting me over to them. Mallory had her head in a book. Well not in it, I guess. She was laying on it, like she had given up.

They had one table off to the back side of the room, close to the windows. I wondered if they picked it to be able to easily spot me when I came in. There were only two other tables in the room. Along the wall were shelves filled with young adult novels. I wasn't able to read any of the titles when I walked up, but the sections above indicated that the girls were by the graphic novels.

"Thank goodness I saw you when I did," Jessica said, pulling me into a hug. I was embraced by vanilla and sugar cookies, with a small hint of horses.

"Yes, thank goodness," I agreed as we let go. I gestured my head down towards Mallory.

"Oh don't mind her," Jessica said brushing it off, "She is trying to learn the material through osmosis."

Jessica let out a little laugh and I instinctively followed. I didn't understand why I did it, but it felt like something to do. Mallory rolled her head slightly to one side, allowing the side of her face to be visible. She groaned in response to our laughter.

"Mr. B was teaching us about it, so why can't I use it to study?" she argued, but after a moment longer she lifted her head and just sighed. "I wish it was easier for me to understand."

"Don't worry about it," Jessica slid into the chair next to her, reassuringly wrapping her arm around Mallory, "We'll study until you understand it. Right, Charlie?"

Jessica flashed a bright and hopefully smile at me. I wasn't as confident about our study date as she was. If Mallory was resorting to osmosis for studying, I really didn't think I could help her.

"Well when is your mom coming back to get you?" Mallory asked, looking at me.

I wasn't sure if she was saying that because they saw her dropping me off like a kindergarten or if she was just making an assumption about how I got here. Either way, it stung for some reason.

"She said she'd be back at 2pm," I answered, finally settling down into a seat across from them. I hadn't realized I was still standing until then. I was starting to worry about what they were thinking. *Freak girl needs her mommy. Why is freak girl just standing there?*

I tried pushing the thoughts out of my head, distracting myself in my backpack. I slowly pulled out the material they had out. The class textbook, a notebook, and an assortment of highlighters and pens. I could see Jessica was still on the eager train, but Mallory was slowly falling off.

"Have you guys been here long?" I asked. It was only five minutes past noon when mom and I pulled into the lot, so I couldn't imagine this was what happened after a few minutes of studying. Maybe I should have told mom to come back at 1pm instead.

"Sadly, no," Mallory groaned.

"Someone just wouldn't listen to me last night," Jessica interrupted and bumped herself into Mallory, "and decided to stay up way later than we agreed."

"Oh fun night?" I asked.

"Not really," Jessica shrugged, "Just a movie night, honestly."

"Oh to be a fly on the wall for that," Emily said next to me.

Wait next to me?

I sat back in my chair, glancing out of the corner of my eye at her. I didn't know how long she had honestly been there. I thought she had left once mom ran into her. I thought back to walking into the room and she wasn't by me. She must have just come back from that, but why? Why is she here?

"Ready to get studying?" Jessica broke my concentration.

"Uhh," I replied, still trying to understand what was going on. "Yeah, I'm good." I finally said, shaking my head, shaking me back into reality.

"You good?" Mallory asked, looking me up and down, "Kinda looks like you saw a ghost."

"Yeah I'm fine," I said trying to hide my annoyance, "I just got a whiff of those kids again."

I pointed in the middle schoolers' direction before waving my hand over my nose. I hoped they would go with it and move on. I watched Mallory's lip curl in disgust, but was it for me or them, I didn't know. Jessica was unfazed by it all, her smile never wavering. I wondered how she did it, staying happy all the time.

"So what chapter do you want to start with?" I said to break the silence. I leaned forward over the textbook, slowly flipping through pages as I waited on a response.

"Who wants to study when there is gossip to dish?" Emily practically purred in my ear, as she leaned onto the table, too. I shifted my weight over to be more with Jessica.

"I think we should start with chapter nine," Jessica said, opening her book, "Mallory, that's where you get lost, isn't it?"

"Yeah chapter nine makes no sense to me," Mallory groaned, slamming her head into the book again for a moment before flipping to the chapter.

I moved closer to Jessica, getting my book open to the same page as her's. I eyed up towards Emily, hoping she would understand not to keep pushing. I must not have given the hint enough, because Emily pushed herself closer to me. I watched the chair move closer to us, but assumed that was just a trick of my mind, until I heard the gasps.

"Did you just see that?" Mallory asked, her hand slowly moving to her mouth.

"See what?" I asked, still not fully convinced we saw the same thing. I knew she wasn't seeing Emily.

"That chair just moved," Jessica finished, but her face wasn't as shocked.

"Oh, no I didn't realize," I tried shrugging, but I could see Emily's eyes as she processed what Mallory was saying.

"Don't mind Mallory," Jessica said, swiping her hand through the air.

"Oh?"

"She has always been into supernatural things," she replied, nodding, "and thinks everything is that."

"How do you explain the chair moving?" Mallory questioned, throwing her hands in Emily's direction.

"The floor probably isn't level," I quickly jumped in.

"Yeah, there's always an answer that isn't supernatural," Jessica included, "Can we get back to studying?"

I nodded, pulling out my highlighter. Mallory groaned but continued watching the chair, probably hoping it would move again. Leaning over, pretending to read my text, I glared up through strands of hair to watch Emily. She sat frozen, staring back at Mallory. They continued staring at one another, I was wondering if Mallory was able to see any of Emily sitting there.

"So Mallory," I said, trying to grab her attention, "What part of these chapter do you need help on?"

She didn't move, not even a glance in my direction. They were definitely holding eye contact, but did Mallory know that? I could feel the sweat starting to form on the back of my neck. I wanted to kick Emily under the table, but I knew that wouldn't do anything.

"Mal!" Jessica yelled, "Pay attention."

That got her to break her stare, but just barely. Her head slowly turned to look at Jessica, but her eyes stayed glued to the chair for as long as they could. I knew my secret was out. What will Mallory say about it? Will she tell everyone in school? My heart raced as more thoughts flooded my head.

"Uh," Mallory finally said when looked over at us, "I swore I saw something."

Mallory pointed back to where Emily was sitting. Jessica followed her finger. I did the same even though I knew Emily was sitting there. I didn't want to look suspicious by ignoring it. But I was shocked to see the chair empty. Emily wasn't there.

I almost started looking around for her, but I caught myself before looking too much like a spaz. Instead I looked back to Jessica and Mallory. Jessica's face lacked any amusement, so I was pretty sure she didn't see anything.

"I don't see anything," I shrugged.

"I guess I was just seeing things," Mallory said with a sigh.

Mallory had given up and we were able to get into the study material. It seemed like Emily got the message and took off. Jessica had made an outline for the chapters, allowing us to easily follow the information. We sat there continuing through the outline. I slowly formed a guide for the next test we had. Mallory's eyes seemed to recognize the information we were going through. I hoped that meant she was understanding it.

Eventually Jessica pulled out a stack of flashcards from her bag. Her fancy handwriting had the vocab words on one side, with their definition on the other. She started passing them in even amounts to Mallory and me.

"Here, we'll start on the vocab now," she said once the last card was given out.

We reach for a little stack in front of us. Jessica mixed her cards up and I watched Mallory do the same to hers. I didn't understand why the cards needed to be shuffled around, but I shuffled mine too. Jessica flashed her first card at me, when I noticed it.

Emily hadn't actually left like I thought. She was messing around with the books behind the two girls. I didn't understand why she was doing it at first, until she read the definition out for me.

"I know you don't really need my help," she laughed behind Jessica. "But it is fun."

The sound of her laugh started to heat my blood. She was right. I didn't need her help. She didn't need to be here, so why was she? It was beginning to annoy me, but I couldn't convey that without the girls wondering why. I refused to give out the answer, instead waiting on Mallory.

"Come on guys," Jessica finally said after the silence engulfed us. "Neither of you know it?"

"I'm stumped," Mallory said, shrugging her shoulders.

"Charlie?" Jessica glanced at me.

I lifted my shoulders up, shaking my head no. Of course, I knew the answer, but I didn't want Emily to have the satisfaction of me playing her little game. She looked at me gob-smacked. Her eyes narrowed though, as she understood what I was playing at.

"Fine," she scolded, "be like that."

Her body slowly faded from view, allowing my body to start relaxing. Once I could tell she was fully gone, I got back into studying with the girls. Running through the flashcards didn't take long, mostly because Mallory couldn't remember the vocab. I thought it was weird that she was good in English class but not good at definitions, since that was most of what we were doing recently.

"So are you ready for spirit week?" Mallory asked as we started to back up.

"I'm so excited," Jessica bounced.

"Spirit week?" I asked. "Isn't it still a few weeks away?"

"Well only two I think," Jessica held up her fingers to indicate the weeks.

"Plus the committee has already listed out the theme," Mallory said, leaning over the table.

I leaned in closer, expecting to get some more information. Maybe Mallory was going to tell us what we should do. I didn't really do spirit week prior, but if I had a group to do it with, then maybe it would be more fun. Mallory continued going over the homecoming plans, going on about the football season. I had engulfed myself in her conversation, so I didn't expect what happened next.

One of the books flew off the shelf, smacking her in the back of the head. The thud echoed through the library, turning all the heads to see the commotion. The yelp that came from Mallory caught the rest of the eyes.

"What the hell?" Mallory asked, rubbing the back of her head.

I looked up expecting to see Emily staring down at us, but she wasn't there. It was just the shelves. We watched as books began flying off each shelf, one by one. All of them coming in our direction. Most of them continued to hit Mallory, but a few slammed into Jessica or myself.

Since our bags were packed, we grabbed them, using them as shields to get out of the teen section. The others in the area, confused, did the same. No one could explain what was happening, but none of us wanted to stay in the room. Outside the room, I could see her.

Emily was tearing each book off the shelf. I could hear the scream ringing through the window. I didn't understand her anger that was coming out of nowhere. I didn't want her help with studying so she was going to destroy the library? Jessica and Mallory quickly left the library, fear rushing them out.

I followed, not wanting to watch the meltdown that was happening. She wasn't going to get my attention on this one. Mom had been waiting in the lot, so I quickly waved goodbye before jumping in. Emily clearly needed to cool down before we talked.

CHAPTER FIVE

I pulled down the skirt I was wearing. All the rowdy students bustling down the hall jostled me around. I moved with the crowd but I felt like I was drowning in school spirit. It was finally the end of Spirit Week. I didn't believe Mallory when she said it was a big deal around here. In Springfield, some kids would participate and others would just mock those kids. That wasn't the case here.

The first day was Cartoon theme. Students had come in body suits to match the blue and yellow characters. Some students used body paint to become their favorite comic book hero. The second day was animal themed and a girl in history class had painted her legs and hair a cheetah print. There was still reminiscent of black and yellow in her hair today, but she had tried to cover it with the school colors.

Emily had begged me this morning to attempt to match the theme. Of course, the last day of the week was school spirit, because our homecoming game was tonight. Kids came in with their faces half red and half blue, one kid even brought a big red and blue afro. The teachers made him take it off almost immediately because it was a distraction but still entertaining.

"What do I even wear for school spirit?" I asked, throwing clothes out of the closet.

"Something red and blue," Emily said with an edge to her voice. We hadn't talked about her little melt down and she refused to speak on it, so I had just let it go. I was hoping she eventually would too.

Jessica and Mallory didn't mention it either when I got into bio class that Monday. Since everyone else was going to act like it didn't happen, so was I. It was easier to just brush it under the rug with Jessica and Mallory. I really couldn't tell them about Emily's melt down and I didn't know what they'd actually believe. The librarian tried to say there must have been some sort of plate shift, but no one really believed that.

I heard mom in the kitchen packing up breakfast and setting out our lunches. That meant I had about five minutes to get ready and I still had nothing close to school spirit on. I tried searching for something, but I hadn't got anything from the school.

So now, I was walking the halls in my last year homecoming skirt and a red Ohio State sweater. It wasn't the worst thing I could have thrown together, but watching the girls having matching red and blue two pieces or near full costumes, I felt less than. Emily had been barely around today, because she was snooping on the more interesting kids. She'd bring me back the juiciest of the gossip.

Students packed into the gym as the marching band played. I was pushed through to the back side of the gym. Girls screamed and squealed as they saw their friends they had been saving space for. I knew there was no one saving a seat for me. I tried to sit close to a wall near the band, so the other students around wouldn't notice if I started talking to Emily. I found a seat and leaned my head on the wall, waiting for the spectacle to begin.

I wasn't sure what to expect with the pep rally. The ones in Springfield were hit or miss. If we had a winning season, all the students would go in and be wild. During our losing seasons, the students would just be present, while the teachers tried to make things entertaining. I looked around to see that different games had been set up around the basketball court. The MC's for the night were two seniors, getting help from the AV club as they were setting up their table.

"Oh my god," Emily said, nearly scaring me out of my skin, "It was so hard to find you in the sea of red and blue."

"I tried to pick somewhere where I could talk to you," I said, bowing my head down. It was getting louder in the gym, but still not loud enough that the other students wouldn't hear that I was talking to the air next to me.

Just then, the Seniors told everyone to take their seats. The crowd collectively moved to the bleachers, settling down so they could hear our next set of instructions. The band stopped playing their music and sat patiently. The gym went from a mad house to a quiet one in a matter of seconds.

"And let the games begin," Emily said with a huge grin as she rubbed her hands together. I just nodded in agreement. It had gotten so quiet that you could have heard a pin drop, so now was definitely not the time to respond to her.

"Ladies and Gentlemen of Twindle High," the male senior started.

"We are so excited for our '08 Pep Rally!" the female senior said, throwing her fist into the air. This sent the calm crowd back into a frenzy. The seniors started chanting 08 over and over again.

"It is our great pleasure that we introduce your undefeated Twindle Warriors," the male said, barely able to hear him over the cheering that was still happening. The football team had erupted from the locker rooms, filling the basketball court. More cheers filled the gym and the band began playing our school song.

"Okay so I heard that Jessica has been giving out the details to the Halloween party," Emily said, waving her hand in my face to get my attention again. "Has she given you any information?"

"Well, no but Halloween is still like two or three weeks away," I said, trying to focus on the relay race they were making the football players do.

"You need to get that information or you won't get it."

"What do you mean?" I asked, feeling my brows furrow together.

"These kids," she said, gesturing to the gym. "Have been going to school together since kindergarten."

"I'm still not really following."

"You don't think they don't already know where Jessica lives," she said looking at me like I've grown extra heads.

"So that means what for me?"

"That means everyone else already knows when to show up and where," she said, smacking her forehead, "leaving you in the dust to find it on your own."

"I know where the farms are," I said, trying to reassure her.

"Yeah but can you tell the difference between the Watson farm and the Johnson one?" she asked "because if you show up at the Watson farm and Mallory's mom catches wind of what's going on, she will be sure to shut it down." Now I was the one looking at her extra heads. "Charlie, you don't want to be known for getting the first party you're invited to shut down."

"I won't get it shut down," I said with a sigh.

She practically screamed, "They'll never invite you to another one," horror filling her eyes. I personally didn't think that would be such a bad thing. The races had finished and now the students from different clubs were playing hungry hippos using baskets and rolling carts.

"You do have Jessica's number, right?" she asked, not allowing me to enjoy the pep rally.

"No but I can get it from her in class, can't I?"

"Yeah, if you want to ask in front of Mallory, I guess you can." Emily had tried to warn me after my lunch encounter with her and Britney that Mallory would never let me into the party. I didn't understand it, but I was guessing that Miss Ghost was eavesdropping on a conversation she shouldn't have and heard something she shouldn't have.

I wondered if those conversations happened before or after her little fit. I knew now wasn't the time to bring that up to her, but she had to see how her crashing all my things looks to outsiders. Mallory was freaked at the library.

"What? Is Mallory going to tell her no with me standing right there?" I asked, eying Emily.

"Probably not, but I still think you need to talk to Jessica, without Mallory," she said, crossing her arms and legs. She wanted me to trust her opinion of Mallory just because the Mallory I've seen in class isn't mean, so I don't understand her problem with her.

"Fine, I'll talk to her after the pep rally," I finally said just to break the tension.

"Yeah, good luck with that," Emily laughed at me.

"Why what's so funny?" I asked, searching for Jessica's caramel hair in the crowd of students.

"Because," Emily started to say, pointing in the direction of the band, "she's that flute player sitting right there." My eyes locked onto Jessica, playing whatever pep music the band had been playing for the games.

"What, can I not talk to the band kids now either?" I asked, looking back at Emily confused. I could see Jessica clear as day, and she was almost right in front of where I was sitting. As soon as we wrapped up, I could run straight down and talk to her while she was putting away her instrument.

"You really are just a silly city girl, aren't you," Emily said, adding a twang of country to her voice.

"If I could smack you right now I would," I said, once again wanting to shoot useless daggers at her.

"They'll dismiss you by grade and then by anyone in the pep rally," she said. "Usually Cheer and Dance Team, Football players, then band."

"Why do they do it that way?" I asked.

"Because the football players shout down the hall and the band plays the school song back to class," she said, shrugging. "School figured it would be less of a distraction that way."

"Shit, well I can still see her afterwards when we walk back to class," I said, trying to think on my feet.

"That's an option." Emily started thinking. I could see she was formulating a plan, the wheels rapidly turning in her head.

"Or you could always go to the homecoming game tonight," she said finally, shooting up like the idea bolt hit her.

"I'm not going to that," I protested.

"Excuse me but why not?" she said, practically rolling her eyes at me.

"I'm not a big sports person." I tried defending myself. I definitely didn't like football because I never understood any of it. Plus I hated having my Sundays held hostage by football season. It would annoy me when I was a kid who just wanted to watch her cartoons before having school again.

"You're never going to survive here."

"And why is that," I scoffed at her.

"Most the people who go to the football game aren't sports people," she said, shifting her whole body to face me. "It's what you do in a small town that has nothing to do."

"Are you saying everyone goes to the football game?" I asked not being able to imagine 40 and 50 year olds attending a high school game.

"For the homecoming game? Oh you bet your ass everyone is gonna be there," she said, slapping her knee.

"Well I still don't think I really want to go," I protested.

"Fine, but it's your funeral," she said, turning to give me the cold shoulder "Trust me, people will notice you weren't there, even if you don't think they will."

"I'm completely invisible to these people," I said to her but she started to vanish from sight, actually giving me a cold chill down my shoulders. When she completely cleared from my vision, I realized a freshman boy had been staring at me, making me realize I wasn't as invisible as I thought. I didn't know how long he had been staring, but I was hoping it wasn't the whole conversation with Emily. I quickly averted his gaze and focused back on the rally.

"Before we bring out our homecoming court," the girl MC said.

"It is time to announce the winners for the Best Teacher award," the boy replied.

"The students have picked three teachers to recognize based on a number of things," she continued. "As we call the teachers, we will read a quote left by one of their students."

"Can we get a drum roll, please?" the boy asked, pointing to the band.

On queue, the drummers rattled on their drums. The students around me did the same on their knees. The room buzzed with anticipation. I didn't know there were any teacher awards, and they definitely didn't ask me to vote. I tried to think of the teachers I would have even listed, but I drew a blank as the drums continued in my ears.

"Our first teacher is," the girl said, reaching for an envelope. "Mrs. Weathers who teaches junior and senior literature." She handed the next envelope to her partner as she continued reading. "Mrs. Weathers is my vote for Best Teacher because she has always been so patient with me."

"That is very sweet," the boy replied, tearing into his envelope.

"Let's give a hand to Mrs. Weathers."

A medium built woman made her way down the bleachers from the teacher section. She was grinning from ear to ear, but her face was bright red. Her long skirt flowed as she crossed the court to stand next to the Emcees.

"Our next teacher we want to recognize is Mr. Blackford." The boy paused as he read the name. "I think Mr. Blackford should get Best Teacher because he has given so much back to the community and he makes science fun."

"That he did," the girl said, clapping her hands together. "Give it up for Mr. Blackford."

He was sitting opposite of where Mrs. Weathers was, but he followed her path down to the group. He reached out to shake her hand, as their mouths moved in a pleasant conversation. He towered over her as their conversation continued.

"And our final teacher for Best Teacher is…" the girl fiddled with the envelope, leaving everyone on their seats. "Mr. Wright," she yelled into the microphone.

The senior section jumped from their seats, cheering. They hollered as Mr. Wright made his way down to the other teachers. He was an older man who hunched when he walked. His scrunched face caused him to frown. The boy read off the reason he was chosen, but the senior class celebrated too loud for him to be heard.

The teachers were each handed a small clear plague and a medal that the emcees took turns putting on. When they got to Mr. Wright, they both grabbed the ribbon around the medal and placed it around his neck. Once they were finished, they embraced him into a hug. Seniors ran down to do the same, before being ushered away with Mr. Wright.

"Alrighty crowd," the girl said. "It is time for the final event."

The homecoming court was being brought out. Four boys and four girls from each grade were nominated to be on the court. At the football game they bring the seniors out during half time and announce who won Homecoming King and Queen. At least that was what Emily was telling me a few weeks back when nominations for it had opened. She suggested I throw my name in the running and I laughed at her.

After the court walked back to their area, the MC's announced that was the end of the pep rally. And as Emily had said, they released the freshman class back first, then mine and so on. I got up when they said I could go, but I could hardly take my eyes off of Jessica. If I could get her number before school ended, I wouldn't have to go to the football game.

I didn't realize how little I was paying attention to where I was going, until I nearly missed a step on the bleacher. I stumbled for a second, attracting a few eyes but not as many as if I would have gone tumbling down the steps in front of the majority of the school. I followed the sea of students down the hall, walking slowly. The whole sophomore class had passed me and the juniors were starting to as well.

I heard the beat of the drums first, then the loud trumpets, followed by the rest of the band. Jessica had finally left the gym. I turned down a corner and waited for the rest of the juniors to pass. The seniors and football players came almost together, one group celebrating their potential win, the other celebrating their potential freedom. The band was next.

Unfortunately, the flutes were on the other side of the hall. Jessica was nowhere near me when she finally passed. I had waited this whole time and I wasn't going to miss my opportunity. I could see her high pony bouncing away from me. I took the first step when someone called my name.

"Miss Weber, I don't believe that's the way to your home room," a teacher called from behind me.

There was no arguing, so I turned down the hallway heading to my home room. I realized the teacher was Mr. Gantz which was how he knew I was going the wrong way. I flopped into my chair has he followed behind me back into his classroom. We didn't have much time left of school so most of the students were still up, ready to bolt out the door.

When the bell rang out, they exploded into the hallway. Knowing I would be waiting for mom, I grabbed my books and slowly made my way to the lockers. The chaos was dying down as more students left the school. I got everything I needed out of my locker, slung my bag over my shoulder and headed out to find mom.

Mom had her hair in pigtail braids with red and blue ribbons in it. She was more prepared for spirit week compared to me. She had told her class if they participated in the spirit week they would get extra credit. Of course, she wanted to be in the spirit with them.

She spent most of the car rides back home telling me how crazy her students were getting with their spirit costumes. Today was no different. We exchanged stories of the wild spirit people had. I had told her about an afro man and she told me about a paint boy. We both laughed at the image of what the other was saying. It felt like no time before we were back at the apartment.

"Do you think you will participate more next year?" she asked, pointing at my get up.

"I don't know. We'll have to see, I guess," I said shrugging. I probably wouldn't go as far out there next year but maybe I would draw whiskers on my face for animal day. Something to show a little bit of spirit.

"Are we going to the game tonight?" she asked, holding the front door open for me.

"You wanna go to that, too," I groaned.

"Well, no I guess I don't if I'm going to crimp your style," she said putting her hand on her hip and giving me a look of offense.

"That's not what I meant," I said, throwing my hands up in defense, "Just some kids at school said everyone goes because in a small town there's nothing to do." Mom nodded her head and gave me a look similar to the one Emily gave when she told me that.

"I just wasn't expecting us to go," I said.

"We don't have to if you don't want to," she said relaxing her posture, "I just assumed you would be bored on a Friday night. I mean we watch TV everyday."

I knew I needed to go to the game, but it was only to get Jessica's number. I didn't really want to be there for the whole game. I knew mom wouldn't want to just be there for a few minutes, but I also knew that mom wouldn't not go with me. So I guess we were going to the game.

"No actually," I said, "I don't want to be bored in the apartment tonight, let's go to the game."

"You aren't going in a college sweatshirt," she said walking past me and back to her room. I followed her not understanding what she was getting at.

"Why not?" I asked, "I don't have any school merch." She ignored my question and started rummaging through her dresser drawers. Whatever she was looking for wasn't there.

"Somewhere I have a Red Warriors shirt that you can wear tonight," she said, going into her closet.

"What are you going to wear then?" I asked. She had a red shirt on but it had a big blue T.M.S. that stood for Twindle Middle School. She had made the shirt herself for spirit week, so I didn't think she planned on wearing it after today or for the game.

"Can I not wear this?" she asked looking down at her shirt.

"I mean it is a high school game," I shrugged, "I wasn't sure if you wanted a middle school shirt." I put air quotes around "middle school."

"It doesn't really bother me," she said going back into the closet, "A lot of my students have older siblings so I'm sure I will see them." She reappeared with a red bundle in her hand.

"Here you go," she handed me the shirt.

"Thanks."

"Go get ready and we can go see if there's any tailgates happening," mom said, grabbing her makeup bag. She already had blue and red eyeshadow on, so I didn't know what more she could do.

"What type of makeup do you think I should try," I asked her when she walked into our bathroom. She looked at me in delight.

"Let me do it for you when you're dressed," she got all giddy like a schoolgirl. I went into my room and switched my skirt for jeans. I picked my shredded jeans in case it was too hot for them. I figure once the sun started to set it would be perfect.

I took off the Ohio State sweater in exchange for mom's. I didn't realize that it was going to be a v-neck. With the bra I was wearing, my boobs nearly fell out of the shirt. I readjusted the top to cover more, but it started to show my waist line. I was more comfortable with some cleavage over people seeing my underwear.

I walked back to the bathroom, where mom was still applying makeup. She had touched up her face makeup so she didn't look as shiny anymore. She added just a small wing to her lid. She was adding another layer of mascara when I came up. She saw me in the mirror.

"Are you ready for your makeup," she asked. She set the mascara down and looked at her watch. "I could do a natural look with some red and blue football player lines." I nodded my head and sat on the toilet lid so she could start doing my makeup. Once she finished up, we took one last look at ourselves in the mirror before gathering our stuff and heading to the game.

At the game, the air was filled with hot dogs and popcorn. My stomach groaned, longing for a hot dog. I could tell by the way mom's head turned when she exited the car, that she had the same feeling. We both passed looks of agreement that we were going to find the source. Younger students scampered past us, apparently recognizing my mom.

"Hey Miss Santos," they said, "You wanna see us play ball over there." One boy pointed over to an empty part of the lot where other boys had been throwing a football.

"Maybe in a bit," my mom said, patting the first one on the head, "I'm hungry so I need some food beforehand." They all agreed and said something about seeing her in a bit.

"I didn't realize you went back to your maiden name," I said, puzzled by the kids name for her.

"Oh yeah, I changed it back for teaching," she said like it was no big deal.

"What? Why?" I was more confused by her answer when I think she meant to provide clarity.

"I didn't want to be associated with your father anymore," she said shrugging, "plus more people in town recognize me as a Santos anyway."

"You didn't think to tell me?" I asked, a little frustrated to learn my mom didn't share my last name anymore either.

"I assumed you would have been supportive of my decision," she said, taken aback.

"It isn't that I'm not supportive. I'm hurt to learn through your students that we don't share a last name anymore."

"Have you not checked any of the mail?" she asked, her hand on her hip, "Everything has said Carrie Santos, not Weber, for months."

We had arrived at the source of the delicious smells, our hunger distracting the fight. There was a small line of people standing by a blue pickup truck. On the other side was a grill and a dad wearing his Warrior team shirt. He was grilling burgers and hot dogs. Perpendicular to him, who I assumed to be his wife, offering plates, buns, and topping for both meats. There was a small sign on her table that said what the price was.

"Do you want a burger or hot dog?" mom asked, turning back to me once we got closer to the front of the line.

"Um, I think I want a hot dog," I said, tapping my chin. The thought of a mouthwatering hot dog occupied me more than the thought of mom's name change.

"Good I was going to get a burger," mom said, looking at me.

"Oh my lord, is that Carrie," a shrill voice said. My mom and I both turned to the voice. It was an older lady, maybe mid 60's. She had some gray streaks peeking through but mostly the hair was an auburn color.

"Mrs. Crawford," mom said, looking at the woman as if she was trying to place her.

"Yes!" the lady threw her hands in the air and came closer to us, embracing my mom in a hug. "It's been years dear!"

"I know it has." Mom begrudgingly took the hug. "I think I was probably my daughter's age." The lady looked my mother in the eyes, hers wider than the moon.

"You have a daughter?" she asked, "How are you old enough for that?"

"Yes, this is my daughter," mom said, grabbing my arm and pulling me in, "Charlotte."

"Next," said the grill guy's wife. We were the next ones.

"Okay, dear well I'm going to go inside and find me and we can catch up," Mrs. Crawford said.

"Yes, I will," mom said to her, "One of each," she said.

We found seats near the student section. I had noticed that the band was still inside practicing like the football player. There was still at least ten minutes before the game actually started. The perfect amount of time to eat our food before I went to find Jessica.

I had finished my hot dog and mom returned from the trash right as the kick off was happening. The band was on the field playing loud notes. I wasn't a music person but I really didn't think they were playing a song or tune. Once the football game actually started, the band moved to the bleachers.

I waited a few minutes after they got settled to go over there. Of course, once I stood up they started playing. I leaned down to my mom to let her know I was going to say hello to a friend real quick. She seemed excited that I had friends and shooed me there. I went over to the band section. The ramp was being blocked by two moms wearing Red Warrior Band Mom shirts. I tried to pass by them.

"Where do you think you're going?" one asked, putting her hand on her hips.

"Um to see a friend real quick," I said once again trying to pass.

"Only band and guard kids in this section," the other one said blocking me…

"Not even to say hello," I said, adding an extra pinch of attitude.

"No, not even," the one started.

"They need to focus, now go," finished the other.

I walked away in disbelief. They seemed super rude and the band wasn't even playing at the time. I was going to need a new plan if I was going to get Jessica's number tonight. I walked back to where mom was and luckily, it was in a good spot where I could see Jessica and the other flutes. I would just wait for her to leave the band section.

I waited through the first two quarters without Jessica moving. Finally she got up, but I realized it was with the rest of the band to perform the halftime show. I didn't know what to expect after the halftime show. The cheerleaders left the sidelines and the band took the field. They're performance was good but there were only about 40 to 50 kids on the field.

They all came back to the bleachers and slowly got their stuff situated. I was staring at each kid as they put their instruments away and changed out of the top part of their uniforms. Jessica took a few seconds to get up to the flute section. Her parents had stopped her and taken pictures before she could change. She gathered her flute friends and left the bleachers. They headed to the concessions and bathrooms. Now was my chance.

"Hey mom," I said standing up, "I think I am gonna run to the restroom real quick while nothing is happening." She agreed that now was a good time to go since most people went during the performance parts.

I didn't want to run to Jessica because I knew my mom would question that and I didn't want Jessica to see me running at her. I just walked with a purpose to where I saw her head. All the band kids had their long hair in tight little buns on their heads. It was hard to tell who was who from the back.

I searched the crowd looking for Jessica. I didn't know if she went to get food or if she ran to the bathroom. I was starting to panic because I didn't want to miss my opportunity. I also didn't want to hear Emily complain that I didn't get her number.

I was so consumed with panic that I didn't realize there was a girl on my left. We collided shoulders into one another. She was taller and nearly knocked me down. Luckily she grabbed me before I could topple to the ground. I looked to see and it was Jessica!

"Oh hey," I said, way too excited. "Thank you for catching me." I tried to calm my voice.

"Oh hey girl," Jessica said.

"I'm so sorry I was looking for my mom and not paying attention," I lied.

"You're totally good," she assured. She started to turn to go back to the forbidden band section. I knew I need to act quickly for the number.

"Oh hey real quick," I rambled, so she would turn back. "I realized after our study date, I didn't grab your number.

"Oh shoot! You're right." she said, reaching into her pocket, "Here give me your hand and I can write it down." She licked the pen to get it writing and wrote her number down on my hand.

"Thanks," I said, looking at the back of my hand.

"No problem, but hey I got to get back to the section or I'll get yelled at," she said, turning back to the band. We waved goodbye and went our separate ways.

I went back to sit with mom. She noticed the number on my hand and I had lied and said it was from earlier when I said hi the first time. It was a lie since those band moms denied me but I didn't want her to realize I just left to stalk a classmate so a dead girl wouldn't bully me over the weekend.

I sent Jessica a text so she would have my number. She responded with:

Hey, I realized I didn't give you information for the Halloween party.

Address is County Rd 600, in case you need it. Party won't start til 9pm. Can't wait to see your spookiest costume!

CHAPTER SIX

After scoring my invite with Jessica, I needed to secure my permission with mom. I didn't think she would really have an issue with it since it was Jessica, but Emily had been hounding me about a costume since we came back from the football game.

"So what are you going to wear?" she asked, sitting on my bed as I flipped the light on.

I let out a scream, thinking it was an intruder at first. Once I realized it was only her, I knew the scream was going to raise alarm bells. Mom came racing down the hall, peering in the doorway over my shoulder. She was looking directly at Emily, but I knew she couldn't see her.

"What's the matter?" she asked, cradling me in her arms.

"I saw a spider but it ran when I screamed," I lied.

"Oh god." She shuddered. "Was it big?"

"Huge."

"Well come into my room for now."

Mom had saved me from Emily's questioning that time, but she continued to follow me around, wanting to know what my plan was. She would throw random ideas at me, whenever they popped into her head. I knew I needed to get something figured out soon, before she drove me mad. Emily was a great friend, but definitely a pushy one sometimes.

"I'll ask mom tonight over dinner," I murmured, "Then we can plan costumes."

"Fine, but I want you to know that everyone is going all out," she huffed at me.

"Have we been eavesdropping again?" I chuckled.

"Halloween is a serious event," she said, stomping her foot.

"Well let me get that permission." I pointed towards the living room. "Before we get too serious," pointing the same finger between Emily and myself.

"Well then go do it," she urged me.

I knew she was right and that no time would be better than now. Swinging the door open, I was welcomed with the clatter of pots and pans. The warm embrace of nostalgia took over as cumin, chili powder, and garlic filled my nostrils. The air was thick with savory steam wafting from the kitchen. I loved mom's homemade tamales, so I let the smell carry me there.

Simmering meat masks my steps, or maybe mom was too focused on the corn husks. She was working her magic, adding the masa then filling. I inhaled deeply as the corners of my mouth turned up. The air filled a sense of tradition I didn't know I was missing in the moment. The apartment had never felt more like home then right now. The rich flavors complimented by the love of mom. I yearned for one, as she continued folding and tying the tamales.

"What do you want?" she asked, immediately knowing my agenda.

"How did you know I wanted something?" I asked, trying to evade her question.

"Because I'm your mother and I can always tell when you want something." She was right about that.

"Jessica is throwing a small party for Halloween," I said in a rush.

"And you think you're going to get to go?"

"Well Jessica did invite me," I tried justifying.

"But I didn't give you permission."

"I know," I started, "But I am asking for permission now."

"I don't know Charlie," she said, rubbing the back of her neck. "Bad things happen on Halloween."

"Mom, that is just some superstition," I said, trying to reassure her, but mostly trying to get her to let me go.

"I'll have to think about it," she said.

I had to leave it at that. I knew from previous times of asking her for things that I'll have to think about it meant I needed to give her time to rationalize whatever her irrational thoughts were. If I kept bugging her about it, she would end up saying no. So I took it as a yes for now, planning a costume with Emily.

"What did she say?" Emily asked, bolting up from my desk chair as I came into the room.

"She needs some time to think about it," I replied, plopping back onto my bed.

My stomach growled in response, too. Sadly, mom still needed to steam the tamales so I knew I was going to have to wait on those. I wanted a distraction from food, Emily was getting ready to be the perfect distraction.

"Do you want to search up costume ideas?" I asked.

Her head spun faster than a starved cat hearing a can of food, hands clasped between her chest. Her smile was barely contained as she jumped over to me. I pushed myself off the bed, going into embrace before the cold chill broke through my reality. She didn't let it phase her though as she continued bouncing between her feet.

"What are you thinking?" she asked. I moved to my desk, booting the laptop.

I thought back through my previous years of costumes, trying to remember the last time I actually dressed up for Halloween. The only one I could think of at the moment was a generic princess costume that the store had. The tiara had flown away before I made it off the driveway. *Cheap paper crap.*

"I don't really know." I shrugged, "what wouldn't be lame?"

"I have made plenty of suggestions," Emily said, her eyes rolling.

I ignored the sarcasm in her voice as I tried thinking through options. I wasn't really sure what the Halloween store would have, so I thought maybe we should go there before getting my hopes up too much. The basic options she provided would definitely be there, but I wasn't sure I wanted basic.

"Is there a Halloween store?" I asked, realizing I didn't know where I would actually get my costume from.

"Hmm," Emily replied, too busy checking herself out in my mirror. "Oh, yeah Twindle has the Twindle Terror in the main square."

"The Twindle Terror?"

"Yeah, it's next to the little boutique. I think it's Zoey's Boutique."

"Mom got a few of her blouses from there," I replied, remembering the terrors of school shopping. "But I don't remember a store called Twindle Terror?"

"It's only called Twindle Terror during Halloween," she said, waving me off.

"So they just rent for Halloween?" I asked, still confused by it. "Do they really make enough to rent the space for a whole year?"

"It isn't closed during the other months." Emily fixed the out of place curl, "They're a seasonal store."

"Seasonal store?"

"Yeah the Terror part of the sign is replaced with whatever month or holiday it is."

"One stop shop," I chuckled.

"Exactly, that's where most students get their books."

"Wait, Twindle books?" I asked.

"Yup, that's the one." She said, snapping her fingers at me.

"Is it close enough to walk?"

"How far is downtown from here?"

"Not walking distance sadly," I replied.

I wasn't fully sure how to convince mom to let me go Halloween shopping for a party she hadn't fully said yes to. Emily paced in front of me, causing my brain to stir. Even if I could get there, I wasn't sure I had enough saved from birthday money for a costume. Searching for the little pink snout, I went to my shelves to see what I was working with.

Grabbing the plastic pig, I flipped him over to pop the bottom off. Green covered the hole, which I hoped was a good sign. In the past, I've shoved bunches of one's in here. When I came back to open it, I would like to hit the jackpot, only to realize there was about ten dollars. I learned my lesson, shaking the wad of cash loose onto the desk.

There were twenty, a five, and a few dollar bills. That should have given me enough to get something basic. Emily didn't think it would be smart for me to go as out as the other kids, since it was my first party. I didn't argue with her, because I knew that her gossip skills were really my ticket to having a social life at this point. A knock came from my door, as mom slowly pushed her way in.

"Hey," she said. "I've got some errands to run in town. Would you want to come with me?"

It was as if she had heard my prayers. I glanced towards Emily, watching her head shake with enthusiasm. I had the money and now I had the way.

"Of course," I replied. "Do you think I could walk around the little shop area?"

"Sure, that's where my shopping is," she replied.

I grabbed the money off the desk and shoved it into my back pocket, following mom out of my bedroom. I figured Emily would trail behind us. I threw my shoes on, while mom gathered her necessitates.

"Keys, wallet, phone," she repeated over as she moved through the kitchen. "Ready to go?" she asked once she acquired everything.

"Let's hit the road," I said, bouncing up from the cushion.

Getting to the main square wasn't a long car ride. When the town only has 5 stoplights, most things aren't a long car ride. Mom listed off the errands she needed to run today. An envelope and some boxes sat in the back seat with Emily.

"Donating some clothes?" I asked, pointing to the box.

"And some other things," she replied. "What are you shopping for?"

I wasn't sure what to tell her. She hadn't fully agreed to let me go to the party but I couldn't really wait for her to say yes either. I also didn't remember all the stores over there.

"I think I am going to try to find something to wear for Halloween," I said, realizing the longer I stalled the more likely mom would realize I was trying to lie to her. "Since it is on a Friday, the school has been talking about letting us wear costumes."

It wasn't a lie. The school was considering it, but talking with Emily, it sounded like they always considered it before agreeing to it. The administration just creates new costume guidelines to give out based on what the previous year was willing to push. .

"That must be a fun time," mom replied. The middle school didn't allow costumes because it was too much of a distraction for them. "What did you have in mind?"

"We'll see what the stores have to offer," I chuckled.

The main square parking lot was fairly empty for the weekend. There was a spot near the front stores that was shaded by one of the town planted trees. Getting out of the car, I helped mom grab the box from the back. The donation center wasn't too far from the front shops.

"I'm going to run this over," mom said, hoisting the box onto her hip. "Do you want to go shopping and meet back at the car in an hour?"

"Do you really think it will take a whole hour to shop?"

"Maybe not for you," she replied, laughing. "But for me, yeah."

"Okay, an hour it is," I said.

"Please be safe and don't leave the square," mom called over her shoulder as she walked away.

"You be safe too," I called back.

The square only had four main shops and the other buildings were town buildings. The town hall sat in the back of the square, but was taller than any of the other shops. The donation center was technically a second building to the town hall. It would only take someone five minutes to walk around the square, so I didn't really worry about getting lost.

"Do you know which way you're going?" Emily asked.

"Yeah, I think so," I replied, walking to the direction of the stores.

Luckily, there was a giant black and orange Twindle Terror sign once we turned the corner. All the stores had added their Halloween decorations out, so the walk felt like a night of trick or treating. Well without the bonus of candy. One of the stores had a little motion sensor witch that cackled when we walked by.

"That has to get annoying," Emily said, turning back to look at it.

"Hopefully you can't hear it from inside," I replied, pulling open the shop doors.

We were embraced by the spooky Halloween immediately when we walked through. The black and orange combo was plastered on all the walls, making it hard to easily tell where things were. The top parts of the walls had labels, but their color matched everything else. The sea of black and orange caused my head to spin.

"Where to first?" Emily asked as she glanced around.

"I guess the teen section," I replied, pointing to the words now that my eyes were adjusted to the view. I quickly dropped my hand back to my side, realizing I was pointing for the air to the employees. I maneuvered around the scary black cats and censored monsters to get to the costumes.

The shop really had more decoration and accessories, not a lot of costume ideas. A handful of options hung in plastic packages on the racks. The back wall was covered in different colored accessories. Wigs, gloves, and tutus in each color of the rainbow were available.

"What do you think I could do with those?" I asked, pointing at them.

"You could be an M&M or maybe a crayon," Emily replied, looking over at them. "It doesn't look like you'll have many choices."

"No, I guess not," I said, pulling the different plastic packages apart to see what the costume photo was. There were the standard suggestions that Emily had already made like cat and nurse, but there were a few better options as well. I pulled the Goddess costume off the shelf and moved over to one of the mirrors that hung off the walls.

"What do you think of this?" I asked, holding the package over my chest, photo side out. I was trying to envision what the long gown would look like on my body. The model looked like an Amazon woman, so I was probably only half as tall as her.

"Not sure it would be a good idea," Emily called from behind me.

"Why not?" I asked, turning to look at her. She moved closer to the mirror so we both looked into it. My reflection was the only one to return the gaze. Moving the package up, I reposition the photo over my body.

"It's white," she replied. "And it is a barn party. You will most definitely get it dirty."

"Well, I'll probably only want to wear it once," I said, trying to justify it. The gold detailed rope that wrapped around the torso of the model hugged her in the right curves. I wanted to look like a goddess like she did.

"Check the price," Emily said, her head cocked to the side.

I flipped the package over, looking for the little barcode. My eyes felt like they were going to bulge out of my head when I saw three digits underneath it. I definitely didn't have enough savings to afford that and there was no way mom would agree to it.

"I guess that one is a no," I said, reluctantly putting it back on the rack with the others.

"Come look at these ones," Emily hollered from the corner next to the rainbow wigs.

She was looking at some makeshift costumes. There were face paint options, jewels that could be added to the skin, and fangs in tiny clear coffin boxes. It was another accessory section but there were also clothes like a cute little blue overall skirt. It had tutu ruffles underneath to help poof it out. There were also some This is my Costume shirts available.

"If all else fails, I can get that." I laughed as I read the shirt.

"Are you talking to yourself?" asked a cold voice from behind me. I turned around to be blinded by the neon orange of the employee shirt.

"I didn't know you worked here," I replied once I recognized the jagged haircut.

"So does that mean you were talking to yourself?" Britney asked again.

"Just laughing at the shirts," I replied, hitching my thumb in that direction. "I needed a costume."

"You still go trick or treating?" she asks, chuckling.

"No, it's for Jessica's party."

Her eyes narrowed as a bitter smile took over her face. She stepped a little closer, bringing her head closer to mine when she spoke. Not expecting it, I took a step back, bumping into the accessories. They clinked in response.

"Jessica's party," Britney repeated. "She invited you to her party?"

"Yeah why wouldn't she?"

"Because you're a bitch and a freak," she replied, pulling back and crossing her arms.

"Excuse me?" I asked, my jaw falling to the floor.

"You heard me," she answered. "I don't like you and Jessica should stay away."

"You don't like me," I repeated. "This is like the second time we've talked." *And if anyone was a bitch then, it was you*, I thought.

"You're using this party to climb the social ranks at school, aren't you?"

"What social ranks?" I asked, truly confused by where she was coming from.

"I know what game you're playing little girl," she replied, leaning in. She pointed a sharp red nail at me. It looked like a blood soaked dagger.

"Ask her why she's friends with Jessica," Emily said over Britney's shoulder. Her arms were crossed and a smirk sat on her face. "Gone on, ask her."

"Why are you friends with Jessica?" I asked. Britney blinked as her head shook at my question.

"What?" she spat.

"I asked, why are you friends with Jessica?"

"Because we've known each other forever," she scoffed, waving her hand dismissively.

"And not because she wants to get back with her brother?" Emily asked. "She's using Jessica to try to get close to him again."

"So it has nothing to do with her brother?" I asked, raising my brow and trying to imitate Emily's smirk.

"What did you ask me?" Britney asked.

Her voice was hot as her nostrils flared. I watched her chest heave up and down as she planned what insults she wanted to hurl at me. I wasn't sure repeating Emily was the best idea but I didn't like Britney trying to project herself onto me. I wanted to be friends with Jessica because she seemed nice, and more normal than talking to a ghost.

"Everything all right over here," a woman stepped in.

She didn't look to be too much older than me, but she had her eyebrow and lip pierced so I assumed she was at least in her twenties. Her short hair had been spiked up with gel, almost standing straight up from her head.

"Everything's great," Britney said, bouncing up. She replaced her scowl with a bright and chipper smile. "I was just helping this customer find something."

Just like that, the cloud that was casting over Britney was gone. Her eyes almost seemed to sparkle under the pressure of the woman. I watched her back stiffen as the woman continued to eye her.

"That's great to hear," she replied. "You don't want anyone making complaints."

At the threat of a complaint, Britney shot me a nasty look. I wasn't the type to leave reviews and I really didn't want to dig myself in deeper with Britney. I figured it would be better to just try to keep my distance from her.

The woman and Britney walked off, leaving me alone with the assorted costumes again. I tried shaking Britney off, remembering the reason I was here. Emily moved back to my side, close enough that wandering employees wouldn't hear us this time.

"What about that?" she asked, pointing to one of the packages.

It had a shorter girl on it with a straw hat. We agreed to do something cute and simple, grabbing the package and heading up to the front. The costume was perfect and would probably leave me with enough money to get something else with mom. The associate who stepped in between Britney had moved behind the cash register.

"All set?" she asked.

"I think so," I replied, setting everything down for her.

"Sorry about Britney," she said, scanning the items. "She's working on her attitude."

"No worries."

"But you should definitely give her the name of your stylists," she said, pointing at my head. "Few months back she had a bad botch, came out oranger than the orange."

"Oh really," I said. "Luckily, this is natural."

She handed me the bag, letting Emily and I escape from the weird tension that was growing over us. I could see Britney hiding in the rows to watch the check-out interaction, but I wasn't sure if she was actually close enough to hear anything. Makes sense why she was so mean the day in the courtyard. *Britney is Pumpkin Head.*

CHAPTER SEVEN

"You're not really going to go out in that, are you?" mom asked, looking me up and down with a disapproving look.

I could feel my heart drop to my stomach. I was sure mom heard the thud as it fell. It had taken her so long to actually agree to let me go and now because of my costume, I'm going to lose that. I looked back in my mirror, the blue ruffles from the overall skirt were still in my hand.

"I mean yeah," I said, grabbing the little skirt and looking at myself. "What's wrong with it?"

"It's a cute costume, honey." She hesitated before rushing to my side to assure me, "It's going to be in the low 40's tonight. I think you'll just be too cold."

"Is it really going to be that cold?" My eyes practically bugged out of my head. I stupidly forgot to check the weather while Emily and I were costume hunting. It was a cute orange and white off the shoulder crop top. It would have shown stomach, but the overall skirt covered it. Mom was right, it would definitely be too cold for this outfit. I didn't have a replacement though.

I could feel my heart begin to race. I was kicking myself for not looking at the weather beforehand and for not picking something warmer. My brain felt foggy and my eyes got watery, blurring mom from my view. I didn't have back-up plan and I really didn't want to still be that freak girl who wouldn't wear a costume to a Halloween party.

"It'll be okay. We will figure something out." Mom came to my side and consoled me. This only unleashed the gate. Tears poured from my eyes and I crumbled into her arms. She didn't say anything, she just let me sit there and let my emotions out for a minute. She always knew what I needed, even if I didn't.

I let out my final tear after about 10 minutes of being curled in her arms. I took a deep breath in and finally accepted what the situation was. I had enough clothes that I could pull something together and still be a scarecrow. Different articles of clothes raced through my head.

"What do you think we can do?" I finally asked. Mom gave her angelic smile and I felt much better.

"Well why don't you go into your room and start looking for options," she said "I'll go into my room and see if I can't find anything plaid or warmer for you."

"Plaid? Would that be a good option?"

"Do you still want to wear that shirt? Because I can find a cardigan or shawl," she offered. I looked down at the shirt again. It was super cute but since it was off the shoulder, I feared that a jacket or something over it would make the sleeves uncomfortable. Plus the cropped aspect of it didn't seem appealing when I knew it would be almost cold enough to snow.

"No, I think you had a good idea with the plaid," I said, rethinking the whole costume, "I think I am going to find a white tee and jeans." She smiled and we both headed off to our rooms. I came back into mine to see Emily where I left her.

"So what did your mom think of it?" she asked. I frowned.

"It's gonna be too cold, so we're changing it up."

"What's the new plan?" she asked, moving to her feet. I shrugged, unsure how to answer. I knew I wanted to find my best bell bottom jeans, but I wasn't sure if I had actually unpacked them. I had a few boxes in the way back of my closet that I hadn't fully unpacked. I hadn't missed the clothes in there so I never cared, but tonight was a big night.

I pulled the first box out into the bedroom, plopping on the floor. I tore through the box as witch sisters sang their spell songs on my TV. Emily had asked for a Halloween Mixtape so she could dance while we got ready. I had put the Halloween CD mom used for when she passed out trick or treat candy into my CD player.

The box didn't really have anything of use in it. It was mostly old tee shirts from my old school. I shoved the clothes back into the box and went to grab the other one. I did the same motion while Emily looked through my makeup collection. I didn't have too much there, just some foundation, pencil liner and mascara. She had scolded me when she realized that.

"What kind of scarecrow makeup do you plan on doing with these?" she asked.

"I was just going to ask my mom," I said pulling out a few pairs of jeans, "She has a few different palettes so I'm sure one of them will work."

"Good. This night needs to go perfect," Emily said, putting an emphasis on perfection. I agreed with her, finally finding the perfect jeans I wanted. I threw the extra clothes back in and out the box away. I had already ruined my clean room trying to get ready and I didn't need to make it worse by throwing a whole box of clothes on the floor.

I ripped the overalls off and threw the shirt into my laundry basket. Slipping into the jeans, I tried to remember where I put my white slutty tank top. If I couldn't wear the cute skirt, then I was going to wear my spaghetti strap tank that laced up in the front. It showed just enough for me to still feel comfortable. Mom came in with the perfect pumpkin orange flannel.

"I found this," she said, putting it in the air for me to get a clear view.

"That'll be perfect." I screamed. I jumped with joy all the way to her to grab it from her. I slid my arms through the plush softness of the velvet sleeves.

"Good, and those are the jeans you're going to wear?" she asked, pointing down at them. I shook my head and she confirmed it was a good choice.

"Do you think you could do a scarecrow face on me, momma?" I asked, batting my lashes at her, hoping she'd take the bait.

"Oh, darling," she said. "Of course, I can do that." She started listing off the different types of products she would need to achieve the look. As she continued to rattle things off she walked away, presumably to the bathroom to gather everything together.

"What do you think of this outfit?" Emily said as she spun around in a shepherd girl's costume. It didn't look bad but I was hoping she didn't assume she would be at the party. Her stunt at the library had put a crack in my trust for her. I knew she wanted to live through me, but she was going to ruin my social life if she continued following me around when I hung out with the living.

"I like it, but where are you going to wear it?" I asked. I saw it, it was there for only a brief second, but I saw the anger flash across her eyes after I asked. It was the same anger she'd give when I brought up her death. I knew it too well for her to try hiding it.

"I'm wearing it to the party," she said, flipping her hair behind her like she was the main guest people were waiting to see that night. "Do you think I get all my best gossip by sitting at home and watching crime shows with you and Carrie?"

I knew she only flung it back on me because she couldn't really experience the party the way I was going to. I should have assumed she would follow me, I knew she didn't get her gossip from just listening to the kids at school. I didn't want her thinking I want to talk all night when I want to make friends with my living peers. I appreciate her, but I'm tired of people staring at me for laughing at a joke she told, or having to pretend like I'm calling old friends.

"I guess you're right," I said, softening my voice. "I can't expect my best journalist to get her story here in this apartment."

"Damn right you can't," she said, crossing her arms. "I'm still not sure what I should wear." My mom started calling me from the bathroom, signaling she gathered what she needed to transform me. Emily waved me to go.

"I'll bring potential ideas to you as I come up with them," she said as I walked out of the room.

Mom had all her products laid out across the bathroom counter. It looked like a bigger mess than the one I made in my room. I sat on the toilet seat like I have always done when she does my makeup. I wasn't going to question her ideas, she knew my costumes and I trusted her skills. She started with cold creams on my face and then tickled me with brushes and powder.

Once she finished my face, she moved onto my eyes. She told me she was going to use orange and neutral colors to create a smokey eye. I agreed with whatever she wanted to do and kept my eyes closed. I enjoyed getting to bond with my mom when she did my hair or makeup.

It used to be a special time between us when I was younger. We would have a spa and for her wine Wednesday, where we would just take time to pamper ourselves. As I got older and started doing other things, we did spa nights less frequently. Now that it was just the two of us, I wanted to ask her for it again but I rarely got Emily free Wednesdays since she actually did enjoy watching those night shows.

"Okay keep your eyes closed because I'm going to spray your face down," mom said, warning me of the cold mist that rained down on my face.

"Thank you, momma." I said, finally being able to blink.

"Can I braid your hair into two pigtails?" she asked, twirling a string of my hair in between her fingers. I wasn't really feeling the pig tail look, but I didn't want to stop the bonding. I shook my head and readjusted in my seat, knowing that I would probably take it out shortly after getting to the party.

She got to work, moving the strands through her fingers quickly. I didn't sit much longer before she was finished with the two braids. She kissed the top of my head, maybe missing the bonding nights, too.

"Aha," she said, pointing her finger into the air and walking away from our moment. Clearly a thought had hit her. I got up and followed her to her bedroom to see what the thought was. I could hear her digging around in the back of her closet for something, but I couldn't think of what she could possibly have back there.

"Found it," she called from the depths of her closet. She emerged with a straw hat that looked similar to the one the scarecrow from Oz wore. She rested it on my head and positioned me in her bedroom mirror so I could give my approval.

"Mom, this is perfect." I was so happy we were able to avoid my costume disaster and now I feel ready for the Halloween party.

"Do you think I could borrow your boots for tonight, too?" I asked. She went back into the closet to retrieve them. They were her nice faux leather boots. The intricate stitch forming pretty brown roses. Once she brought them out she set them on the floor next to her bed, giving me the option to put them on there. I sat down and did just that.

"We probably want to get you out of here soon so you aren't late," mom said, grabbing her jacket and keys from her dresser. I shook my head in agreement, bouncing up from the bed to show I was ready. I took one final look in the floor length mirror mom had. Mom had painted a stitched scarecrow smile on my face, my nose matching the orange of mom's flannel.

We walked down the stairwell and heard the kids running up and down, door to door, to collect as much candy as they could. We passed goblins and knights and ghouls and even a few ghosts. Emily rolled her eyes at each ghost we passed.

"A bed sheet for a ghost," she whispered into my ear. "I mean are you serious, kid?" I chuckled at her comment, sure six year old Timmy didn't want to dress as the high school girl ghost for Halloween.

It was chilly outside, so I'm glad mom recommended the change. I wrapped the sun kissed flannel tightly around my chest, shielding me from the harsh wind. Mom started the car and turned the heat on. I told her it was on a county road. I let her drive, playing her Halloween CD that she took out of my player before we left. It was a good thing to get me into a party mood and settle my nerves for the party ahead.

"So are you excited for your first high school party?" Mom probed.

"More nervous honestly," I said, not letting her know this wasn't actually my first party.

Ashley got me to sneak out from her place one time. After Springfield won the basketball championship, one of the players decided to throw a big party. His parents were some super rich couple who normally traveled for business. I think he threw the party more out of spite, because I remember him trashing anything he could that night, encouraging his friends to do the same. He had told the whole school to come, that had been the only reason we got the invite.

"Come on," Ashley begged, her black hoodie already over her night clothes.

"What if your mom catches us?" I whispered.

"She won't," Ashley said, waving away the thought, "You know Fridays for wine and wine only."

Her long caramel hair was slicked back into a pony, hiding under the hoodie like her clothes. With the dim lighting in her room, her green eyes started to seem more cat like than human. That night should have told me she wasn't trustworthy. Her scheming eyes had begged and pleaded until I finally agreed to sneak out.

I spent that night worrying about getting caught by one of our mothers. The feeling never shook off, not allowing me to enjoy anything. It didn't help that Ashley decided to throw herself at the seniors, immediately leaving me to the dust. Of course, they threw her back at me when she proved that she couldn't actually handle as much as she thought she could.

I was looking forward to spending tonight's party without that guilt of lying hanging over me. I did worry about the extra guest sitting in the back seat. Emily didn't actually need to ride with us to the party, but she was hardly leaving my side anymore. She would be sitting at my desk, waiting for me to wake up, talking me back to sleep at the end of the day. I peered at the mirror, seeing her eyes staring back at me.

Mom's tires squeaked as her car rolled up to Johnson's sign. I could see cars in the drive and lining the road, but I didn't see any kids outside. I could feel the butterflies immersed out of their cocoon into my stomach. What if I was wrong about the date or time? What if Britney or Mallory made Jessica trick me? My heart raced.

"It's okay," Emily said, leaning forward in her seat. "If you listen you can hear the music coming from the barn."

"Are you sure this is the right spot, honey?" mom asked, looking for the kids, too.

"Yeah, I think I hear music coming from the back," I said, my voice shaking a little. I unbuckled my seat belt and went for the door handle.

"Wait," mom said, preparing to give me the high school party speech. We had agreed on the drive over that I would be able to stay the night. Jessica had sent a group text to a bunch of girls saying she had the basement open for us to crash in.

"I know to be safe and not take drinks from strange boys," I said, giving her a look and half-heartedly laughing at the comment.

"I know you're a smart girl, but still stay aware of the people," she said, placing her hand on my shoulder, "There's scary people out in the world, and not just the ones in scary costumes." I gave her a tight hug to try and reassure her. I was never really able to go out in Springfield because the big city scared her. She had loosened her grip a little since we were in a small town and I didn't want it to come crashing down.

"I know, momma," I said, letting her go. "I'll be safe, I promise." We both ran our finger over our hearts in an X to show our promise. Again, I went to the door handle and this time she let me go.

"I'll pick you up tomorrow at 10 am sharp so be ready," she called as I waved back to her.

The Johnson home was nestled behind the other farms rolling hills of crops. I ran up the drive to the front door. The house itself was a nice modern house, nothing too big or fancy about it. The single story silhouette matched the vast expanse of the sky. Behind it though, was a massive plot of land with different barns and sheds on it. A paper sign with sloppy writing indicated the party was around back.

I rounded the house to see a group of kids by a fire pit. I watched as the boys hunched over, messing in the pit. I assumed since the night was beginning to creep in, they wanted a warm area. The two boys were dressed as ranchers. A girl dressed as Tinkerbell had been trying to get herself a beer from the keg while her other two friends sat in chairs around the fire.

I realized one of the girls was Britney. Her body seemed slimmer, pushed into a skin tight black jumpsuit. I wouldn't have known she was anything but as I got closer I could see the cat ears and black liner she used to draw whiskers on.

"Sexy black cat." Emily laughed in my ear.

My body jumped a little, remembering she was with me. She probably had been right on my heels, but no one else could see that. Quickly, I turned to look at her. I hoped the kids at the fire pit didn't notice, trying to avoid a scene before even getting in. She was wearing my costume! She had the off the shoulder crop top on and twirled in her overall skirt when I finally noticed her. I could feel my face getting red.

"What?" she asked, trying to play innocent, "A good outfit like this shouldn't go to waste, and you know ghosts don't get cold."

Her laugh burned in my ears, lighting more fuel to my fire. Closing my eyes, I inhaled before turning back to the group. I wasn't going to let her ruin my night. If she wouldn't get my cold shoulder hints, then I would just pretend the music was too loud.

"Uh, a scarecrow," came a rough voice. I turned to see it was Britney. She had gotten up and started walking towards me. Emily was gone when I turned back to look at her.

"Yeah, a scarecrow," I said, turning to Britney. I hadn't noticed it before, but as she got closer I started to smell it. She brought the lit cigarette to her lip and took a long inhale.

"It's cute," she said, blowing the smoke at me with a clip in her voice.

"Brit, don't scare off the guest," one of the ranchers said. He pushed himself off the ground, and the fire started. Britney rolled her eyes at him, but snaked her body around his as he got closer to where we had been standing. His body stiffened at her touch. It seemed like his eyes rolled at her.

"I'm Jacob," he said, extending his hand out for me. So he wasn't dressed as a rancher, he was just a farm boy.

"Jessica's brother," I said, grabbing his hand and shaking it. I could practically hear the growl come from Britney when our hands touched.

"Ahh you're one of Jesse's friends," he said.

"Yeah, we have a bio together."

"Cool, her and Mallory are out back in the barn," he pointed to the big red barn that was farther away from all the other barns. It looked miles away from where we stood by the fire. Tinkerbell walked arm and arm with the other boy who I assumed was Jessica's other brother. *Josh? Maybe John?* I thought to myself. I didn't remember his name, but knew all the kids' names started with J.

"Something spooked you walking up?" he asked, turning back to face me.

"What do you mean?" I asked, a little shocked by the question. Had he seen Emily next to me?

"I work with horses, little lady," he continued, tipping his hat in my direction, "I know when I see fear."

"Oh, I caught a hole walking down and almost tripped," I lied, trying to brush him off.

"Here you go." The girl offered me a red solo cup, foam spilling. She was a stranger but technically not a boy, so I took the cup from her hands and sniffed the liquids. I have only tried my dad's beers once or twice in my life and wasn't sure what to expect. It wasn't like my dad's beer, which usually tasted like gross bread. This went down smoother.

"What is this?" I asked, surprised that I actually enjoyed it.

"It's yuengling," the other brother said, coming back into the conversation.

"It's not bad for beer," I said, taking another swig.

"Thanks, I picked it," Tinkerbell said. "Annabelle."

She grabbed my free hand to shake it in hers. I really looked at her for a minute. I hadn't seen her around school before. I assumed she wasn't in the same grade, but still I should have seen her walking around the school. I had seen the friend who was sitting with Britney around school even though I didn't know her name.

"Do you go to our school?" I asked, after staring for too long.

"Oh god no," she laughed, practically doubling over, "Justin and I met in college and he wanted to bring me home for his family's Halloween Party."

His name was Justin!

"Oh, your parents are here, too?" I asked the brothers.

"No," Justin answered first.

"They go to the Sheriff's Halloween party every year," Jacob finished.

"Apparently it's easier to get away with partying if you're friends with the Sheriff," Annabelle winked at me.

"I think it's time for the kid to go to the kiddie party," Britney harshly cut in. She made it very clear that she wasn't a fan of mine.

"You don't have to be so mean, Brit," Annabelle said, rolling her eyes. "But if you do wanna see Jess, she is in the back with her other friends," she said, turning to face me.

"Yeah, I should probably go see her," I sheepishly said. I knew I didn't belong with them and Brittney would make sure I wasn't welcomed if I tried to stay longer. I walked back towards the barn where the others were. As I got closer, I could hear the music getting louder. Kids were outside giggling and having fun. Some of them had beer cans but most had the red solo cup with foam spilling out the sides like mine.

With everyone in costume, it was hard to tell who was who. I wandered aimlessly hoping this wasn't a forecast of how my night would go. I didn't see Jessica anywhere and really wasn't sure what she'd be wearing. Would she just be dressed in her farm get up, like her brothers, or would she actually dress up?

"Oh my god," squealed a voice behind me, "You actually came."

I turned around to see who it was and I was engulfed in a big hug from two girls. One was dressed like little Bo peep and the other wearing a red cowgirl hat and matching outfit. I finally recognized the girls to be Jessica and Mallory. Mallory's hair was curled, making her the perfect Bo Peep. Jessica had straightened hers, two pigtail braids dangling from her head.

"Yeah," I said, when they let me go to breathe. "I got a little held up with your brothers." I pointed to the bonfire that was actually getting pretty big compared to the smoke it was just a few moments ago.

"Don't you be like Britney and go after Jessica's brothers," Mallory slurred, her finger wagging. She hung onto Jessica, both girls struggling to stand straight. I could smell the booze coming off both their breaths as they giggled.

"Trust me, I won't," I said defensively, throwing my hands up, spilling a little bit of my beer. Both girls doubled over in laughter and I couldn't help but join them, the few sips making my head feel light.

"Come on, let me show you around," Jessica said, wrapping her free arm around me and pulling me into the barn.

Other students were milling around in there, drinking and having a good time. I could see a few different tables set up with drinking games. The football players crowded around the flip cup and pong tables, while many of the girls sat at tables trying to flip quarters into shot glasses that were being passed around. This felt like the parties you'd see on tv and definitely not the small town party my mom thought I was going to.

"Do you wanna play a game?" a jigsaw boy asked us. I thought it was part of his costume until he handed Mallory a ping pong ball. The girls walked to the other end of the table, leaving me with jigsaw.

"I guess we're partners," I said, looking at him with a bit of confusion. Even though I had watched numerous parties thrown on my shows, I had never been before and really didn't know how to play beer pong. Jigsaw nodded and turned to face the other girls.

Since Mallory had the ball, she and Jigsaw threw first. He explained to me that this was how we would see who got to go first in the game. Mallory's ball wasn't even close to the table and again the girls erupted in laughter. Luckily for us, Jigsaw got his ball in the middle of the pyramid.

"It was fine that I hit that cup for this round," he explained to me, "but you don't want that to be the first cup to hit."

"Why not?" I asked, puzzled. "I thought the point of the game was to get all the cups."

"It is, but that's a pitch cup," he said.

"Pitch cup?"

"The city doesn't do pitch cups?" he sounded a little shocked but laughed it off. I didn't know what the city did, but I wasn't going to let him know that.

"If you hit that cup before any of the other cups you either have to pull your pants down and leave them down until you make another cup or call your mom and tell her you're a bitch."

I tried to hide my horror in that thought, but judging by his laugh, I didn't hide it very well. I made a mental note to not aim for that cup as we both prepped to throw. Jigsaw threw first and made it square in the pitch cup. He groaned but begrudgingly dropped his pants.

"Momma didn't raise a bitch," he whispered in my ear as I threw my ball. It had missed and bounced off of Jessica. The two girls were hardly paying attention to where they were throwing. Clearly they had been drinking while setting up because they were more drunk than the rest of the party. It made it easy for jigsaw and I to wipe the floor with them.

Once we won, Jigsaw picked me up and spun me in victory. In the air, I was able to watch a hockey mask grab the attention of Mallory. She ran after him, leaving Jessica alone. Her hands dropped to her sides, eyes wide as she watched. Back on the ground, I grabbed for my cup, ready for a victory swig. I looked at my almost empty cup. Jigsaw noticed it, too.

"Here let me get you a refill," he said, grabbing my cup. I would have normally protested, hearing mom's warning in my head, but seeing Emily pop up behind him threw all logic out the window. She was grabbing his shoulders, trying to show her approval. She was still in my costume and now she was touching on my guy. I could feel the blood boiling in my body. She had crossed too many lines tonight.

I caught glimpses of her wandering the party during the game, but I was intent on ignoring her. She clearly assumed I was just engulfed in the game, because I watched her making a b-line to us when Jigsaw had me in the air.

"Yes, please," I said, trying to keep my cool so he wouldn't see what a freak I really was. "I'm gonna head to the bathroom."

I marched to the bathroom, which wasn't much since it was the barn bathroom. I slapped the door behind me, knowing she would just walk through the closed door anyway. I could feel her presence, but we both just sat there in silence. My hands white knuckled on the bathroom sink.

I only had two drinks, but I could feel the liquid in me mixing with my emotions. Anger and confusion swam through my head, the silence allowed all my thoughts to rage. I wanted a normal high school experience. I wanted to not be the freak everyone was trying to make me out to be. I wanted to not see Emily.

"Why are you here?" I managed to ask, not lifting my head to look at her.

"How do you think I get all my hot gossip," she laughed. Her laughter only increased my anger towards her, like somehow her laughter was a mockery of me.

"You're still in my costume," I snapped. I felt the rage continuing to creep up my throat, ready to let the beast out. My brain was no longer in control, the filter ready to come off.

"Is that what this is about?" she asked. "Because I can change."

"No, it's the fact that you're here." I said, spinning to face her. "You're always around me!"

The words were finally out, words I didn't know I had been holding. The part of me that was still sober knew those words couldn't be taken back, but at that moment, the drunk me was in charge and she didn't care about feelings. Not tonight. Tonight was supposed to be my night to experience normal, not her night to live it through me. I wasn't her puppet any longer, cutting the strings of that bond.

"You're the only one who has been able to see me in years," she whispered, lowering her head. It finally broke the silence that I hadn't been hearing. My brain was screaming, trying to tell me she needed to know how I was feeling. My stomach dropped.

I didn't know how to respond. Her words cut through me like a knife. Now there was nothing inside my head, nothing but guilt. My pride was stronger though, keeping words behind my sealed lips. We both stood there in silence, until a knock on the door made us jump. Emily vanished as I left, letting the next girl in. I knew she'd be back in the morning, who else would she dish all her gossip to.

Leaving the bathroom, I went back to find jigsaw and my drink. He handed me the beer and I drank as much as I could, wanting to forget the bathroom ordeal. I imagine the liquid drowning the memories in my thoughts instead of it sliding into my tummy. He pulled me out onto the makeshift dance floor. Twirling around each other, we danced until I couldn't see straight. We danced and drank the night away. For the first time, I felt like a normal girl, living the normal teenage dream.

Chapter Eight

The midnight sky spun around me, the stars circling slow. I couldn't tell if they were actually moving or if the alcohol was starting to catch up to my brain. I looked around, a clouded fog erasing where I was for a moment. The soft grass under me felt like a velvet comforter, ready to wrap me to bed.

Bed sounded nice but it didn't feel right. I sat upright, trying to find the barn or maybe the campfire. I needed to find other people. The alcohol warmed my blood as the cold air blew through my pigtails. One was looser than the other, more hair wildly flying around. I could hear the music still coming from the party, but my head was spinning so the sound surrounded me.

I couldn't remember how I had gotten outside. I tried to piece the memories together, blank dots forming instead. At least I knew where I was. Mostly. I didn't imagine I had wandered too far. Some memories slowly drifted back as I gathered myself up. The Jigsaw boy didn't stay, but he had asked me to say goodbye. That was how I ended up out here.

I turned to face the music, my stomach churning with it. I didn't feel stable on my legs as they wobbled between my steps. Getting closer to the barn, I realized that most of the party was working on heading out too. Laughter carried people's goodbyes to me, but I watched others still pouring drinks for themselves.

"What's going on?" I asked, my speech slurring as it fell out. In the darkness, I really couldn't recognize the people who were. I hoped that meant they wouldn't recognize me either.

"The boys are leaving," a girl replied. She was wrapped around a taller figure who chugged their beer.

"It's lame," he belched, finishing his drink.

"I know, I'd rather go home with you," she purred, snaking her body around him.

"Is the party over?" I asked, my head still spinning.

"Just for the guys apparently," the male voice replied. "Don't forget my paper is due Tuesday."

"I'll have it for you Monday," the girl replied.

Crunching of leaves under heavy boots faded in and out of my ears. My lids were getting too heavy to hold and the night breeze tickled my nose. I was ready to go in, but I wasn't sure I could make it in the right direction.

"Are you planning on staying out here?" asked the girl. The barn light was just close enough to make out her costume. The shepherd hook looked more like a weapon in the dim evening. Or maybe it was morning now? I looked around again trying to remember how long I had been out here.

"Did you hear me?" Mallory asked. I wanted to respond but my tongue couldn't move, my jaw barely opened. Instead, my stomach churned. Each slosh inside feels like a million turns. Trying to push myself to my feet, my limbs shook under me. I collapsed back to the grass.

I rolled up to my knees just before the bile wormed its way up my throat. Greasy pizza chunks burned as they mixed with my stomach acid. I hurled my insides onto the grass in front of me. Once I felt that everything was up, I gave a shaking thumb back to Mallory.

"I'm right behind you," I croaked.

Mallory's shadowing figure disappeared back towards the barn. Music softly drifted to me, but it had changed from the dance club music that played earlier. Boy bands bounced through the grassy field to get to me. I mustered the strength to get to my feet, but my legs were still a little shaky under me.

Each step felt like I had cement in my shoes. The barn didn't seem to be getting closer, no matter how many steps I took. I could feel the stomach acid trying to force itself out of my mouth again. I pushed it down, as I treaded forward. But the acid eventually won the battle.

I collapsed to my knees again. This time rough rocks dug into my skin when I hit the ground. I must be getting closer. More stomach acid poured out of my mouth, some seeping down my nose. Hot tears ran down my face in response. I hated puking and something about this time was worse. I wanted to curl up into bed.

"Oh my," a voice called. "Are you okay?"

I tried to look up, but the barn lights blinded me. Suddenly it felt like daylight again. I knew it was only my imagination, but the harsh contrast of the light was too much for my eyes to handle at the moment. I watched the girl move down closer to me.

"Do you need help?" Jessica's dusty doe eyes stared at me.

"Do you think we could get some water?" I asked.

I sat back on my knees, the rocks underneath digging further in. It felt like they were rubbing against my bones, I moved to sit on my butt, swinging my legs off to the side. I shoved myself away from the vomit that was taunting me with its smell.

"I'll grab you some," Jessica replied. "Do you think you can walk?"

I can barely speak, let alone walk, was what I wanted to say but instead I shook my head no. Examining my knee, I pried rocks from my ripped jeans while Jessica hurried off to the barn. My body felt heavy again, the weight causing me to tilt to one side. My view crooked for a moment. My body felt the cool touch of the jagged rocks and sharply shot up.

Heart racing, I felt like I had just missed a brush with death. The head rush from sitting up lifted the sleepy curse that was taking over my body. Slowly breathing, I came into my surroundings again. Trying to remember what was happening before I came out here. Blinking fast, I searched for Jessica.

"Here you go," Jessica said, rushing a cup into my hands.

"Thank you," I said, but the words were slurred together.

I gulped the water down, letting the icy liquid soothe my throat. It helped clear my head a little, but now my body craved more. I tilted the cup completely back. Trickles of the water ran down the side of my lip and onto my shirt. Once the cup was empty, I took a long inhale.

"Do you think you want another glass?" Jessica asked.

"Couldn't hurt," I replied, shrugging my shoulders and lifting the cup to her.

"Are you steady enough to walk now?"

I looked around to see how many people were still outside. I wasn't really sure if I was steady enough, so I wanted to make sure minimal people saw me if I took another tumble. Everyone has either gone inside or left, leaving Jessica and me to stand outside.

"I think I can," I said, slowly pushing myself up.

"Just far enough to get to the water," Jessica said. "We don't have to go back into the barn just yet."

"Thank you. I think I've been social for two lifetimes tonight."

"Yeah I noticed you and that one boy seemed to be getting along pretty well," she chuckled.

I was slightly taken aback by the comment, mostly because I thought Jessica was too drunk to notice that. I wasn't sure how noticeable I was being with my flirting when we were playing pong together, but clearly it was enough. I felt my cheeks heat up, even though the wind was tickling my face.

"I didn't realize you were paying attention," I lied. "Did you recognize who he was?"

"No," she shrugged. "With the face paint and dark lights, anyone can be anyone."

"Anyone can be anyone?" I repeated.

"Yeah, it's Halloween night," she said, as we made our way to the hose that was attached to some fancy hydration system. The contraption was a little taller than Jessica, but multiple nozzles hung down allowing for easy access.

"This seems nice," I said, my hand reaching to grab one of the nozzles.

"It's to help keep us hydrating when we're out here working on stuff," she replied, handing a full glass of water to me.

"Thank you," I said, starting to gulp the sweet water down again.

"Want to go sit up by the fire?" Jessica asked, after a long pause.

"Is it still going?"

"It looked like a little smoke was still coming from it," she said. "I could get it up and go again."

"Do you not want to go back to your party?" I asked.

Jessica looked back towards the barn. The music was louder since the water station was closer to the barn. I could hear giggles coming from the barn with others singing out of tune karaoke. Singing wasn't my strong suit so I didn't mind missing out on all that. Plus the music didn't sound familiar to me, so I doubt I could sing whatever the lyrics were.

"Not really," she said, finally looking back at me. "I'm starting to sober up and the music is kinda loud."

"Yeah it's pretty loud now, I don't think I could handle it any louder," I agreed.

"The fire will keep us warm," she said, guiding me down the slope. "And if we want to start drinking again, my mom's wine coolers are closer."

She locked her arm around mine as we continued walking down. I wasn't sure if she did it to help with my balance or just because she wanted to, but I enjoyed the gesture. The warmth that radiated off of her was a nice contrast to Emily's cold presence.

"So how have you been liking Twindle?" she asked, breaking through my thoughts.

"It has definitely been different from my last school," I said, not really sure what else to say.

"Is different bad?"

I had to think for a minute. I didn't really think different meant bad, but different meant a lot of things that felt bad. Dad wasn't here, but I hadn't decided if that was bad or not. I didn't have David, which now I had moved on from, but in the moment felt bad. Or I didn't have Ashley and that one still stung, but having Emily helped fill that a little more.

"I don't think it is bad or good," I answered, finally.

"Explain."

"Well, I think the school is good and I like the people," I started. "But, I don't have my dad with me and that's been an adjustment. And, I don't really talk to my old friends."

"I can understand that," she said, halting.

"You do?" I wondered.

"Yeah, I was the new kid too once," she replied, staring at me.

"Wait, you didn't grow up here?"

"Not necessarily," she shrugged. "We moved here in sixth grade."

"Why did you move?"

"Mom got remarried, so I guess my dad is out of the picture too," she said, giving a cold laugh. "I'm going to go grab those wine coolers I mentioned."

She sat me in one of the chairs around the dying fire. The older kids had left but I didn't know if they went inside. The house seemed quiet with little lights shining through the windows. Jessica briskly walked to a fridge that sat on the back patio. I watched her reach into it and pull out a case of pink bottles.

I moved closer to the embers, trying to get whatever heat I could. The beer was starting to run out of my body, leaving me vulnerable to the night air. I felt my body shiver as I watched Jessica make her way back to me. She handed me one of the bottles and took the seat across from mine.

"So where is your father now?" I asked.

"He died," was not the answer I expected to come out of Jessica's mouth. The liquid got stuck in the back of my throat as I processed what she said.

"I'm so sorry," I said, in betweens little coughs and gasps.

"It's okay," she shrugged, grabbing a stick off the ground to poke the fire. "I've been in a lot of therapy to help process it."

She took a sip of her bottle, her gray eyes peering through the smoke lifting from the fire. I wasn't sure what was causing it, but it looked like a storm was forming in her eyes. The gray twisting into a dark cloud, ready to unleash a lifetime of rain. She titled the bottle up like I had done with the first water. She didn't get any on her cheeks.

"How do you stay so happy?" I heard myself asking.

It caught her off guard too. I watched as she almost choked on the wine, but gracefully pushed it down as she cleared her throat. Once the bottle was empty, she stared down at it and the pit that housed the pathetic fire.

"I didn't really think of myself as someone who stays happy," she answered, still looking down at the embers.

"You always seem happy around me," I said. "Well I guess I don't see you letting life get you down."

"I try not to let the things I can't control get me down."

"How?"

"Just look on the bright side," she said, flashing her pearly whites. "My granny always says you make breakfast with broken eggs."

"What is that supposed to even mean?" I asked, laughter bubbling up.

"I think it's supposed to mean that even cracked things can create something yummy," she replied. "My granny has some saying for pretty much anything in life."

"Sounds like a wise woman," I said, tipping the wine cooler in her direction in a semi toast fashion.

"She is more wise than anyone I know," Jessica replied, popping open another bottle.

I didn't have much left in mine. The bottles weren't much bigger than my hand, so I didn't imagine there was too much alcohol in them. I tipped it back, getting the last drop in my mouth before flipping it right side up.

"Do you mind if I have another?" I asked, lifting the empty bottle to her.

"Go for it," she said, handing me another one.

"Do you see your Granny often?" I asked, taking it from her.

"I wish we saw her more," Jessica replied, her head moving to look somewhere else. "She's my dad's mom, so since my mom remarried, we don't see her as much."

"Why don't you get to see her as much?" I stupidly asked, the alcohol clearly not fully out of my brain.

"My mom says she's a painful reminder of my dad," Jessica admitted. "It makes her too sad to go back."

"So none of you can see her?"

"Not until I get my license." She shrugged, "Justin goes a few times a month if college isn't too busy."

"Well I'm sure once you can drive, you'll be able to see her all the time," I said, hoping to put a positive spin on things.

"Yeah, I'm sure you're right," she agreed.

"So did Mallory leave?" I asked, trying to change the subject.

"Hopefully," she replied, coldly. Jessica took another long pull from her bottle, leaving me speechless. "I don't know where she went."

"You guys okay?"

"Not really," she said, shocking me. "Mallory has kinda been only focused on herself lately."

"What do you mean?"

"She's just blowing me off to go hang out with stupid people," she huffed. "It's honestly stupid."

I felt like I closed one bad door only to walk into a hornets nest. I thought the fire would lead to fun gossip, but that wasn't what it was turning out to be.

"Well let's change the subject," I said, trying to think on my feet. "Do you want to play two truths and one lie?"

"Okay but you have to go first, since it is my party after all," she laughed, taking another sip.

"Okay that seems fair," I said, rubbing my chin. "I got it. I am a Libra, my favorite color is purple, and I just moved here."

"Well I guess I know one is true," she giggled, followed by a hiccup. "I'm going to guess that your favorite color isn't purple."

"It is," I grinned. "I'm an Aries."

"Hmm," she said, putting her hand to her chin. "I really don't know much about astrology."

"I'm not too big on it, but I think the horoscopes are fun."

"Horoscopes are definitely fun," she agreed. "My turn, I am the only girl. I'm allergic to chocolate and bees."

"Are you really allergic to chocolate?" I asked, my eyes almost bulging out.

"How did you know it was chocolate?" She answered my question with her own.

"It was a guess but that sounds awful."

"Your turn."

I took a long chug of my drink. I wanted to get closer to Jessica. She had let me know about her dad, so I wanted to tell her about mine. I wasn't really sure the best way to do it, but my two truths, one lie, decided to pull it out.

"My dad has a gambling problem, my dad was arrested, and my dad hasn't spoken to me in over a month," I said. "Oh wait, none of those are lies."

I slammed the bottle back, finishing the little bit that was left. It felt good to finally grieve my issues with my dad and Jessica felt like the right person to do it with. I had discussed it with Emily in the past and she always brushed it off, but I felt Jessica wouldn't.

"I'm sorry," she said in a low voice. "Dads can suck sometimes."

"They really can," I agreed.

"My dad died from a drug overdose," Jessica managed to say. "Sometimes the addictions get the best of us."

CHAPTER NINE

The sun was barely peeking over the horizon, but the light still burned my eyes. Using my hand as a shield against the harshness, I peered down the long driveway. Please mom just get here soon. As if she could hear me, her car split the light as she drove through the neighborhood streets, working her way past each house to get to me. I couldn't be certain, but mom's car looked to barely move. Maybe she was trying to remember which house, or maybe my head was just still reeling.

Her car finally stopped in front of me, waiting like a school bus. I heard the click of the car as it unlocked. I scrambled in, needing to curl into my own bed. I could tell by mom's face that I probably reeked of booze. I had woken up and thrown my head into a toilet so I'm sure my breath wasn't pleasant.

"Thank you, momma," I said as she was turning around in their driveway.

"Mhmm," she murmured. This was the tale tale sign that she wasn't happy but also wasn't ready to say anything. The conversation would come later, probably for dinner tonight. I placed my head on the window and tried to sleep a little, but I could feel all the bumps along the way home. My head throbbed and stomach churned. I couldn't wait to be home. I prayed I would be able to make it home without getting sick again, each turn of the car feeling like the tilt-a-whirl.

I felt bad that I needed mom to come get me, but I didn't want anyone to see the way I looked when they woke up. Granted, I didn't know what I had looked like when I went to bed last night. I didn't remember getting to bed, I just remembered the thud of my body hitting the couch when someone threw me on it.

Jessica's family had given us the basement, which was filled with a plethora of couches. When I woke up, I was in a room filled with other girls, mostly in our grade. I ran to the closest bathroom and after I got sick, realized how awful I looked. I stared at a red and white mouthed scarecrow, barely recognizing that it was me. I realized that the red and white had come from jigsaw boy. I didn't realize in the dark that his paint was smearing on my face.

I had tried to clean it off before mom picked me up, but I knew that I didn't get all of it off. Mom would give small glances my way and bite her cheek or give a small sigh. I could tell she wanted to say something, but had waited too long. We were pulling into the apartments. I could see the village sign.

As soon as mom pulled into a spot, I yanked my seatbelt off and pulled on the handle. The door wouldn't budge since mom hadn't put the car into park. Once the click happened, I pushed the door open and my body pushed what I hoped was the last of the beer I had at the party. Mom didn't even turn to check on me, she just walked to the apartment.

I was only a few steps behind her but I could barely do the stairs. My feet felt so heavy and each step made me feel nauseous again. Mom held the door open for me and I kicked off her boots, crashing onto the couch for a second. My head started to spin again. I felt like I was still drunk.

"Um hey missy," mom said, grabbing her boots, "I don't care if you treat your shit poorly but don't treat mine like it."

I could feel the heat radiate off her as she stormed past me. Great I pissed off Emily and now I've pissed off my mom. The slam of her bedroom door confirmed she was pissed.

I laid down on the couch, waiting for the next wave of sickness to carry me to the bathroom. I opened my eyes and the ceiling twisted. That was all I needed. I pushed myself off the couch and ran, barely making it to my target before my guts came up.

My arms collapsed under me and I rested my head on the toilet seat. I just needed a minute to collect myself before I could crawl into my bed. I felt a cold chill run through my body. I knew I needed to apologize for how I acted last night, but I didn't realize Emily would be ready to do it this early. My head wasn't going to be able to handle this.

"Hey, Em, about last night," I croaked, my voice horse and sounded almost like a stranger. Sober me trying to remember what all drunk me said. "I'm sorry for how I acted," not fully ready to admit to the words. My whisper echoed in the empty bathroom. Pulling my head up, I realized it was really empty.

I was met with nothing. She wasn't there, it was just a normal cold chill. I had had Emily by my side for so long that I didn't realize I would just assume the supernatural whenever something happened. It sent a pang through my heart that she wasn't there. My words rush to my head, ready to slash at my already hurting heart. Now ready to remind me of how vicious I was to her.

I was ready to curl up into a ball and cry myself to sleep. I didn't know why but I just felt awful for everything, not just last night. All my emotions were ready to explode, I just needed to get to my bed for it to happen. I finally pushed myself to my room, feeling the flood gates start to crumble as I heard a small whimper escape my lips.

Mom had made my bed last night before she went to sleep. She had put my favorite bear in between the pillows. Seeing my childhood bear stare back at me was the final straw I needed. I fell into the bed and wrapped my arms tightly around the bear. I didn't bother taking the clothes off or getting under the blankets. I just needed a minute. My eyes filled, the tears flowing freely. I could feel the top of Teddy's head getting wet with my tears.

I laid like this for a long time, until I felt like I had cried out all of my body's water. I finally decided to get under the covers and close my eyes. My head was still pounding and the sun was getting brighter and brighter outside. I threw my blanket over me and squeezed my eyes tight.

I didn't realize I had fallen asleep until mom came into my room. She had brought something that smelled delicious in. Shaking my shoulders, she let me know it was lunch time. I blinked my eyes, trying to figure out why it was still dark if it was lunch. Mom pulled the covers off my head and gave me life. I could see that lunch was her chicken and rice that she made with corn and her famous salsa.

My stomach growled in response to the smell. I couldn't help but run for the bowl she had. I practically downed it in minutes. My stomach slowly settled back to normal. I was hoping she made more for us because her food was incredible.

"Could I have another?" I asked, tilting the empty bowl towards her. She stared for a little bit. I wondered if she was still upset or if she was ready to talk about it. She grabbed the bowl and went into the kitchen. I would have followed her but she was back before my brain could process that she had left.

"Thank you," I said when she handed me the bowl. I could see her biting her lips, almost ready to spill what she had been thinking.

"So how much did you have to drink?" she finally came out and asked.

"I think six beers," I said. I learned a long time ago it was better to be honest with her and take the punishment than lie and get double.

"Where did you get them?" she asked, putting her hands on her hips. I could tell she was ready to scold me last night. I watched as she glanced around my room. I could imagine all the different scenarios running through her head. Did I have a fake ID? Was I pimping myself for booze?

"Jessica has two older brothers," I said. "They got a keg for the party," putting her mind at ease.

"And did you make sure that you poured all your own beers?" she asked, starting to loosen up. She was probably remembering what trouble she got into at my age.

"If I didn't pour it, a girl did," I said.

I realized it was a lie after a few minutes remembering that I let Jigsaw get me one of those beers. Glimpse of Jigsaw played through my mind, sending my stomach into a frenzy. I tried pressing my lips together, avoiding a smile.

"And what red face boy were you kissing on?" she asked, pointing to my face.

Guess I didn't hide that very well. I realized I still hadn't cleaned my face completely off. Looking down at my pillow, there were little red stains. I wondered if my face would have matching stains for school on Monday.

"Oh he was a boy in my bio class," I lied, realizing I had no idea who the boy was.

"Does he have a name?"

"Jackson," I said, coming up with the first name I could. She eyed me suspiciously. I knew I wasn't very convincing, so I just went back to her bowl of chicken and rice. That seemed to be good enough for her because she changed the subject.

"Don't think that just because we moved to a small town that I'm gonna let you run wild," she said, pointing a finger at me like I was some sort of criminal. I nodded my head. She already started her lecture on the dangers of the world. I let her get her speech out instead of trying to argue or defend myself. She was trying to look out for her only child, even if I thought she was overstepping sometimes. I was drinking, not running the streets like a criminal.

"Anyone can be dangerous," she said, trying to hammer in my head how "not safe" the world was.

"I know that, but it was just kids, mom," I said.

"Kids can be dangerous too," she threw up her hands, "I mean anyone. Teachers, students, anyone."

She was almost yelling at this point. I didn't understand the aggression. It was a harmless party, no one got hurt. I still wasn't going to argue with her reasoning. She had always had an irrational fear of being kidnapped. I think it was embedded into her. Grams had always joked that she would be scooped up, because her small stature made her an easy target. She took it incredibly seriously, expecting every stranger to try to grab and run.

"Also you're grounded for two weeks because of the drinking," she said, getting ready to walk out of the room.

"Wait two weeks?!" I said before I realized I said anything.

"If you argue with me, I'll make it longer," she said, leaving my room. That shut me up real quick. I really didn't have anywhere to be so it didn't matter that I got grounded but it still made me feel lame.

I felt a buzzing coming from my back pocket. I pulled my phone out and slid the screen to see who had texted me. I realized that Jessica had put me in a group chat with a bunch of other girls from school. Probably the other girls who had been sleeping downstairs when I woke up. I scrolled through the messages, trying to catch up from my nap.

Most of them were telling Jessica thank you or saying something about the party. I quickly responded to something to the same degree. I also apologized for running out. My message was followed up with question marks and people asking whose number it was. I let them know it was mine and went back to the other messages.

Jessica had started the group chat by asking if anyone wanted to go ride horses with her. Most of the other girls had said not after their hangovers, but a few did say it would be fun. I didn't see any horses on Jessica's farm last night so I didn't know if they had gone somewhere else or not. I remember seeing multiple barns, so maybe they kept them somewhere else. Somewhere where drunk hooligans couldn't steal them to get injured later. I wasn't in the farm scene so I didn't know where all the farm hang out spots were. The farm lands took up the entire eastern side of town, so they probably had options.

Horse back riding sounded fun, but I didn't think I could successfully sneak out with my grounding looming over me. I knew mom had been excited about me making friends here, but that didn't mean she would go back on her punishment. I wasn't going to say anything about it in the chat. Plus I didn't want anyone to know I got grounded because of the party. I left the group chat alone and decided to pull out some homework.

While I was reading for assignments, the group chat buzzed a few more times. It was just the different girls telling Jessica that they had made it home from riding. It seemed like I was maybe starting to get a little friend group. Jessica had said she was going to stay just a little longer.

I went back to my homework, trying to get what I could do so my Sunday night could be nothing but pure laziness. I wanted to be able to watch cartoons and binge on sweets without the linger of homework over my head. I did feel like I was slowly drowning in assignments, too. I needed to stay on top of my grades or I knew mom would extend the grounding. I continued working my pile until there was practically nothing left.

I left some work for the week, but it wasn't anything due until Wednesday. I knew I would still have time. I felt like my assignments were in a good place now. Pushing myself from my desk, I gathered everything into my brown school bag. I left it on the floor next to the desk, easy for me to throw everything back in before the next day.

I worked my way around my room, setting up for the new week starting. I pulled out clothes for tomorrow. Feeling a new boost of confidence, I decided to go with something a little more flattering. The jockey comments about my hoodies swimming through my head. The thought made me yearn for Emily.

She would have let me know if the rhinestone studded jeans were as cute as I thought they were. I held them up in the mirror, letting the back pockets glint under the overhead lighting. I had stolen a shirt from Ashley back when I still lived a normal life. She had better style and a mom with a shopping problem. I was pretty sure she hadn't noticed it missing, and if she had figured it out now, she knew she wasn't getting it back.

I threw the jeans onto my bed, before heading back into my closet. I knew the shirt was buried in the boxes. The feelings and memories of Ashley are buried with it. I caught a glimpse of the forest green when searching for my jeans yesterday. I knew it wasn't in the jeans box, so I pushed past that one. I pulled the farther box closer, ripping the cardboard tabs open.

It was a skin tight t-shirt, but it was magic in a cloth. The material was softer than butter, gliding onto your skin, but it sucked everything in. Ashley had sworn there was no padding in the chest area, but I swore my breast always looked two times as big in it. It was the perfect shirt to show off the butterfly that came out of my cocoon at Jessica's party.

That night, I slept on a cloud. The vision of sexy, a vision I could never see myself in, coming together when I laid everything out. The brown of my bag complements the green in the shirt. My runway evening helped to ease the pain of missing Emily.

S.B. Dunn

Chapter Ten

I was awoken by my alarm clock screaming its sirens at me. My brain sent panic through my body, as it tried to take in my surroundings. My room was still mostly dark, with just a hint of light creeping in through the blinds. I wasn't ready for the morning to begin, so I threw my hand onto the snooze button. Silence went through my room as my heart started to calm back down to a normal beat. I could hear mom's alarm going off in the room next to me.

She turned hers off, but didn't snooze it. I could hear her rustling around in her closet trying to get herself ready. She opened her door and came to mine. Giving my door a light tap, she called to confirm I was moving. I made a noise in the direction of my door to indicate I was at least awake.

"I am going to hop in the shower. You better be getting ready when I get out," she called. I could hear the bathroom door opening and closing as she got her stuff together. My snooze would only allow for another five minutes to sleep, but mom wouldn't take more than ten minutes in the shower. I shut my eyes tight, trying to hold on to the little bit of sleep I had.

My alarm started screaming at me again. It was sadly time to get up. I wasn't ready for another week at school, all the ambition from last night drifting away on my cloud. My head was still hurting a little bit from the Saturday night party and I hadn't seen Emily all weekend. A funk crept over me, my readiness to tackle the world barely there.

I could hear the squeak of the shower turning off. I drag my feet across my room to find the clothes I laid out. I opened my bedroom door so mom would know I was up when she walked by. I didn't fold my laundry yesterday so it was still sitting in the basket. I dug through it trying to find all my good bras. I was hoping putting the clothes on would help put the facade back on. I was glad I had prepped last night, because I felt scattered. Having my school stuff ready was checked off, letting the scattered feeling loosen.

Mom finished getting ready and was in the kitchen making her normal cup of coffee. I could hear the beeps as she pushed each button to get her perfect blend. I knew I only had a few more minutes before we'd be out that door and off to school. I peered around the room one last time before leaving, hoping to see Emily at the mirror applying lip gloss or on my bed mocking my appearance.

I had decided to switch from the normal sweatshirt and jeans look today and I would have appreciated her input. She wasn't there to tell me if the shade of green I picked brought out too much of the red in my hair. I'd have to survive school without her today I guess. I wasn't sure how long she was going to give me the silent treatment so I will just have to make do with the silence.

I tried ignoring the weird feeling her absence left in me. She had pulled the silent treatment before so it wasn't the first time I would tackle school alone. I remembered the first day jitters I had without her. Those same jitters trying to wiggle up my spine now. I shuttered, trying to shake them off. Something about Emily missing felt different this time though. It felt weird. I pushed the worry that I may never see her again to the back of my mind.

"It's time to go," mom called from the kitchen. I hadn't heard her coffee sputter out to indicate it was done. I was too lost in my own thoughts, I barely heard her calling for me. I grabbed my backpack and headed towards the front door. Mom was standing behind the island shuffling her papers together, probably her lesson plans.

"I'm ready," I said, hoisting my bag onto my shoulders after I had finished tying my shoes. She grabbed the door knob and we headed out. She was taking bites of her bagel and sips of her coffee in between each step we took. She used to grab me a morning bagel and butter it, but I enjoyed going and grabbing breakfast from the cafeteria. They normally had mini cereal bowls and morning pastries.

Once at school, I headed straight to the cafeteria. My stomach was finally starting to wake up and I was ready for breakfast. I could smell the sausage through the halls. I grabbed a small thing of corn flakes and went into the line. Staring down at the links, my stomach growled in anticipation. They sat on the other side of the cafeteria glass, enticing me to get them. I caved, hearing them whisper in my hunger stricken delusion. I took my little breakfast and headed to my first period.

I plopped my food bundle onto my desk. Grabbing for one of the links first, I dug into my breakfast. Since mom was a teacher, I was normally one of the first kids in class. I waited there and watched as students poured into history class. Most of them barely awake with crust still covering their eyes. There was a handful who had probably been up since four or five in the morning helping with farm chores.

A boy who looked oddly familiar walked in. I had never really noticed him before, but I knew that he wasn't a new kid. I watched as he took his seat in the same spot he had probably been sitting in all year. I stared at him until the bell rang, scaring me into thinking I had been caught red handed. I quickly turned back to face the front of the classroom, feeling my cheeks burned.

Without Emily, you're still a freak, ran through my head. I swear it felt like everyone had been staring at me. I was probably crazy but I could feel their eyes burning lasers into me. Finally the teacher walked in and greeted the class. The heat seemed to die down. I looked around. No one seemed to care about the crisis I felt like I was having. It was probably just in my head.

Ms. Sheets started going down the list, doing a mental roll call of each student in her class. Once she had marked the absence of students, she got to work teaching today's lesson. We breezed through the conversation. Most students opted out of participating today. Probably because they still felt like shit from the party, too.

"Wasn't the Stamp Act in 1765?" the familiar boy said with his hand in the air.

"Yes, that is correct, Max," Ms. Sheets said, continuing with her lecture. It was Jigsaw boy. My mouth practically fell to the floor when I realized. He had had his hair slick back and black for the Halloween party but now I could see he had brown curly hair that came to his ears. He turned to look at me. We made eye contact and I froze. I didn't know what I should do. He winked at me and flashed a smile. I tried to smile back, but just turned to face the front of class again.

When the bell rang, I bolted out of the class. I didn't want to give jigsaw, or I guess Max, the opportunity to talk to me. I tried to focus during my other classes but I couldn't stop thinking about Max and the Halloween party. I was trying to jog my memory of what happened that night. I remember Max and I on the dance floor kissing but he left before I even went to bed.

Before I realized it, it was time for biology, which was good because I really wanted to talk to Jessica. Since Emily had been giving me the cold shoulder, I hadn't really talked to anyone about the party and now I had gossip to dish out. I walked with a purpose to Mr. Blackford's class, but stopped short when I walked in.

Mallory was sitting there, alone. Her face was buried in her phone. Jessica must have decided to skip school today. I was pretty sure her and Mallory had the same class before this because I would see them walk in together. The only time one of them was early to class was when the other was home sick. I tapped on Mallory's desk.

"Hey, how are you?" I asked. Her face shot up to look at me. Her eyes stained red.

"Oh," she said, her voice catching in her throat a little, "I've been good, you know." She shrugged trying to hide the fact that she had been crying. Maybe her and Jessica had gotten into a fight at the party, too.

"That's good. Where's Jessica?" I asked, pointing to the empty desk next to her.

"She's probably at home resting her massive hangover." Mallory tried to laugh off what she had said but I could see the concern fill her eyes.

"Yeah probably," I said, trying to make her feel better. I didn't know what more to say to her, so I walked to my desk and sat. I didn't dislike Mallory but she was not who I really wanted to be talking to anyway.

Mr. Blackford had split us into groups for a lab project. Mallory sat a few lab tables over. I watched her checking her phone repeatedly throughout the class period. I assumed she was texting Jessica updates on the class work for Biology, but something seemed off. I tried to stay focused on my lab work, but my eyes would occasionally look over at Mallory.

I tried catching her as we went to lunch but she never packed a lunch so Mallory headed straight for the cafeteria while I still needed to run to my locker. I hurried that way trying to spare a little time. Mallory's concern grew over the course of the class and I wanted to talk to her again. If her and Jessica were fighting, maybe we could offer each other advice on how to mend the friendships that were being threatened.

Of course, I knew I couldn't fully confide in Mallory, but it would be nice to talk to someone. I said some bad things, but maybe Mallory would understand me. I was just starting to feel suffocated. Maybe Jessica felt suffocated by Mallory, I thought. Whatever their issues were, I just knew talking with Mallory would make me feel better.

Once I got to the cafeteria, I headed to the courtyard. It was still nice enough for the administration to keep it open so I assumed Mallory would still be eating outside. I looked around but only saw Britney. She was with the other girl at the party who wasn't Annabelle and another junior girl who I remember seeing at the party. I wanted to walk over there and ask Britney if she knew what was going on. I knew that would probably be social suicide on my part, but I wanted answers.

She caught me walking her way and stared. Her other two friends didn't seem to notice and I could tell she wanted to keep it that way. I was just some lowly sophomore who wasn't worth her time, at least that was what her eyes were trying to convey. She didn't want me coming over there and ruining whatever she had going.

Her eyes continued staring, her head slowly moving side to side. She looked more like a viper than a girl. Her body stiffen at the threat of danger, sending her warning call of a poisonous end. I took the hint and went back inside to try and look for Mallory. Britney was at the "adult" party so she probably wouldn't know anything that happened between Mallory and Jessica anyway. Plus I didn't remember seeing her name pop up in the group chat that Jessica had made, so I didn't think the three of them were really on good terms.

Jessica was probably pissed at Britney for picking Jacob over her at the party. Mallory's slurred warning ran through my head. I couldn't understand how Jessica and Mallory could have gone from laughing drunks to silent friends.

Thinking of the group chat, I remember I could see when Jessica was last active there. I pulled my phone out and read through the different messages. A few of the girls were talking about what they had planned to wear today, but I hadn't seen anything from Jessica. I scrolled back further to Sunday. The last message from Jessica was saying she planned to stay late at the horse stables.

I don't know why but in that moment panic raced through my body. I think it was the concern that was on Mallory's face in Biology. I ran to the bathroom feeling like I was going to get sick. I couldn't help myself, but I could feel something was wrong. I pulled my phone out again and sent a quick text to Jessica.

Hey girl, I saw you weren't in Bio and I wanted to check in on you.

I waited in the bathroom for a response. I stared at the phone until my eyes started to cross. I wanted Jessica to respond and tell me everything was fine with her. The bell to signal that lunch was over went off, breaking my staring contest with the phone. I went to my next class hoping to see a response by the end. I waited the rest of the day for Jessica to respond, but she never did.

I decided that the next morning I would wait outside bio class. It was only the first day back, so I didn't need to be worrying as much as I was. Plus, Jessica and I just started texting. I don't really know how long it normally takes her to respond. I played reason after reason why Jessica hadn't responded.

I continued playing those reasons over and over in my head while I waited for her outside of bio, but Mallory walked up to me. That means Jessica wasn't here again today. Or maybe the two of them were fighting so Jessica walked alone. I tried finding her in the sea of students behind Mallory, but she wasn't there. I stared at Mallory, willing her to come to me. I could see her eyes were still puffy. Maybe she hadn't been sleeping well. I wondered what happened between her and Jessica and I was going to find out. As she walked closer, I pushed my body off the wall, getting in her way.

"Hey," I said, blocking her from getting closer to the class, "Do you know where Jessica is?"

"No, I don't," she said, trying to push past me.

"Haven't you talked to her?" I blocked her again.

"She hasn't answered my text," Mallory spat.

Mallory shoved past me, nearly knocking me into the wall I had been leaning against. She wasn't the viper like Britney had been at lunch. She was definitely still on the predator side of things. I knew if Jessica hadn't brought me into their group Mallory would have eventually devoured me alive.

No she wasn't like Britney, ready to attack because I was getting too close to her nest. She was more like a wounded dog or a trapped bear. Scared and lashing out at anyone coming near. Not sure who is there to help and who is there to hurt her. I didn't know how to get her to trust me, but I knew how it would go if she was a wounded animal.

I gently walked into the classroom, after I had collected myself. Making my way to Mallory's desk, I tried to present a friendly demeanor. Mallory's puffy eyes registered she was my target, quickly trying to avert away from me. I needed to speak with her, though.

I got closer to her desk, kneeling to be eye level with her. I didn't want to draw the attention of the other students, but I could see a few heads turn to look in our direction. I ignored them, but I could see Mallory's eyes darting between them and me. Maybe she was trying to plead with them. She really was just a scared animal.

The thought sent chills through my spine. I didn't know what Mallory had to be so afraid of, but her fear only worried me more. I was hoping she was in on whatever game Jessica was playing at, and just scared to get caught. I needed to rationalize my thoughts, before I spoke to Mallory.

Inhaling, I collected my thoughts into a nice bubble, ready to only let out what Mallory was ready to talk about.

"I didn't mean to upset you," I whispered, calmly to Mallory.

Most of the wandering eyes had gotten bored, but I didn't want listening ears to pick up our conversation. She barely glanced up from her notebook. She wasn't writing in it, in fact, it wasn't even open. She just wanted to not engage with the world. I understood her feelings, but that was why I needed to talk to her. I was pretty sure I was the only person who really understood what she was going through.

"I don't want to talk to you Charlie," she said through gritted teeth.

"Okay," I started to say, but the bell cut me off. I wanted to say so much more but I knew there wasn't the time. Mr. Blackford would be coming in any minute now, telling me to get to my desk. So instead, I just settled with, "I'm here if you want to talk."

Chapter Eleven

It took the rest of the week, but Mallory did come around. I didn't push anymore after Tuesday's bio class, but I smiled on Wednesday and Thursday, trying to show I was still there for her. Jessica's absence was causing more worry to grow. I wondered if her parents were down Mallory's throat. She gave me the opportunity to ask.

Thursday towards the end of the day, I got a text from a number I didn't have saved. I knew who it was from the message, "r u still down 2 talk?" I recognized the number had been in our group chat, which confirmed it was Mallory for me.

Always, was all I sent.

Ur moms a teacher, right?

Does that mean you can stay after?

I didn't know how Mallory knew mom was a teacher, but I wasn't going to respond with that.

Yeah, I'll tell her we're studying. Courtyard?

Too cold. Library.

Okay see you there

Thx

Waiting for the bell to let me go, my legs shook under me. Once the bell finally did ring out, I bolted. I didn't need to go straight to my locker if I was planning on staying later. Instead, I headed down the middle school hallway, trying to remember which way to mom's class specifically.

Luckily, I didn't have to remember. Barely taller than the students she was saying goodbye to, mom stood in the hallway, a smile brighter than the lights shining to the students. Catching sight of me in the hallway, shock took over her face. She normally was the one waiting for me out of the car, but today was different.

"I need to stay after for a little bit," I huffed, finishing my sprint to her.

"What?" she said, shaking her head.

"I need to stay after," I repeated, not sure if she couldn't hear me.

"Why, though?"

"Mallory needs help with something," I pleaded.

"Who?"

The commotion around us was drowning out my voice. The middle schoolers were more ravenous than we were. I heard a loud scream come from the end of the hall, which resulted in louder yells from others. I followed the sound, shocked by the almost howl-like sound coming from a group of jersey wearing boys. The colors looked like school ones. Rolling my eyes, I turned back to mom.

"Is it always like this?"

"Yeah, normally," she said, shrugging, "It gets worse at the end of the week."

"Gross, but Mallory needs me to stay after," I said.

"I have some tests that need grading," she said tapping her chin, "but it won't take me longer than probably thirty minutes."

"That should be plenty of time," I said, turning to leave, "We'll be in the library."

I turned back, quickly giving her a hug before leaving the chaotic animal kingdom of middle schoolers. The howl had died down, but they had started heading towards the bus doors, banging on their chest. I couldn't get to the library fast enough after seeing them.

Mallory was already sitting at one of the small reading tables. Her phone was in her hand and had all her attention. She must not have heard the library doors open or my steps as I came up to her. Her phone clashed to the table as she jumped out of her skin when she realized I was standing there.

"Jesus," she said, grabbing her chest. "Why are you so quiet?"

"Sorry," I said, my cheeks getting hot. "I thought you heard the door." I hitched my thumb towards the library door, another student coming in almost on cue.

"No, it's fine." she brushed off. "I've just been a little jumpy since the party."

At the mention of the party, I watched her body tense up. She tried playing it off with a stretch, but it couldn't hide the worry in Mallory's eyes. I slid into the seat across from hers, reaching to calm her shaking hands. She hesitated the embrace, but let it happen anyway.

"What happened after?" I asked in a rush. Mallory averted her gaze, shaking her head.

"I don't know," she cried out. "Jessica gave me the cold shoulder that morning. I don't know what I did."

Tears filled Mallory's eyes, but she tried shutting them in. I gave a light squeeze to her hands while letting her collect herself. By her fragile demeanor, I could see she was barely holding it together all week. The cracks were finally starting to show and I must have been the only person willing to reach out.

"So I'm sorry, but I don't know," she finally said, just barely above a whisper. Her head was down, so I couldn't see her eyes, but I saw the little puddles forming on the table.

"It's okay," I tried reassuring her, my thumbs rubbing the back of her hand like mom would do to comfort me. "Do you think her parents grounded her?"

Mallory's head gave a small disapproving nod. I had never met the Johnson's so I didn't know about their parenting style. I tried probing a little more, careful not to scare her off. I knew she was real and in front of me, but I feared that one wrong move and she would vanish before me like Emily did at the party. My heart aches with her absence, causing me to hold Mallory a little closer.

"What are they like?" I asked, "Jessica's parents."

"They were nice," she started, "but since they think I know something, they've been so aggressive." I could hear her voice croaking under sobs.

"What do you mean by that?"

"They're convinced I told her to run away." Mallory threw her hands up in the air. "Told me I was always a bad influence and that they should have never let me into their family."

As her words registered, the sadness crept back over her. She slumped into her chair, releasing my hands. I watched her get lost in her own thoughts, but I couldn't figure out what she was thinking. Maybe she was replaying the conversation over in her head.

"I remember the first day I met Jessica," she said, as if she knew what I was asking, "It was the first day of horse camp."

Her eyes stared off somewhere behind me, like she was watching the memory play off in the distance. I wanted to turn to see if I could see it, too, but I knew the thought was silly and I didn't want to make Mallory feel embarrassed. I didn't know why she was telling me these things, or why she wanted to confide in me, but I wasn't going to let the opportunity for answers go.

"We couldn't have been older than ten," she continued, "I had been so scared of the horses, but Jessica, she wasn't afraid of anything."

"So she's always been a horse girl?" I asked half-heartedly. I got into a more comfortable position as Mallory continued her memory.

"She was born to ride," Mallory said, "is born to ride." She corrected herself. "She's still out there," Mallory whispered.

"I'm sure she'll come back," I said, letting Mallory know that I believed her whispered thoughts.

"I know she will," Mallory said, finally breaking her vacant stare to make eye contact, "Of course she will come back."

"So born to ride?" I tried moving the subject back to her memory.

"Yeah," she half smiled, "They didn't let us ride the horses right away, but Jessica still tried saddling one up while we were broken up for lunch."

"How did she manage that?" I could feel my eyes getting big at the thought of tiny Jessica and a massive horse.

"She technically didn't," Mallory laughed, "but with a little help, she was able to get on a pony."

"A little help," I raised my brow, assuming Mallory was that little help. She threw her hands in the air defensively, but was still laughing.

"Hey, I said I was afraid of the horses," she said, "but I didn't say anything about the ponies."

"So how far did you two get?"

"Oh, not very."

For some reason, this sent both of us into laughter, drawing a few eyes towards our direction. Even a shhh from one of the librarians that was pushing a cart around. It felt nice to hear laughter though. Clearly they didn't understand the stress of the world Mallory and I were in. Both of our closest friends had just up and left us, without a word. We needed this time to forget that.

"So where do you think she went?" Mallory asked, her voice losing all the joy it had a moment ago.

"Honestly, I was hoping you'd have a clue," my mouth spoke before my brain could filter what was said.

"What?" Mallory tried to register what I was saying, "Do you think this is some Nancy Drew thing to solve?"

Now it was my turn to throw my hands up defensively. I hadn't come to this with some plan to solve anything. I wasn't even sure there was a mystery to solve, so I didn't understand what Mallory meant by that.

"No," I started, "I just meant that I don't know Jessica as well as you do, clearly by the pony story." I tried using her story to re-lighten the mood, but I could see in her eyes it was too late. Maybe I wasn't the only one at school who had reached out, and the other students just wanted a story they could run with.

"So then, why did you offer to talk?" she asked, her arms folded over her chest.

"A close friend and I just got into a fight," I started confessing, "I think really I just wanted someone else to talk to. You know, get an opinion."

I didn't know why I was telling Mallory about Emily, but it felt right to do. She had opened up with her story, so I felt open to do the same. And it was true. I was hoping Mallory would be a listening ear for me, if I was one for her.

"I know it's silly," I continued, "but I thought you and Jessica had gotten into a fight. I hoped we could help each other out with our issues." I paused to see if she had anything to add. "But I don't think we can." I stared down at my hands, letting my words register with me, too.

We sat in silence for a moment. I didn't look up. It was my turn to have a moment and let Mallory reassure me. I hoped that she would, but I assumed she was weighing her options. She seemed to enjoy talking, but did she care that it was with me. The new girl freak. I could never tell her who the friend was or she would really believe the new girl freak label that I felt I was getting for myself.

"What was the fight about?" Mallory asked.

"Something stupid." I tried brushing it off, before realizing that wasn't helpful. I let out a big sigh. "Actually, I was a big jerk," I admitted.

"You?" Now it was Mallory's turn to raise her brows.

"Yeah, me," I said, rolling my eyes. "I may have had a little too much to drink."

"Wait, was it at the Halloween party?" Mallory leaned forward, clearly now more intrigued.

I let too much out. I didn't know how to take it back and I didn't know how to go forward. My hesitation only furthered Mallory's suspicion. Her Cheshire grin taking over as she set her chin over her hands. She suddenly looked like a kid on the edge of their seat waiting to hear back from Santa.

"Yeah, kinda," I lied.

"I didn't think you had any friends here." She let out a slight chuckle before realizing what she had said, "sorry."

"No, you're right," I agreed, rolling my eyes. I knew I couldn't try to come up with someone at school that I could have fought with. Plus, I figured if I did that, Mallory would run to get their side of the story on Monday. They would probably think I was trying to start drama, which I really didn't need. Instead, I used the same scapegoat I had been since Emily came into my life.

"Her name is Ashley," I said. "She was my best friend at my other school."

"Was?" Mallory asked, one brow still raised, "Do you not think it is fixable?"

I knew my friendship with the real Ashley couldn't be fixed, so I sprinkled bits of her story in with my fight with Emily. I told Mallory that I had been pretty sure that she was seeing my ex boyfriend and in a drunken slur, I had confronted her about it. I explained that was why I had been in the bathroom for a while that night.

"Jessica thought you had gone, but didn't know where," she said when I was explaining that part.

"Yeah, I had gotten really heated and needed a moment to collect myself," I lied, as the memory of the fight started playing over in my head. The alcohol had made parts of it a bit fuzzy, so some pieces were still missing.

"In the bathroom, I called her and unleashed," I rambled, "I really can't remember what I said." That was the truth. I felt like my words had been harsher than my memory was willing to let me know.

"Well honestly, she sounds kinda like a bitch." Mallory's words cut through my fogged thought.

"No, Emily isn't," I heard myself saying, "I meant Ashley. Sorry, my thoughts are all over the place at the moment." I tried to recover.

I didn't think Mallory actually believed that. She probably thought everything I just said was a lie. It technically wasn't a lie, I was just combining two people's stories. That rationale didn't really make me feel any better about it, so I tried dropping it. Maybe I could move it back to Jessica. I hoped my slip up didn't cause Mallory to go back to distrusting me.

"Who's Emily?" she finally asked.

"Emily was the other one in our group," I lied, "She was the glue I guess. She sided with Ashley though, so I lost her friendship, too. That's what I was thinking about."

I didn't know if I was giving too much information to make it believable, but the words came out almost like vomit. My mouth is unable to keep anything sealed at the moment. Mallory just stared for a while, probably trying to decide what to believe.

"I didn't realize," she said.

"Didn't realize?" I asked, looking up puzzled by her comment.

"Yeah, didn't realize that you had no one." She said it so nonchalantly, but somehow it slashed through me, making me realize it too. I had no one. Emily was gone and something about the way Mallory had said it, it felt like she was never coming back.

"Yeah," I quietly said, really ready to be done with this conversation now. I hoped mom would come to my rescue soon, but I really wasn't sure that would happen. The silence grew louder over us, as we made awkward glances at each other. Neither of us knowing what to say, hoping the other would just speak. I thought Mallory was just going to get up and leave.

As she leaned down for her bag, one of the books fell off a shelf near us. It caused Mallory to jump back into her seat, dropping the bag. She yelped as she cowered under her hands. The few eyes still left in the library looked at the commotion, but the librarian was too shocked to shush her scream.

"I'm sorry," Mallory said, trying to collect herself. "It's just flying books and me don't really mix well as you know."

She tried laughing it off, but she wouldn't take her eyes off the book that laid on the floor. I couldn't help but stare at it too. I knew the books at that library had been Emily. I looked around to see if she was somewhere in the library, but my hope was quickly extinguished.

"It probably wasn't pushed all the way back," I said, pushing myself up from the table to put it back on the shelf.

"Yeah you're probably right," Mallory agreed, "but just to be safe, I'm going to head out." She already had her bag over her shoulder and was up from the table. "You know, before things get crazy." She laughed it off, but I could still hear the worry in her voice. Clearly Emily's meltdown had impacted her, even if this is the first time she's been willing to acknowledge it.

"Sounds good," I called over my shoulder, leaning down to grab the book. "I'll talk to you later."

"Talk to you later," I could hear her calling as she walked towards the door.

Grabbing the book, a cold shiver went through my hand and down my spine. Dropping the book, I looked up expecting to see Emily. She wasn't there, no one was. I was alone, leaning over a book. There was nothing special about the book, I tried rationalizing to myself. It probably wasn't pushed all the way back, I remembered.

I picked it up from the ground again, sans the cold chill, and put it back onto the shelf. I was putting myself on edge by trying to force Emily into my life. I wanted every little unexplainable thing to be her. I was honestly probably looking for more "signs" and blaming completely explainable events on her. I knew I was trying to fill her void, but it was starting to make me feel more crazy.

Mom pushed through the heavy library doors, her frame almost swallowed in the doorway. She had come to save me from the crazy thoughts that were clouding me. She had some sort of mom sense that always knew when I needed to be rescued. Moving quickly to close the gap between us, I tried putting distance between those thoughts.

"I need to grab my stuff from my locker," I told her.

"Okay, I will meet you at the car."

Chapter Twelve

Commotion from the kitchen carried the scent of chicken and bacon into my room. My stomach growling in response. I sat alone pushing into my bed, while my mind raced. I tried to focus on getting my homework complete, but every pop of the pans clanging together in the kitchen sent me into a spiral.

It had been about two weeks since Jessica's party and she still hadn't shown up. Her parents had come to school and pulled Mallory out of class Wednesday after we had talked in the library. That's when the rumors decided to run rampant. Kids in class started to whisper about Jessica's drug problem that she didn't have.

"She must have gotten caught up in the wrong dealer," one student said, shaking their head in disbelief.

"I'm sure she OD'd in the middle of the woods," another student said.

They were filling in the blanks where the officers wouldn't, making it impossible to get a clear understanding of what was happening. I knew the gossiping teenagers needed something to talk about, but the way they turned Jessica into a villain was unexpected. Mallory had been red-faced in most of her classes that week, and the whispers attacked her too.

"I bet Mallory had something to do with it."

"She was always jealous of Jessica, I wouldn't put it past her."

Mallory may not have been the nicest girl at school but she definitely wasn't the meanest either. People blamed her for Jessica's disappearance, saying if she was a better friend Jessica would still be here. I could see Mallory's heart break a little more each day that Jessica didn't show up. I knew what she was feeling, because if I was a better friend Emily would be here.

I wanted to reach out to Mallory again, spending nights staring at her number on my phone. After we talked, I thought we had built a little more of a friendship, but the following Monday she pretended it had never happened. When the girls in our chat realized that Jessica was missing, the chat went silent. Eerily starting with Jessica and ending in a way with her. She must have been the glue holding a lot of people together.

Everyday that I didn't see Emily sitting in mom's back seat or in classes ready to gossip, my heart broke a little more, like Mallory's. She didn't know it, but we had more in common. It was my fault that Emily was gone, but it probably wasn't Mallory's fault for Jessica. I just wish I could figure out how to bring them both back. This had been the longest I had to go without Emily by my side since school started, and it showed me how truly alone I really was.

A soft knock at my bedroom door sent all thoughts out the window. Mom was standing in my doorway, steam rising from the chicken that was on her plate. I hadn't realized how lost in thought I had been. My homework assignments and textbooks were still in my bag, untouched.

"Dinner's ready," mom said, extending the plate to me.

"Thanks," I said, pushing myself to my feet and grabbing for the plate.

"I thought you were coming in here to do homework," she said, pointing at the still closed backpack that sat on my floor.

"I planned to," I said, turning to look at the enemy, "I got distracted by my thoughts." I tapped the side of my temple and tried to push a smile through.

"Are you worried about that girl?" mom asked, concern clouding her face.

I nodded my head, dropping my eye contact with mom. I knew she meant Jessica and I was worried about her, too. I was more worried about Emily at the moment, though. I didn't know anything about the other side really and had steered away from asking about it in the past, mostly because I didn't want to think of the morbidity of death.

Now, I felt like I could kick myself because of it. I didn't know if Emily had the power to cross over whenever she wanted. I didn't know where Emily could go when she wasn't with me. I felt like I didn't know anything, which started making my head spin. I stared hard at the floor, trying to will the tears back. It was becoming harder and harder as mom talked. She was telling me about how nothing bad happens in small towns, so Jessica would turn up any day now.

"Honestly, she was probably upset that her parents grounded her so she went to stay with a friend for a few days." Mom continued to ramble as she walked in the living room where her dinner plate was waiting.

I knew if mom was right about Jessica, Mallory wouldn't still have puffy eyes. She was Jessica's closest friend, so she should know where Jessica would run to hide. I didn't understand mom's complete one-eighty she was doing. Just a week or so back, she was ready to rip my head off over stranger danger, and now she was trying to convince me nothing bad could ever happen.

I wanted to believe the optimism she was trying to radiate in the apartment. But the grim reality would creep in, mom's eye flashing with worry with the latest new reports yielding nothing. My spiraling must have been more noticeable than I assumed, so she thought she needed to be the stronger one of us.

I followed her, trying to push all the thoughts out of my head. I imagined stacks of papers in my brain, each one representing a stress in my life. The mini me inside my head tried to push them off a little cliff I had given her. She was pushing and trying, mostly clearly all the stacks.

When mini me got to the ones marked Emily and Jessica, she shrunk, allowing the stacks to tower over her. I wasn't going to let myself get defeated. I forced my mini me to shove those stacks with all her might, but they wouldn't budge. I kept seeing this scene over and over in my head, as I stabbed the potatoes, trying to stab out the emotions I was having.

After dinner, I helped mom clean the kitchen as we made small talk. It was really my attempt to silence my thoughts. I would ask about her classes and which ones were her favorite and why. I had learned pretty quickly that she didn't enjoy her after lunch class because they were full and ready for a nap, so they hardly paid attention.

She went on and on about her second period class. She mentioned names of kids that I wouldn't remember and how they would bring her gifts or crafts to try and brighten her day. She was passionate about teaching, but I knew mom really appreciated it when her kids showed appreciation. She finished loading the dishwasher as she finished telling me the wonders of teaching.

"Have you given any thought to what you want to do?" mom asked, seemingly out of nowhere.

"Not really," I said. I really hadn't thought about my future or what job I would enjoy. I didn't think I could be a teacher like she was. Some of her stories would send me into a psychotic break. But, I didn't want to be a car salesman like my dad, so I didn't ever really think about it.

"Haven't they done any job placement training in school?" she asked, interrupting my thoughts.

"We had a finance game once," I said, remembering my freshman year back at Springfield. "But we didn't get to really pick jobs, they had a list and you got to pick based on your grade."

"Well it's something you may want to start thinking about," mom said while drying her hand. "I have a few things I need to grade. Are you going to start your homework?"

We both gave a half chuckle since I was supposed to start with it before dinner. I nodded and we both walked to the bedrooms. I split off at my door and watched mom continue the two feet to her room. She turned to me and we both gave the sailor salute as we went to tackle our papers.

Once in my room, I quietly shut the door and leaned against it. The world felt like it was sitting on my chest, needing a minute, I slid down the back of the door and crumbled at the floor. My emotions had felt all over the place the last few days and I still wasn't fully sure I was okay.

I tried to collect myself, but if I allowed my brain more than a second to think, I would be wrapped back into my armadillo ball. Racing between hoping that Jessica was okay, hoping Emily would come back, and just wishing I felt normal, my body ached with stress and pressure.

Shaking, I finally pushed myself away from my door towards my bag on the floor. Tears still poured down my face as if someone was letting a bucket fill before watching it tip over and spill water over my cheeks. I knew I wasn't going to be able to do any homework in this state, but I was hoping movement would give my brain the distraction I needed.

I climbed to the side of my bed, pulling my body up by the comforter that hung off. Once I finished the Everest long climb, I pulled my bag up to be my companion. I sat with it folded into my chest for a long while. The weight of the bag prevented me from floating into my thoughts again. I felt like removing it would send me into a world wind spiral that I wasn't prepared for.

The sun was shining through my windows, bringing heat into my cold room. The days since the party had been sunny and bright and today was no different. I peered out the windows and saw no clouds in the sky, just the sun demanding to be seen. It felt like a mockery of my life. It seemed beautiful and bright at the moment, but the longer you stood in the sun, the hotter and more uncomfortable things became.

I went to sit back on my bed, tired of watching the endless sky. With how bright it still was outside, I couldn't curl into a ball, closing my eyes until tomorrow's alarm went off. I began a staring contest with my bedroom door. I didn't want to leave and risk mom seeing me but I didn't want to sit in here, suffering in silence.

I finally decided to turn my brain off. I was going to flip my TV on, hoping to find something stupid to watch. I really enjoyed watching the Simpsons when I was sad but I wasn't sure if they would be on. I was hoping to find something with the same type of humor so I didn't need to think about my falling world.

I was aimlessly flipping through each channel, stopping long enough to register what was playing and skipping it once I realized it didn't fit my criteria. My overhead light flickered, like someone was turning the light on and off. I half expected to see mom messing with my light when I turned around, but nothing. The switch wasn't moving to indicate some demon moving it.

I stared up at the light that was still flickering. It must be close to needing a new light, but I wasn't going to change it tonight. With the sun still out, it was bright enough that I didn't need the light on anyway. Swinging my legs off the side of the bed, I decided I was going to turn it off. Once it started getting darker, I could turn on a movie and wallow in my blankets and pity.

The light finally stopped having its seizure, light from the window still keeping my room illuminated. Since I was up, I decided to lay out the things I would need for tomorrow. I didn't really take anything out of my back pack, so I left it still sitting on the bed. I would throw the pens and pencils back in and set it in my desk chair when I was ready to crawl back into bed.

I moved clothes around in my closet, trying to play God and determine what the weather would do tomorrow. I figured I would get a T-shirt and bring a hoodie in case the weather changed up on us. I was looking through my hoodie option trying to pick one.

I pulled out an old black one that had my middle school dance team logo printed on the back. I really liked this one, but I could hear Emily saying something snarky about it. I brought it back out to my room and threw it next to my pants.

"I can't believe you're going to wear something from middle school," Emily said from behind me.

Wait! Emily? I stopped dead in my tracks, her voice finally hitting my brain. I turned very slowly, afraid that sudden movement would scare her away, like a deer. I didn't believe that she was actually there, but she was standing with her arms crossed looking at the hoodie with disgust. A brown curl hung in her face. She was actually there.

Her cold figure watched me collect myself. I was so excited to finally have Emily back, that I immediately threw my body into her, expecting she'd catch me in a beautiful hug. I was so caught up in my excitement that I had forgotten she was a ghost. She did try to catch me but I just went flying. I had bounced off my bed and landed on the floor with a thud.

I could hear mom mute her TV and move around in her room. She was coming to investigate the sound I just made. Quickly thinking on my feet I moved some books to the floor. When she burst through the door, I didn't want to have to explain I was over zealous from my dead friend coming back.

She flung the door open, hitting Emily in the process. Emily's body exploded on impact. It was as if she was just paint being splattered on the wall, but her body slowly re-materialized while mom stood in the doorway. I tried to gather my composure while mom eyed the situation in my room. If only she could see everything going on.

"What happened?" she asked, looking around. "I thought I heard a noise."

"Yeah," I said, stepping aside to show the mess of books on the floor, "I had my textbooks in my bed and accidentally kicked them off the bed."

Mom stood in the doorway, eying me and the textbooks suspiciously. I tried to plaster innocence on my face, but I wasn't sure it was really convincing her. She didn't have any reason not to trust me. The textbooks were on the floor and no boys were trying to hide under my bed. She finally gave up and retreated back to her room.

Once the door completely closed, I looked around for Emily. I could finally talk to her, ask her where she's been and finally spill the gossip to her. Since she had vanished during the party, she didn't know about Jessica's disappearance or how quickly the school had turned on Mallory.

"Where have you been?" I whispered, still going to her for another hug.

She stared at me wildly and didn't move. It was like she didn't know who I was. I felt like she was just showing herself to put me in more agony. We stood like this for a long time, just staring back at each other. Her eyes wide like a scared deer who would bolt at the first sign of trouble. I was afraid to blink, thinking she would disappear while my eyes were shut.

The silence only echoed the pain her presence caused. She continued standing, never moving. I worried that she was just a figment of my imagination. I started questioning my sanity, questioning if she was ever really there to begin with. Memories with her replaying in my head, trying to confirm if she was there, or worse, just something my brain created. But why would she be what my brain created? Was she a trauma response that I made up? Convincing myself she was just a ghost to hide the fact I was losing my mind.

"You can see me again?" she asked, finally breaking the silence between us.

"What do you mean?" I asked, confused by her question, "You've been gone since the party."

"No I haven't," she said blinking at me, "I was waiting in the car Monday morning, but you looked right through me."

It suddenly clicked. I thought I was feeling her presence throughout the weeks, but I never saw her. I assumed my imagination had been trying to fill her place, making me cold or seeing things move when there wasn't anything.

"Wait, were you messing with the lights?" I asked, realizing that she was trying to get my attention this whole time.

"Yes." Her voice raised an octave as she threw her hands down in frustration. "I've been doing everything to get you to notice me, again."

"I'm sorry," I said sheepishly, "I didn't know you were there." I felt incredibly bad because I had been mentally begging her to come back and she was with me the whole time, I just didn't realize she had been.

"It's not your fault," she finally said, "The whole afterlife rules are weird anyway."

"So, why can I see you again?" I was happy to finally see her again but I didn't want to screw up.

"I don't know how the rules work," she said, raising her shoulders to her ears. "I can't remember anything about my past life, but I can remember every day I aimlessly walk through those high school halls."

She wandered around the room, messing with the things on my desk and shelves. I never really thought about how death had affected her thoughts and memories. I stared at her, hoping if I looked hard enough the answers would appear out of thin air like she did. Nothing happened, she just stared back with questioning eyes.

"But you're back," I said to break the tension.

"For now," she said nonchalantly.

"What do you mean by that," I asked, panicked. I didn't know if that meant she was just coming back to give it to me for being rude at the party and leave.

"I just told you I didn't know how the rules worked," she started, "I don't know what even happened to make you see me again."

"Have you been here this whole time?" I asked, thinking of my breakdown that I had been having. I was hoping that she would say she wasn't there watching me lose my shit over not being able to see her.

"I mean not this whole time. Sometimes I would visit the neighbors just to see how they were living," she said sitting on my bed, her body not creating a dent in the bed like mine did.

"So if you've been with me the whole time, does that mean you know about Jessica running away?" I asked, a little sad that I wouldn't actually be able to spill anything to Emily.

"She didn't run away," Emily said coldly.

"How would you know what happened?" I asked, crossing my arms. I didn't think Jessica had run away either but there was no way Emily knew what was happening.

"I saw her," Emily said. Her eyes were wide as if she was seeing Jessica in my room now.

"Seeing her doesn't mean anything." I said, "You saw her everyday in class." I tried to justify what she was saying to me. "Honestly, seeing her proves that she didn't get taken, right?"

Emily looked at me with somber eyes. It felt like she was going to tell me my dog went to live on a nice farm upstate. I was right, if Emily saw Jessica walking around somewhere, then Jessica wasn't trapped in some weird guy's basement. That had to count for something, she probably got in trouble for the party and left to cool down.

"I'm pretty sure she saw me too," Emily said. She waited for me to realize what it was she was trying to say.

"So you're saying she's dead?" I asked, not fully believing what I was hearing. Mom's voice of nothing bad happening in small towns racing through my head.

"I mean, I think so," Emily said, rolling her hands into each other, "I didn't stop and try to talk to her or anything, but we made eye contact."

"How do you know you made eye contact if you didn't talk to her?"

"Because she gave me the same look I gave you the first time you saw me," she said, trying to give her death experience to Jessica.

"Well that doesn't mean anything," I said, shrugging her off, "I can see you and I'm not dead, maybe whatever she's going through has given her the special gift."

"Charlie," she said, putting her hands through my shoulder, "She doesn't have some special gift. She's dead."

"Oh yeah? Then where's her body?" I asked, folding my arms. Emily had been nothing but a gossip since I got here and she was just trying to push the rumor mill like the kids at school.

"How did I respond when you asked me how I died?" She mimicked my gestures. Clearly, she wasn't enjoying any of the attitude I was giving.

"I just can't comprehend what you're trying to say," I finally said. There were a million other things I wanted to say to her. Why are you lying? Why are you being like this? I can never have real friends. I could only think about these things, because I knew starting a fight would only make her leave again and that wasn't what I wanted.

"I'm just telling you what I thought I saw." Emily had turned on her motherly voice that she frequently used on me.

"So you could be wrong?" I asked, trying to hold onto hope. I could see her thinking about it. Maybe Emily had moved something near Jessica and it caught her attention.

"I didn't talk to her so who knows," Emily pushed herself off the bed and started pacing. I just stared at her as she made circles into my carpet. She had her chin in her hand probably running through the scene with Jessica.

"See, so maybe you just thought you guys made eye contact," I said, moving to sit cross legged on the bed, my stomach sinking. The room seemed to tilt as Emily's circles had gotten wider. Her brows furrowed into a line, spinning on her heels she moved her circles the other way.

"Maybe," Emily said, raising her index finger, turning to face me. She paused for a long moment. "She's been able to see me all along, but didn't want to say anything."

"You don't think she would have said something if she could see you?" I asked.

"I mean you don't shout it from the roof top, do you?" she started, "You use your phone, or excuse yourself from an area, or tell people you're jumpy." She ticked off each finger as she listed the ways I had kept our communication secret.

"So she made eye contact with you to let you know that she can see you?" I was still questioning the idea of Jessica being able to see Emily. Why not send me a text about it? Or even just pull me aside to talk about it?

"It's a possibility," she said, coming back to the bed, "It was the first time I've seen her without you around."

"Well, and are you even sure it was Jessica?" I asked, realizing that Emily probably saw the back of someone's head and assumed it was her.

"It could have been someone else," Emily said laying back on the bed, putting her hands on her head. "I really don't know at this point. I probably am wrong." She stared at the ceiling while speaking.

"She's going to come back any day now," I said, laying down too.

Emily didn't understand the rules of the afterlife, but wanted to try to convince me she had some special gift to see the dead. She had never mentioned seeing other ghost until now. Come to think of it, I wasn't sure if she did see the ones on the other side. If she did, wouldn't she have a family she'd want to see? Not gossip amongst a small town?

It didn't make sense to me. I spent the night telling myself over and over again, Jessica will be back. I rationalized the sighting Emily had. I could picture Jessica fuming at a cousin's place, somewhere hidden from school and life. She was probably making her way back home when Emily saw her. Emily never did see where they ran into each other.

I used these thoughts to cloud over my worry, trying to fall asleep. Trying to shut my brain off for the night. I was able to slowly drift to sleep. Night surrounding my overactive thoughts, blackening them from view.

CHAPTER THIRTEEN

I threw the olive in my mouth, smashing it between my teeth as I reached for another one. Mom had set out some of the pre-Thanksgiving snacks and since she had been starving me all morning, I couldn't help myself the second her little platter was put out. Grams would be here any minute and then we could actually start dinner.

The gurgling of my stomach had only increased throughout the day. It had started when I came out of my room to mom making a whole feast at ten in the morning. Since Emily came back a few days ago, I had been more focused on her, completely forgetting about Thanksgiving. I had asked mom what we would have for lunch as she was prepping.

"It's Thanksgiving," she said, waving around one of her spatulas, "The only meal you eat today is at dinner." She turned her back and continued stirring whatever it was she was making. I smelled cranberries as the smoke lifted, so my tongue was ready to flop out of my mouth for her cranberry sauce.

"So I'm just supposed to snack on olives and deviled eggs?" I asked, picking one of the green olives, sucking the pit out before eating the whole thing.

"Dinner will be ready in a few hours or so," she said, over her shoulder. "It will be fine, plus I'm sure grams will bring her Chipotle-spiced sweet potatoes."

"I do really like her sweet potatoes."

I watched as mom's mouth started to salivate at the thought of them. She had definitely gotten her cooking skills from Grams. That was clear by her speed in the kitchen. Watching her move from side dish to entree was like watching a painter move colors on a canvas, creating artwork. Grams was the master when it came to the kitchen, though. Her cooking was like heaven touching your tongue. Her secret ingredient is always being love, according to her. I thought her extra care to each ingredient was the real secret.

"Good, maybe she'll let you have some when she gets here," mom said, adding her mangoes to the burning concoction.

I looked around the kitchen. Mom had the ham already cooking in the oven. The stove looked filled with different pans of food. She was working on her cranberries, while also stirring the gravy. A different pot had broccoli steaming inside, while the green bean casserole sat off to the side, waiting for oven space. The rolls were the only thing missing it seemed.

"Are the rolls in the fridge?" I asked, getting up for the bar stool. "I can start prepping those if you want."

"Yes, honey, they're in the fridge," she said.

I went into the fridge and rummaged around until I could find them. Mom didn't do anything fancy for rolls, just heated up store bought ones. Mom's thoughts on it had always been that she was making everything else, so the rolls could be store bought. I didn't care, but I knew dad's dad used to make comments about how he was used to having freshly made rolls for Thanksgiving. Apparently, my paternal grandmother was a homemaker, making every meal fresh from scratch, at least, that was normally his comments.

I never met her, because she died before I was born, so I really didn't know what she was like. I often forgot her name, my mind now trying to search for it. Remembering her nickname was Connie, I couldn't remember if it stood for Constance or maybe it wasn't short for anything.

I really think my parent's relationship was doomed from the start. My dad's side of the family never approved of mom's southern border ways and often stated how they didn't like their son being with a Mexican, never caring to realize that Grams is from Peru. Grams didn't really appreciate his family trying to white wash over the culture she wanted me to see. This used to cause my parents to fight a lot, but once mom realized that dad never cared about her culture, she stopped trying to include him in things. That is where the cracks started.

Mom started our Wednesday nights after that, using it to keep me connected with her heritage. Of course, then dad was jealous of the "girls club" and would go hide in his room upset. He would pout, later throwing this in her face when I wanted to stay with her instead. There wasn't really much of an option, but she wanted to at least hear my thoughts during their divorce.

"You're turning her against me," dad snarled on drunken nights.

"If you think someone is turning her against you, you need to look in the mirror," she snapped back. She was right. His actions drove me away from him, not anything mom said.

They had a few more fights like this when first moving to Twindle. Mom screamed into the phone that he knew where I was when he wanted to be a dad. The fights stopped after that one. Now, there is just the occasional text from him.

The oven was already preheated for the rolls. Mom had pulled the ham out and left it sitting in the warmer. Once I got the rolls out of their little bag, I pulled each row apart. Placing them onto the cooking sheet, I thought back to last year's Thanksgiving. That was right before the big incident with my parents. They were trying not to fight in front of me, but I could hear it all from the living room, where I would watch the Macy's parade. I didn't realize then that it would be our last family Thanksgiving, but I should have seen the signs coming.

Mom had barely done any prep that year. Most of her meal was store bought and she didn't make her mango cranberry sauce like she is this year. When we were eating, no one spoke, it was just the sound of our silverware clinking on the plate. Afterwards dad stormed up to his room and mom took me to see her family. I tried ignoring it then, letting dad have his tantrum.

Completing my job, I moved to the living room. The parade was coming to an end, but I still heard the broadcasters discussing their favorite balloons from this year. Glimpses of that balloon would replace their faces, as the network showed previous parts of the parade. Getting cozy on the couch, I waited for the end.

The parade paused for a moment as the channel panned to a press conference. It was a man and a woman standing at the podium. I noticed that the two boys who stood back were Jessica's brothers. The woman had pulled out a photo of Jessica and tears streamed down her face.

"Please, we just want our baby girl to return home." The woman stood, her hand starting to tremble so the photo wobbled.

"We will pay if you have her," the man said, wrapping his arm around the grieving mother.

Jessica's mother broke down in her husband's arms. Her sobs begin echoing through the room. It was just her sobs and camera clicks for what felt like a thousand years. Finally, the sheriff helped pull the two off stage and began releasing some information, like Jessica's height and weight, and what she had been wearing when she was last seen.

Jessica was last seen at some horse ranch her parents took her to. She was wearing a pink ruffled shirt and jeans. As the officer continued providing dates, I realized she hadn't been seen since horseback riding with the girls after the Halloween party. She decided to stay longer and someone must have been watching, deciding that was when to take her.

"If you have any information regarding the whereabouts of Jessica Johnson, we urge you to call the Twindle Police Department," the sheriff said, the number for the department flashing at the bottom of the screen. "As of now, we are investigating all the leads that come in."

The reporters in the conference room threw their hands up in the air, hoping to be called on for their question.

"Do you suspect there was any foul play involved," one reporter asked, hand lowering as he said it. The sheriff looked back at the grieving family before he continued.

"There hasn't been any reason to assume that yet, but we cannot confirm that at this time," the sheriff rushed out in one breath. His knuckles were turning whiter with each second the camera sat on him.

More hands flew into the air, but the video cut back to parade, those reporters laughing over something. They had not a clue about what was going on, about the press conference. No care about missing Jessica Johnson. Sinking my weight into the couch, I felt my heart ache.

Mom continued her clamoring in the kitchen, probably never realizing that the parade changed. She was enthralled in the world around us, while my world was slowly crashing. Trying to focus on my last memory with Jessica, I thought back to our night under the moon. The last night she probably got to see the moon. I pushed the thought away from my mind. No longer ready to accept anything from the press conference.

The buzz of our apartment door startled the both of us. Neither of us had guests over often, so we were still getting used to the buzz instead of a knock. Seeing that mom was still busy with her stove of food, I went to the intercom box and pressed the door button. This unlocked the front door for Grams but she would still need our front door unlocked once she got up the stairs.

I waited by the door, not sure if she would use the elevator or the stairs. Faintly, I heard the chime of the elevator on the other side. I pushed my ear up against the cold door and listened. Huge mistake, as grams pounded the door down, each hit with her fist bouncing into my skull. It took me a second to refocus on what was happening, before I opened the door.

Grams embraced me in a bear hug. I would count it more like a cub hug with her tiny body. She was definitely still a mighty woman, but her age had started to brittle her a little bit. Her hug was as tight as she could make it, but it felt like any other hug since she lacked her strength.

"Oh my dear darling," Gram said, brushing my hair down with her hands, "I swear you've grown at least two inches since the last time I saw you."

In reality, Grams had probably just shrunk those two inches, not me hitting a weird growth spurt. I never wanted to point out her aging, so I just agreed with her as I helped her remove her coat. The weeks leading up to Thanksgiving had tricked everyone in town into believing we'd have great weather until December.

The midnight snow storm that rolled through on Tuesday night had crushed everyone's hope of that happening. The town went to sleep expecting some light rain to bless their Thanksgiving, but woke up to a white Christmas a month early. I personally loved the snow, so when I realized it had snowed, I ran to the balcony and danced in the flakes still falling from the sky.

"Grams, do you want me to get you a drink or anything?" I asked, coming back from the hall closet.

"No honey bun, I've got my diet coke," she said, pulling a tiny can out of her purse.

The can didn't look any bigger than her hand so I hoped she brought more in her purse. Her purse had always been filled with nonsense. As a child, I thought it had a black hole inside and whenever Grams was reaching inside, she was making trades to get her goods. Once I got older and realized how wild my imagination could be, I learned that Grams just packs a lot into her purse.

"You never know what you're going to need," she would say, pulling random things that no one needed out.

Grams walked around the kitchen, each food item needed her approval before it could be plated and served. I could see mom trying to avoid her as they danced around each other. Mom would take a step back and bump into Grams, or Grams would check the oven and hit Mom with her hips. Either way, I could tell too many chefs were in the kitchen.

"Hey Gram," I said, walking to grab the remote. "Do you wanna watch the game with me?" I flipped through the various channels until I found the cheering crowds.

"Oh yes dear," Grams' head spun around so she could see the TV.

I walked back over to the couch, the smell of the kitchen had started to really get to me. I feared if I stayed in there much longer, my animal instinct would take over and I'd start tearing into the ham. Emily appeared cross legged on the sofa, staring at the screen.

Her eyes looked glossy, like a layer of water was over them. I stared at her for a long second, afraid she would see me and bolt. We had mostly mended our friendship, but I could tell that there were times where she'd rather be somewhere else. I didn't know where she was when she wasn't around me, but I felt like she had been spending a lot more time there.

Grams came to my side, her arm lightly bumping me. I didn't hear her walking over so the touch of our skin sent me through the roof. I slammed my hand on my chest, trying to keep my heart in there. Grams moved so quietly from the kitchen, I could have thought she was just a ghost, too.

"Who is that sitting there?" she asked, pushing herself onto her toes so she could whisper it in my ear.

I saw Emily's head snap to look at us. She wasn't looking at me though. Emily was staring at my Grams and it looked like Grams was seeing her there. I didn't know how to respond.

Grams had always believed in ghosts, I knew that. She would swear that her late husband would come to visit her before bed. I always thought it was just her broken heart, trying to help her get closure. I never paid any mind to her old wise tales. Emily was the first ghost encounter I had and this was the first time Grams had been over.

"She can see me?" Emily asked, meeting my gaze.

My Grams stood there watching Emily's spot. It felt like my tongue had fallen out of my mouth. I was unable to speak, unable to answer either of the questions just thrown at me. Not sure how to respond without mom hearing us talking about the ghost in her living room.

"What are you seeing?" was all I was able to push out.

"I don't really see much," Grams cocked her head to the side, "But I can tell someone is sitting there." She pointed to Emily's forehead.

"It's Emily," I stammered. I grabbed Grams' shoulders and guided her to the opposite side of Emily.

"Emily is such a pretty name," she said, turning to face Emily when she talked.

"Mom doesn't know about her," I said, putting my finger over my lips as I lowered my voice.

"That doesn't much surprise me," Grams said, waving away the comment, "She tried to ignore these things when she was a kid."

I didn't know what Grams was trying to say. Did our family have some sort of ghost seeing power that mom could just ignore? If I just ignored it, would Emily be gone to me forever? I had always thought that I could see Emily because she wanted me to, not because of some family line gift.

"Wait," I said, my brain clearing enough for me to think. "Does our family have the gift?"

Grams laughed at me, like I was some toddler asking if Santa was real. Emily still hadn't taken her eyes off Grams since she had sat down. I assumed by her laughter that Grams wasn't going to bestow generations of knowledge about being a ghost hunting family on me.

"No dear," she said once she collected herself, "Your psychic abilities come from here and here."

For her first here, she pointed at the spot just above where her eyebrows parted, the second here she pointed to her heart. I didn't get the first reference, but I assumed pointing at her heart meant I wasn't closed off to the world around me, that's what let Emily in.

"Food's ready," Mom shouted from the kitchen.

It had startled Emily, who had become invested in my Grams. Her shock forced her to disappear from the couch. Grams' head moved around, as if she was seeing Emily jump and vanish. I hoped she would come back tonight so we could talk.

Grams and I went into the kitchen and fixed our plates up. We didn't have a dining area set up since mom and I mostly ate while watching TV. I could tell by Grams head swivel that she was looking for the table. Mom walked past the both of us, plate steaming with food, and sat where Emily had previously been. I followed suit and sat in my normal spot.

I sat there quietly watching the TV, while mom and Grams chatted about life. The disappearance of Jessica didn't make it on things for mom to tell Grams about. I was hurt, but I didn't want to talk about it either. My brain raced which caused a throbbing pain to course through my head. The chatter became faint as my mind became more crowded.

I took the plates from them, moving into the kitchen to clean up. I hoped the distraction would help. Thoughts haunted me as I submerged my hands in the scalding water. The distraction is not doing its job. I moved through the motions of putting Thanksgiving away, but my mind was somewhere else.

What was Thanksgiving like at Jessica's house right now? Does she even know that today is Thanksgiving? My heart fell to my stomach. She probably had no idea what was happening. I couldn't imagine she was keeping up with everything. If she had run away, there was no way she saw the local broadcast and if she was kidnapped, I doubt she was anywhere near a TV.

I hoped the next time Jessica's name was mentioned, it would be because she was found. Maybe an anonymous tip would see her at a coffee shop, sending police cars to rescue her. St. Anthony please help the police find her. I sent a silent prayer up once I was finished in the kitchen. Unfortunately, I didn't think the prayer was heard.

After our Thanksgiving feast, Grams headed back to her place. The apartment fell silent, as mom and I stood, staring at the door. It was late and our tummies were full. I was ready to crawl into bed and decompress. I just hoped mom wanted the same.

"What do you want to do?" she asked, turning from the door to face me.

"It's been a long day," I replied. "I think I am just ready for bed."

"I think I'm going to stay up a little later," she said, moving to the living room.

"Okay, goodnight," I hollered after her, turning to go to my room.

"Goodnight," she called back.

Emily hadn't followed me, which I appreciated. I really did just need some time to be alone. I flopped into bed, throwing the blankets over my head. The world around me going dark. My sobs caught in the back of my throat as the tears poured over my eyes. The hot liquid stinging as I tried to fight it back. I laid like this until my body gave up and forced me into a sleep.

I woke up to a crashing thud from outside the apartment, followed by the jiggling of the knob. There was only one thing it could be. I flung the cover off my head, going to the front door. Mom loved Christmas time and could never wait to put the decorations up. I, a Christmas scrooge on the other hand, always forced her to wait until after Thanksgiving to start.

She didn't appreciate this, but she followed it. I had to enforce it or I'd be listening to Christmas music from the first day of November until the New Year. My sanity couldn't handle that much. She had been playing Christmas music since the week of Thanksgiving, claiming there were no Thanksgiving songs she could play instead.

Flinging the door open, mom pushed her box through the door. Looking in the living room, I noticed the bare tree was already sitting in the living room. Mom must have wanted to grab it first thing in the morning. The stress of school had taken most of the Christmas joy away, but I didn't want that to show.

I went to help her get the box closer to the tree. Emily sat on the couch, silently being a part of our family tradition. The lights on Christmas twinkled in Emily's eyes, they changed colors when the lights danced to the next one. I wondered what she was thinking about. Maybe Christmas with her family. I wondered how many Christmases she had missed with her family, what traditions they probably had. Did she have a family still waiting for answers from her? I wouldn't know and didn't dare ask.

I wasn't sure if Emily would remember any Christmases with her family. I stared back at where she sat, trying to imagine her in a house setting up Christmas decor. I watched as she put ornaments on the tree, rearranging them in a perfect order. I tried to imagine her family, but they only formed shadows around Emily. Their form blurred by the unknown. I worried about them, hanging ornaments she probably made in school.

That thought made me hug mom after we got everything set up. I squeezed her tightly, hoping to never be away from her. Emily watched us embrace, her eyes glossed over more, but I could tell it was from a layer of water forming over them. Feeling bad, I moved to sit on the couch near her. I moved the fabric on the couch to get my hand closer to hers. I lightly put it over hers, giving her a look to tell her I'm always here for her.

She smiled at my touch, tears starting to disappear. We stared like this for a moment, I silently pleaded for Emily to be okay, while she was probably wishing to be with her family. Mom turned the TV to the Christmas channel, a fire burning bright while jingles played in the background. I felt warmth take over me, the Christmas spirit finally entering my body. I let the worry of the world slide off as I pushed myself off the couch. I went to one of the boxes of ornaments. Our tree was bare minus some lights. Mom got to work doing the same. We both worked to fill it. I picked through to find my favorite ones.

Mom had replaced some of the plain ornament bulbs over the years, those had their fancy packaging still to protect them. The ones I made over the school years were gently wrapped in a smaller box that sat at the top of the box I pulled from. I sat the smaller box off to the side, ready to look through the creations of Christmas.

I tugged the lid off, exposing my childhood memories. I admired them one at a time, placing them front and center on the tree. The first one I pulled out was from my fifth grade. I only knew because mom would write the year on the back of them. This year's was to make a wreath out of puzzle pieces. I couldn't remember if the teacher brought the pieces or the students, but I remembered the fun of painting them all green. Our teacher giving instructions on how to glue them into a circle played through my head. My fingers tracing each row as the next step rang out. In the center was a picture taken of me from our holiday choir.

I was tiny in the wreath, my braced smile the biggest part of the whole photo. Mom had done my hair that night, trying to recreate the Whoville hairstyle. My neck was wrapped in a black fur turtleneck. I didn't remember the top in the photo, assuming it was probably for special occasions, meaning I wore it once and grew too big before I could wear it again.

I set the puzzle wreath towards the top of the tree. My tiny face staring over the living room to watch for Santa on Christmas Eve. Once the tree was complete we moved on to putting stockings up and some lights around the area to make it more festive inside. Mom added hooks over the mantle for our stockings. I hung them making sure they were evenly spaced. After we finished hanging the last light up, mom grabbed me into another hug and swinging my body around hers. We were dancing in the living room with the music surrounding us.

The living room air filled with our laughter as we continued to spin. The sun was setting, allowing the room to be lit by the Christmas lights. The tree changed between greens and reds. The flashes almost seemed to match the beat in the music. Mom shook her hips while Jingle Bell Rock played. I mimicked her movements, not another care in the world. The candle mom lit flickered in the middle of the coffee table, sending scents of sugar cookies up, mixing with the sounds of Christmas.

This moment was pure joy. I felt the happiness radiating inside, warming me. Emily's smile was bright, almost outshining the lights on the tree. She gave a little cheer towards mom, who continued swaying in the living room. She had gone to the kitchen for a glass of wine, taking small sips in between her sways. With everything that had been going on, I just needed a moment like this to forget the world spinning around us. A moment to just be in a snow globe, a perfect little life manufactured.

Sadly, the moment was short lived, the world making itself known again. The music abruptly stopped and killed our faux fire that was on. Two broadcasters replace our joy. I already knew it was something important. If it wasn't important, they would have waited for the nightly news, they wouldn't interrupt unless it was important.

The two broadcasters were the man and woman who did the nightly news. Both wore disheartened looks as they stared into the camera. They waited silently for their crew to give the sign that their broadcast had made it on air before speaking.

"A body has been found," announced the female broadcaster, her blue blouse washing her skin tone out on the camera.

Mom and I stopped dead in our tracks, eyes glued to the TV. Emily had already moved closer, as if she'd get the information sooner. Or maybe she was reviewing the broadcaster's body language, hoping it would give more details. There was only one person who I could think of, but I was sending a silent prayer that I was wrong. I moved to the couch, and needed to get something stable under me. I felt the world crashing around me and if I stood any longer, I'd be crashing with it. I could see Emily was trembling at the edge of the couch. She had tried to warn me, but I didn't want to listen.

"As of right now, the body has not been identified," the male broadcaster replied. He wore a blue suit that matched the color of his co-star. Compared to the ashy white skin of the woman, his darker skin and darker hair made the blue look like a royal color on him.

Hearing that the body hadn't been identified, I held out that there was still a chance it wasn't Jessica. The air caught in the back of my throat as we continued to listen to the details. Mom turned the volume up, just as intrigued by the new discovery. All three of us sat there still as statues, waiting to get more information.

"The body was discovered earlier this morning," the woman said, "A man was out walking his dog when he made the gruesome discovery."

The camera switched to show the man in question, a young man fear still in his eyes. There was a reporter with him, a younger woman who looked like she could be the daughter of the other woman. Her hair was pulled tightly into a blond pony, allowing her crooked nose and narrow eyes to be on full display for the camera. She wore a similar blue to the others. It must be the newsroom's colors, I thought to myself.

His body shook on the screen as he tripped over what words he wanted to say. He continued running his fingers through his hair. There wasn't much for his fingers to run through. I couldn't tell if he shaved it or had early baldness, but I continued watching each of his moves. I noticed the darker gray stains under his arms. It wasn't a hot day, so I wondered what the nerves were from. Did he get caught in the act of dumping her body or was he really just an innocent bystander. His brown lab continued going crazy next to him during the interview, so I didn't think it was a lie that he found her. Staring at him I couldn't shake a weird feeling that was forming in my guts. A lot of criminals go back to the scene.

I didn't recognize where the news crew was filming the man. I could see houses behind him but they didn't look like any part of Twindle I had been to. I peered over at Emily, hoping maybe she would know it. Her face had lost all color, not that she had much color as a ghost. Mom sat on the other side of me just as glued to the TV.

"Where are they?" I finally asked, hoping either would answer.

"It doesn't look familiar to me," mom said, eyes never leaving the screen.

Emily shook her head and raised her shoulder, signaling that she didn't know the answer either. The man was describing his normal path that he walked his dog. He pointed to something off the screen, explaining that the front of the neighborhood turned into a trail. Even the name of the neighborhood didn't sound familiar. The camera had panned to show the neighborhood sign. The words Village Park barely visible under the overgrown ivies that wrapped around the sign. Was the body even found in Twindle? Panning back to the broadcasters in the office, they began to explain the appearance of the victim.

"The police have informed us that the body was of a young girl," the male broadcaster said.

"She was found on the trail just outside of the Star Horse Riding Farm," the female replied.

That was where the girls went after the Halloween party. I remembered Jessica's text of wanting to ride longer than the other girls. I reached for my phone to see if the girls in that chat were saying anything. No new notifications. The chat sat silent, almost in mockery. No one was ready to make the first jump that the body was Jessica's, but it had to be. There wasn't any other missing girl in Twindle.

"That's where my aunt would take me riding," Emily said, breaking the silence around us. I half jumped at her comment. She still hadn't taken her eyes off the TV that was now panning around the Star Horse Farm to show little girls riding in an open field. Emily's body had color returning, but it was a dark green hue color. She looked like she was ready to hurl. I didn't understand what she meant by her aunt.

She never mentioned anyone outside of immediate family. She couldn't remember anyone, but the ranch must have jogged something. I continued peering at her from the corner of my eye. She wouldn't move but I could see her eyes intently watching the screen. When it panned to the stables, I saw her arm reach out towards one. It sat in the back of the stables, looking abandoned. *Maybe no one has touched it since Emily disappeared.*

CHAPTER FOURTEEN

I stared down at my bare feet, mud protruding between the cracks of my toes. I looked around, confused at my surroundings. Standing behind a wooden fence, I stared at an open field not understanding how I got here. Birds cawed above me, sending my face to the sky searching for the terrors. I couldn't see any birds as I stared.

The sky looked like it had been set on fire, one side simmered a light yellow orange while the other burned a bright red. I couldn't tell what time of day it was. The sun wasn't clear in the sky, so I didn't understand the harsh brightness that poured down.

My heart raced as the sound of the caws got louder, coming closer and closer to my head. I still couldn't see them, but their caws echoed in my ear drum. I tried to convince myself they weren't there, thinking I was just going crazy. That was until I felt it. I felt one of them fly through my hair, lifting a few strings into the air. I felt another swoop down, this one's beak pulling my hair as it flew away. My head yanked towards that direction uncontrollably.

I ducked into a ball as they made their way back to me. My body completely paralyzed by fear. I could feel the tiny pecks on my arm and in the back of my neck. Each one felt like the end of a sword stabbing me. I swore I felt blood trickle down me.

"Help," I tried croaking out. When I opened my mouth, piles of dirt spilled out. Rocks pushing through as if I had been shoved underground. My throat gagged by the debris inside me, silencing my cries for help. I shoved my head back into my legs, tears creating a wet pattern into my fuzzy pajamas. I didn't know where I was, nothing around me looked familiar. I wasn't even sure how I got here, trying to remember what happened before I was staring at muddy feet.

I couldn't remember anything though. It was as if a white wall blocked out any memories I had before being here, but I still couldn't tell where it was. I opened my eyes, but all I saw was the dirt, as my head was still tucked between my knees. I tried pushing past the wall but nothing would come to me. I could barely remember what my name was. *Wait? My name. Who am I?* More thoughts continued racing.

As the thoughts continued through my head, I didn't notice that I was only hearing the thoughts. Not the birds. I slowly peered up from my knees, searching for the little devils. I didn't see them anywhere. I sat completely silent, listening to my surroundings. I was trying to tell where they had flown off to. I heard nothing, like they were never there.

I stared at my arms, expecting them to be in shreds. Pain radiated through them as I moved them, but I was surprised when I looked. They were still intact, no blood pouring down from recently opened wounds. In fact, there was nothing on my arms, not even little marks from the beaks. Once again showing me that the birds weren't there.

Replacing their caws, I could hear horses in the distance. I grabbed the fence post, pulling myself to my feet. Horses ran in the field playing in the flaming light. They seemed like they had no care in the world, like they weren't aware of the angry birds over here trying to attack me. I walked the length of the fence, trying to find an opening to the horses.

The walk felt like it lasted hours, but when I turned back to look at where the birds attacked me, it was only a few hundred feet away. I could probably hit it with a rock if I really wanted to. My legs ache under me, trembling with the weight of a marathon. I couldn't understand how I walked so far, yet so little. I tried pushing past the confusion.

A giant sign read Star Horse Riding Farm. I was at the farm where Jessica had been taken from. Fear conquered my confusion. Who brought me here? I didn't see cars or humans anywhere around me. I spun, digging my heels in the dirt. No one was around. I needed to go home, but the farm looked like it went on for miles in every direction. I couldn't see anything outside of the farm.

"Emily," I shouted. I kept shouting for her. I didn't care if the world knew she was a ghost, I needed her positive outlook to bring me out of this situation, plus she knew the town better than me, so she could get me home. I kept screaming out, each scream only feeling like a whimper though. The air around me was too thick for sound to travel. No one could hear me.

"Emily," I cried again, tears heating my face as they fell down my cheeks. There was a tree in the distance. I thought maybe I could climb the tree and get a better view of where I was. The town wasn't that big, maybe I could see it all in the tree. My brain was trying to come up with solutions, but my heart kept screaming it was useless.

I started walking that way, but my legs felt like they were attached to cinder-blocks. I felt like I had walked a thousand feet but the tree wasn't any closer. The horses were just behind the tree so I focused on their neighs. The louder they were getting, the closer I was getting.

I stared at the tree, not knowing fully if it would help but knowing it was the first step to safety. As I got closer, the neighs had changed. They weren't exactly the same as when I noticed them after the birds, but I couldn't understand how they had changed. I looked away from the tree and looked for the horses, hoping they would calm me like before. They had vanished like the bird, but unlike the birds, their neighs still echoed in the air.

Their neighs came from every direction. It didn't matter where I turned, I could still hear them as if they were right in front of me. Their sounds getting louder made me think I was getting closer.

Searching for the horses, a movement by the tree caught my eye. A dark shadow moved from behind it. It was then that I realized the horses' neighs weren't what I was hearing anymore. The shrill sound ran through me. I could feel the vibration of it on each of my bones, shaking like an alarm was sounding in me. I realized the sound was screams. Girls screamed out in terror all around me. I didn't know where any of them were but once I realized it, the sound engulfed me. It crippled me, sending me to my knees.

I tried cupping my hands to my head, hoping to provide a barrier, but it didn't. The screams continued, getting louder, almost as if they were coming from inside my head. There was no end in sight. I felt hot liquid fill my hands. I pulled one away to see the crimson color cover my hand.

I could feel the cold mud soak through as I knelt there, terrified. The shadow moved closer to me, revealing it was a hooded person. It was too tall to be Emily and if it was mom she would have said something before now. I didn't want to find out who it was. I tried to push myself up but the mud had dried around me like concrete. I was stuck.

The hooded figure moved closer as I struggled with the earth. I squirmed in the pit I had created, feeling suffocated by the dirt. I was drowning. I looked back to the hooded figure, slowly still making its way towards me. More panic shot through my body. Everything went quiet, the screams gone. I couldn't hear anything, not even my own scream as I begged for help again. Then, I heard it. It was barely above a whisper, but it had been close enough I could practically feel lips on my ear.

"Run," came a girl's voice.

As if I had only been waiting on that command, my body finally pushed itself away. I got to my feet and ran. I didn't look back, thrusting my legs into the ground. The screams slowly came back, and I felt as if I didn't move, my scream would join theirs. I pushed everything I had into the ground, trying to propel myself further. I wanted to get away from here. Get away from the hooded figure and the fear.

I finally decided to turn back, hoping to see the hooded figure far in the distance, too tired to chase after me. That isn't what I saw though. The area around me seems exactly the same. The same as it did when the birds attacked. The same as it did when I saw the horses. And the same as it did when the hooded figure appeared. I hadn't actually moved.

I stopped, realizing my lungs had deflated. I collapsed trying to catch my breath, trying to get an understanding of what was happening. I only got to lay there for a moment before the danger bell clanged in my brain. The hooded figure had been closing in on me, but I couldn't run anymore.

I searched for a place to hide, but I was out of luck. The farm was nothing but an open field. My only cover was the tree but I had run the opposite direction of it. Although the hooded figure was my consequence for going near the tree. I couldn't trust it or anything around me. I laid my body completely in the ground, accepting my fate.

I knew I couldn't fight. My legs had turned into noodles after my sprint. I stared back at the fire sky, waiting. White clouds started to extinguish the sky, sending a wave of peace over my body. I closed my eyes and accepted that the hooded figure would be upon me soon. I didn't know what they planned, but my instinct told me it was nothing good.

The red of the sky was still blazing into my eyelids. Since I wanted to hold onto the bit of peace, I tried to control my breathing. I filled my chest before letting all the air out. I tried getting control over the terror that my body was holding onto. I didn't want to be afraid anymore. I didn't want to cower from the situation. I allowed calmness to take over.

A shadow overtook the blaze. I knew the hooded figure was over me. Adrenaline pushed any calmness I was holding onto, making the decisions for me. I lunged my body at them, screaming as our bodies made contact. I felt a sharp pain in my eyes as I rolled away from the figure. I opened my eyes to see the damage I accomplished.

I was in a dark room, stunned. I blinked and looked around. I couldn't make anything out so I wasn't sure where the hooded figure went. My heart beat echoed through the darkness, the only sound around me. Suddenly a door flung open and brightness shoved its way in.

"Are you okay?" came a familiar voice.

I threw my hands up to cover my face, the light blinding me. Spots and dots covered my view but slowly, I realized I was in my bedroom. The familiar voice was mom. She stared at me, hair and eyes wild. At first I couldn't do anything but nod. I was still expecting the hooded figure to appear somewhere.

"Yeah," I said, placing my hand over my chest, "I think I was having a nightmare."

She immediately rushed to my side, putting me in a comforting embrace. I hadn't realized I was trembling until she started running her hand down my hair. Her touch brought me safety again. I was back in my room and not on that farm like Jessica.

"Do you know what it was?" she asked, not moving me out of her grip.

"No," I lied, not wanting to relive any of it. I was trying to push the hooded figure out of my head. Each stroke of mom's hand helped push them out a little further and further. My body finally felt completely here. I looked over to the little green number on my clock.

I had only been asleep for about three hours but my dream made it feel like I didn't get any. I knew it would take a while before the thoughts would stop racing to all the negative things it could. I didn't want mom to leave because I feared the hooded figure would come back the second she wasn't there to protect me.

"Do you need anything?" mom asked, releasing me from under her wing.

I just pulled her back into me. I needed her and that was really all. I contemplated asking her to stay in her room tonight. I didn't want to be an inconvenience to her but I feared I wouldn't sleep in my bed tonight.

"No, momma," I said, now being the one to release her, "I just needed you for a second longer.

"Are you ready to go back to bed?" she asked, moving half on the bed and half off the bed. She would be able to stay if I asked her to but she was also able to push herself and go if I said I was good for bed. I wasn't really ready but I didn't want to keep her up any longer.

"Do you think you could turn on a night light or something?" I asked. I wasn't afraid of the dark, I wanted to be able to see if the hooded figure came back. Mom searched through my night stand, knowing I normally kept my childhood night light in there.

"I can tuck you in too," she said, plugging the sleeping bear in, his cloud lighting up. I didn't answer, I just shimmied onto my back, getting ready for her. When she realized I was waiting she gave a light laugh.

She grabbed the blanket and brought it up to my chin. I thanked her as she pushed the blanket under my body, trapping me to the bed. She gave me a goodnight forehead kiss as her form of "you're welcome." The peace I felt briefly in my dream coming over my body again.

"I love you," she said, walking to my bedroom door.

"I love you too."

She flipped the light off and shut the door. I could hear her footsteps get fainter and fainter as she went back to her room. I stared at my closet door for a long time. It cracked open just the smallest amount. My brain sent anxiety through my body seeing the blackness of the closet. It was telling me that the hooded figure had snuck there to avoid being caught when mom came in.

I knew I wasn't going to be able to sleep with that door open. The blanket felt like a safety net, holding me to my anchor. I wasn't ready to get up, but I didn't want to wait too long. Fearing that the figure was going to jump out, I grabbed one of the text books that had been sitting on my nightstand.

I didn't think I had enough strength to take anyone out, but at least I could get the jump on them. I tiptoed to the door, trying to avoid sections where I knew the floor would squeak under my weight. Reaching the door, I wrapped one hand around the handle and the other getting a good grip on the book.

I flung the door open and swung the book frantically. I heard the sounds of hangers hitting together. Turning the light on, I realized there was nothing but my overactive imagination. I shut the door and a weight lifted with the click. I tried to laugh off my paranoia as I walked back to my bed.

I crawled back in and got comfortable. Knowing I was finally safe, I rolled over to look out my window. I jumped when I saw someone sitting at the edge of my bed. The curly hair giving it away and calms my heart down. Emily was sitting with her hands wrapped around her knees.

"You scared me," I said.

She didn't acknowledge me. Her eyes were filled with terror. She stared past the wall into another world. I looked to see if I could catch a glimpse but there was nothing. It looked like sweat was pouring off her face, but that didn't make any sense. She was a ghost and I was pretty sure they didn't sweat. I leaned up and waved my hand in front of her eyes.

Nothing. She didn't even flinch as I got closer to her. She just continued to stare. That's when I realized. Emily has produced a heat I had never felt from her body before. She always gave off a cold chill when she was near or when she touched me.

This was completely different. It was like the same heat I felt inside my dream. I didn't understand why she was here or what was going on. The fear started to rise in my body again. This time I didn't fear for my safety, but for Emily's. I tried to touch her knees to get through to her. My skin was burned the second it made contact with her. I pulled it away instantly, the burning feeling slowly melting away.

My touch sent Emily into a screaming frenzy. The scream echoed in my ear like the ones from my dream. My hands flew to my ears, expecting the hot dripping blood my dream self-experienced. There was only a pang in my right hand, the hand that touched Emily. A few seconds later she vanished, leaving me there alone. I stared down at my hand, a red burn mark already forming.

CHAPTER FIFTEEN

The chatter of kids was exploding in Mr. Blackford's class. The whole school had been buzzing since the news of Jessica. After the announcement was made on Saturday, the family went to identify the body. Sunday night the top story was the body of a missing girl found. Even though the police stated drugs were not involved, the students were still spreading the gossip that she was a crack addict who was selling herself to get her fix.

Students were talking all day, but this was my first class that Jessica would have been in. Each student warily passed her empty desk as they walked in. The empty desk must have been the conversation starter. In my other morning classes, I could just hear the whispers, assuming it was about Jessica, but this class I heard her name over and over again. I wondered if each of her classes were like this, students talking around an empty desk about the girl who used to be. Of course, they were coming up with all types of ridiculous stories.

I sat at my desk, trying to drown out the noise around me. The two girls who sat in front of me were talking about how they thought Jessica was looking skinny and strung out days before she went missing. The kids to my left were throwing out theories of how she was murdered. The police released little information during their press conference, which let the students around here run wild with ideas.

The noise went silent as Mallory walked through the door. Her eyes were stained red and her cheeks soaked. Her skin looked like it craved water, lips chapped. A lot of heads turned to her, like a flock of birds noticing a predator. The other students tried to avoid looking at her. Maybe they were afraid she had something to do with it. Looking at her, she seemed like she was going to break any minute.

She booked it to her seat, looking over at the empty one next to her. I could see her whole body start to tremble. We made eye contact and held it for a while. They seemed to be filled with anger and rage, all her sadness gone. *Was she angry at me? Does she think I caused this?*

I wanted to talk to her, but she clearly didn't want to talk to me. She turned and faced the front, ignoring the side comments being made under everyone's breath. Luckily, the room quieted down as Mr. Blackford walked into the room. He was usually the last one in, since he supervised the hallways during passing periods. Sometimes he would beat the bell, but today wasn't the case.

I could see he had a little white paper in his hand. He would look down at it and then up at the class, then back down at the paper. He did this for a long while, not wanting to read whatever the paper said. I assumed it was probably regarding Jessica. There had been a morning announcement to let us know that extra counselors had been brought for those that need them.

"Mallory and Charlie, you guys are needed in the principal's office," he said, finally revealing the message on the paper.

Mallory practically broke her neck to look at me, more anger being thrown in my direction. I could feel more than just her eyes on me, each one like a laser beam burning into my skin. The majority of the class was staring at me. I could hear some kids whispering about the "freak girl" being involved with the dead girl. Little did they know, I had been involved with a dead girl this whole time, just not the one they were thinking.

I gathered my stuff, looking up to follow Mallory out the room. She was out the door before I was able to reach down and grab my bag. I tried to catch up to her. Hearing my footsteps, she spun on her heel to glare at me. I had almost stopped at the sight of her.

She seemed wild, something about it reminding me of my dream. Her tousled locks almost formed into tangles. I realized, as strands clung to her forehead, that she was sweating. Her eyes were wide and unblinking, staring through me almost knowing everything already. I watched mania dance behind those eyes.

"Why are they getting you involved?" she spat at me.

"I don't know," I said defensively, "We don't even know what this is about."

I knew that wasn't true, but I really didn't know why they were calling me down. I wasn't really sure what we were walking into. Maybe the principal wants to check and make sure we are handling everything okay. Maybe he wanted to know if we had seen her in the weeks she was missing.

"You know exactly what this is about," Mallory crossed her arms over her chest.

"If it is about Jessica," I started, "I don't know why the principal would want to talk to me. It makes sense to talk to you. You were Jessica's best friend.

At the mention of Jessica's name, Mallory finally broke. The tears poured from her cheek uncontrollably. Her hands rushed to find them, wiping the tears away before they could slide too far. I stared at her in discomfort. I had never seen Mallory get this emotional and I couldn't remember the last time I saw someone have a breakdown, besides myself.

"Why are you just staring at her?" Emily appeared by my side, staring at the mess Mallory was becoming, "Why aren't you comforting her?"

"Well I'm not just gonna pull her into a hug," I said, turning to Emily, not realizing until it was too late that I said something out loud.

"What did you say?" Mallory said in between hiccups and sobs.

"Nothing, don't worry about it," I said, trying to brush it under the rug, "We need to go to the office, instead of just standing out here."

We walked in silence as the hallways seemed to grow longer with each step we took. No matter how many steps we had taken, I didn't feel any closer to the office. Occasionally, I would sneak a glance at Mallory. She had stopped crying for the most part, but she still had hiccups and her face looked as bright as a stop sign.

"If you hold your breath, your hiccups will stop," I said.

She didn't respond to me but I could hear her suck in her breath and hold it. We continued to walk like that for a few more moments. When we finally reached the office doors, Mallory let go of her breath. Her face had hardly changed color.

"Thank you," she said quietly, almost too low for me to hear.

"No problem," I said, holding the door for her. She paused before walking in.

"I'm sorry I yelled at you," she said, holding her arms close to her. "Today has been rough."

"I'm sure rough is an understatement," I replied.

"Thanks for understanding," she said, moving closer. "The school's been turning on me for weeks and today was the breaking point."

"Well if you need a library date again, I'm available." I said, following behind her as we went into the office lobby.

Neither of us expected what we were walking into. The back wall of the administration office was lined with officers. The chairs in the lobby were filled with girls. Some of them I recognized from classes, but others I felt like I had never seen before.

"Thank you for finally joining us," the front desk lady said, staring at us like we were holding up everyone's time.

We stood there, shocked and confused by the scene in front of us. One of the officers gestured to two open chairs near her. I didn't want to sit anywhere near them, but Mallory followed the offer. My feet followed her without listening to what my brain had to say.

"Are you an idiot?" Emily whispered in my ear as I took the seat closest to the officers.

Mallory had taken the other seat so I didn't really have a choice and right now I needed to watch myself. I couldn't talk to her without drawing attention to myself and with the line of officers, I didn't really want to do that.

I knew they had brought each of us down to discuss Jessica in some capacity. I wasn't sure how they caught wind of me hanging out with her, but I didn't want to add anything to their suspicions. Talking to Emily would only label me as a freak to them, and I didn't think freak was a good label to start with. I watched her from the corner of my eye.

Emily stood on the other side of my chair, just between me and the officer. She must have understood my silence, because she decided now was time to size the officers. She moved to stand in front of the officer who had offered Mallory and me the chairs. I watched Emily stare her up and down, unable to understand what she was doing.

She made her way to each of the officers, staring them up and down like the first one. Her face fell flat as she turned back to me. I turned to look over the girls that sat with me, continuing to watch Emily roam through the lobby. She moved to watch the clock.

"What are they wasting time here for?" she asked, her voice growing annoyed. "I highly doubt a student did it."

I tried to ignore her comment, pushing my own down that bubbled up through my throat. Unwillingly, a peep did escape my lips. It was enough noise to draw the attention of everyone's eyes. I could feel the heat in my cheeks, as I dropped my head.

"Did you say something," she sharply said.

"No ma'am," I managed to get out, but barely.

"Good, because this isn't a laughing matter," she practically barked. The other officers nodded in agreement. Most of them also shooting disappointed looks my way. I nodded and turned back to the front, my blood starting to heat. I decided to keep my head low, so I wouldn't witness anything that could get me into trouble.

We all sat there in silence not knowing what was going on. The pieces finally falling into place, I realized these were the girls in the group chat made by Jessica. The girl who sat next to Mallory had been passed out on the couch next to mine the morning after the party. I remember her chestnut hair draped over the armrest. It had been so long then that it almost touched the floor. Now it was shoulder length.

She was holding hands with another girl I remember from the party. She was wearing a witch costume that night, hidden under a big hat and ugly green nose. Without all that, I realized she was a sheepish girl. Her eyes were pure like a rabbit's as she stared at the officers. Her hands were shaking just like the others. I continued looking down the line of girls,

S.B. Dunn

remembering each costume and trying to connect the names from the chats.

So they had called us down to see what information they could get out of us. I didn't know what help I could be to them. I wondered if Jessica's parents had given her phone to the police, or if they found this chat. Was our little chat the last time Jessica sent a message? Still peering at each girl, I tried to imagine what their private conversations with Jessica were like. Did they discuss boys or just school with them? I looked over at Mallory wondering if she really was the closest friend. Everything up until this point made me believe they were, but now looking at the lobby filled with girls, I realize how many friends Jessica really had.

A tall man came out from the principal's office, followed by Britney. She looked at all of us sitting there, clearly surprised to have an audience. I assumed they pulled her down first and the other girls fell in during her interrogation. Without making eye contact with anyone, she walked up to the receptionist to get a hall pass.

"Detective Jones, Mallory is here now," she said, completing the form for Britney.

"Oh good, Mallory, would you come back with me?" Detective Jones asked.

"Can I call my parents first?" Her voice was shaking.

"Yes, you can," he said reluctantly. He looked at the rest of us, deciding which girl to take back next.

"If you need a parent's present, I can call Charlie's mom down here," the front desk lady said, pushing her glasses up her nose. "She works for the middle school."

Great, I thought to myself. I knew the front desk lady was a mother of one of the students, getting a job here because she also helped with whatever club or organization her kid was in, too. Her beady eyes narrowed at me as her glasses slid off her pointed nose.

"That would be appreciated and whichever one of you is Charlie," Detective Jones said, running his finger through the air to point at all of us sitting there, "you can come back with me."

Fear ran through my body, making it almost impossible to get up. I probably would have sat there pretending that Charlie didn't exist, but the front desk lady cleared her throat, glaring at me. I pushed myself off the arms of the chair and got to my feet. They felt unsure of themselves, ready to give way at the slightest pressure.

I could hear the lady calling my mom's class and asking her to come to the high school office. I knew mom was going to freak out and run down here. Detective Jones and I barely made it through the principal's door when she got there.

"What's going on?" she rushed in looking from Detective Jones back to me.

"We need to ask your daughter a few questions about the murder of Jessica Johnson," he replied, waving for us to take a seat.

Murder.

He had said the murder of Jessica. It wasn't stated that she was murdered when her body was found. I had been trying to play dumb over the last few days, hoping it was some freak accident. I never anticipated sitting in an office with a detective for murder. I could feel my heart starting, ready to take laps around the track. I watched as worry flashed over mom.

"Why do you think my daughter is going to know anything?" Mom knew I was at her Halloween party but she didn't think we were super close. I guess we weren't really close but I had wanted to grow a friendship with her before everything happened.

"Your daughter was in a group chat with Jessica and the other girls in the lobby," he started, taking his seat and pulling out a notepad, "We just want to make sure Jessica didn't mention anything important to the girls."

"I don't know anything," I blurted out, not thinking, "I mean to say, I was added to the chat a few days before she disappeared."

"So you guys weren't close?" he asked, starting to put pen to paper.

"We had class together," I started, "but we didn't really hang out outside of school."

"We just moved here this year," mom introjected, "she is still making friends."

"I helped her study at the library once," I started again.

"With another girl, Mallory," mom finished for me. I didn't know if she added Mallory's name to throw her under the bus, or just to make sure Detective Jones had all the details.

"Right, with Mallory," I nodded, "And I saw her in school sometimes, that's how I got her number."

"And how did you get in the group chat?" Detective Jones asked, brows raised and pen still working to jot everything down.

"Well that's how I got invited to the Halloween party," I stammered.

"Ah yes, this Halloween party," he said, moving to look through other notes he had laid out on the desk.

Mom placed her hand over mine, knowing that I wasn't involved. When she picked me up from the party, Jessica was still alive. She had grounded me right after so I couldn't leave and commit murder. I hadn't said goodbye to Jessica when I left, though. I tried remembering what my last words were, but all I could remember was fighting with Emily.

"I picked her up early from that," mom stepped in again, "I already told you, she didn't have anything to do with this horrible thing."

I could see the fury was building up inside of her. She wasn't ready to listen to anything the detective had to say. She was in mama bear mode now, ready to rip out anyone's throat if it meant protecting me. Jessica's disappearance being referred to as a murder must have set off her protective whistles.

"I understand ma'am, but like I said your daughter was in contact with Jessica before she disappeared," Detective Jones said, "We want to cover all of our bases."

He was an older man, but not like a grandpa, more like your dad's older brother that you get to see at holidays and funerals. Wrinkles lined his forehead and gray was peeking through his hair. His jaded crow feet stares intensely at us. He was trying to be pleasant to us, but I could tell years of the job have made it hard.

"I went home after spending the night with Jessica and some other friends," I replied.

"And these are the same friends sitting in the lobby?" he cut me off.

"Yes some of them, but not all of them," I said, remembering how many couches were in Jessica's basement. "The next morning I had my mom pick me up and that was the last time I saw Jessica."

"You didn't go riding with her?"

"No, I went home and napped. By the time I had woken up most of the girls had left."

"But not Jessica, right?"

"No, I don't think so. I'm pretty sure she told us she would stay."

"Did she say who would pick her up?"

I thought back to the text messages. I didn't remember seeing anything about her getting picked up. Maybe she did, but I really didn't remember. I knew her and Mallory had talked about her getting her license after Christmas, so I assumed she didn't drive herself.

"I don't remember, but I don't think she did," I said, feeling the gazes on me.

"So you don't know if she was picked up from the farm?"

"No, I don't really know anything. I'm confused why you're talking to me."

"We want to cross everyone off our list to help make things easier for us," Detective Jones said pointing out towards where the other officers were.

"Are you saying my daughter is a suspect?" mom said before he could ask another question.

"That is not what I am saying, at all."

"Do you have any other questions for her?"

"No, I think she's answered all my questions," he said, closing his notebook.

"Good, then we're leaving," mom said standing up, nearly knocking her chair to the ground.

I followed her, but didn't speak. Detective Jones wasn't far behind me. He handed his card to me in case I could remember any more. I wanted to be far away from here. We walked past the other girls in the lobby, each girl looking at us as we walked by. Mallory had been in the hall on the phone with her parents when we walked out.

"I have to go back to my students," mom replied, "but I will take you out of school if you need."

I did not want to go back to the class and face everyone, plus I already had my stuff with me. I nodded in agreement, ready to bolt out of the school and never look back.

"Okay my free class is after this so I can drive you home if you can wait about," she looked at the clock, "fifteen minutes."

"I'll run to my locker to get everything," I said.

Mom nodded in approval before heading down towards the middle school hallway. I let my feet drag me slowly towards the direction of my locker. I wanted it to take the full fifteen minutes to get to my locker, but I knew the school wasn't big enough for that. I still tried, though.

With the halls empty, my steps echoed around me. I could hear some of the teachers giving their lectures as I walked by, but their voices disappeared almost as quickly as they appeared. The stairs leading to my locker did a half spiral as it moved up. I clung to the railing since the steps were still a little slick from this morning's snowy prints. Most of the steps were dry, but one caught me off guard. I stumbled, pulling my shoulder almost out of the socket as my hands refused to let go. A small cry escaped me as I fell to my knees, the books in my hands tumbling to the ground with me.

I sat there for a minute, staring at the splattered marble print of the stairs. I wondered about what Jessica last saw, before someone took her life. I worried it may have been the face of her murderer as they drained the life from her. These thoughts caused tears to pour over my cheeks, splashing onto the floor.

They sounded like a leaky faucet since my ear was close to the splashing. I gathered myself off the ground, using my good arm to push myself up. A small ache came from my hand as I realized Emily's burn was still healing.

With the ache in my shoulder, I realized each day was bringing a new injury it seemed. I pushed forward, hoping my stair fall was enough blood for whatever vindictive god was playing with me right now.

CHAPTER SIXTEEN

I slammed the door shut with my body, trying to catch my breath from running up all the stairs. Eyes closed, I prayed that I was dreaming a long nightmare. When I opened my eyes, I would wake up and Jessica would still be alive somewhere. Maybe this was all just a bad dream caused by the alcohol. I knew none of this was true, but I kept my eyes closed just a few seconds longer, hoping. I leaned against the door, the cold metal somehow calming me.

"I can't believe they called you in," Emily said, startling me.

She had vanished after I went back to talk to the detective. She wasn't waiting out in the lobby for me when I returned, but finally appeared again. Heavy snow showered the outside world, making the apartment seem darker than it normally was. She was hard to see with the minimal lights. Pushing myself off the door, I went to flick on a few lights.

"I guess they're just doing their job," I shrugged.

"Not a very good one if they're questioning you guys instead of the sick creep that did this," she said, hands on her hips.

"They're trying to gather evidence," I said, coming to the officers' defense. I didn't know why I was so quick to protect them against Emily's rage, but Emily seemed to be bothered by them talking to me and not bothered by their police work.

"Oh please, I could collect evidence a hell of a lot quicker than them," she said.

"And how exactly do you plan on doing that?" I asked, intrigued on how a ghost would solve the murder.

"Well," she said, putting her hands behind her back. She was trying to play innocent, but I knew she was hiding something.

"Well what?" I asked when she didn't continue.

"I have seen Jessica a few times since the first night I told you," she spilled.

"She didn't cross over?" I asked, confused.

"I'm not even sure if there is a crossover, or if we just live on earth in a different plane," Emily said, throwing her hands in the air.

"What do you mean you've seen her?" I asked.

"When I'm not with you, I'm exploring the world around us. Sometimes I like to go into town and look at the new things the stores get."

"So she's out shopping?" I asked, sarcastically.

"No," Emily replied, coldly. "This isn't time to joke."

"I'm sorry, I'm just confused with everything going on," I admitted, "I never realized you could see other ghosts."

"Normally I don't," she said.

"So why is Jessica different?" I asked.

"I'm not sure," she said, shrugging, "I normally see older people who passed naturally. The only other time I saw someone my age was probably about two or three years before you moved here."

"Years?" I asked, astonished. I didn't know how long Emily had been dead, but I knew from past conversations that time moves differently for her. So who knew how many years it had truly been since she saw that person.

"Yeah, she was walking around the school but when she realized she was a ghost, she freaked and I never saw her again."

"So just her and Jessica?"

"Yeah for the most part, like I said, sometimes I can see grandparents."

"I just always assumed that all ghosts could see each other," I said, scratching my head. I didn't know much about the ghost world since Emily kept pretty tight lipped on it. I had made my assumptions based on what TV and movies showed.

"It isn't like how it gets portrayed," Emily said, as if she could read my mind. "No one but ghosts understand the other world, and not even then sometimes."

"They don't give you some type of rule book," I laughed.

"No, sadly they don't." She sighed, "But it would sure be nice if they did." We both burst into laughter.

I walked to my bedroom to unload my school stuff. I could feel Emily's presence following me. I threw my crap to the floor and crawled into bed. I was ready to sleep for the rest of eternity. I just wanted to forget the last few weeks.

"What are you doing?" Emily asked, staring at me from the doorway.

"Taking a nap," I said.

"Why?" she blinked at me, expecting that I had some great adventure up my sleeve.

"Because what else do I have to be doing right now?" I didn't understand what she wanted.

"Umm, I just told you I can talk to Jessica and you don't want to see if she knows who killed her?" Her eyes were practically bugging out of her head.

"You never said you could talk to her," I replied. "You said you can see her and it doesn't sound like you see her often."

Emily grabbed her sun necklace, twirling it in her hands as she was thinking. Clearly, her gossip days had become boring to her so now she wanted to play detective. I didn't want to get involved more than I already was. She wouldn't be the one facing the law if any of her schemes get us caught. She will just vanish, leaving me to take the blame.

"Well, but if I can see her, surely I can talk to her, right?" Emily threw her hands in the air in frustration.

"Have you tried to talk to her?" I asked.

"No, it's like she gets spooked when she sees me."

"So then how do you know any of this plan will work?"

"Because I can feel it, there's something telling me I need to try."

"Okay, let's say your wildly crazy plan does work and Jessica does talk to you," I said, swinging my legs off the bed to face her, "How am I supposed to tell the detectives my ghost friend talked to the dead girl and there's your murderer?"

"Ouch, dead girl's got a name," she said, wincing at my comment. "Or have you already started to forget about her?"

"That's not what I meant and you know it."

"No, you're right. We can't just go to the police and start pointing fingers."

"What if she doesn't remember?" I asked, knowing that Emily barely remembered her past.

"You start to lose memories after you've been dead for a while," Emily said nonchalantly.

"So you did remember what happened to you?"

"No, I don't."

I could see her figure starting to dissipate at my questions. I knew she didn't like to talk about her death, which is why I didn't understand why she felt comfortable trying to get Jessica to talk about hers. I knew I needed to change the subject.

"So how much homework do you think I'll be missing today?" I asked.

"Who cares about stupid homework!" Emily practically screamed. "We need to talk to Jessica!"

"Okay," I said, putting my hands up defensively, "How? I can't make you appear at will."

"No, I guess you can't."

"Plus, no offense but I do not want Jessica to just appear in my room," I said getting freaked out by the idea.

"Well, I usually only see her when I'm in town, so I guess we could start there?"

I wasn't planning on being a part of the talking to Jessica thing. Emily could talk to her whenever and wherever, I know she'll come back and tell me anyways. And we still didn't have a plan for how we would tell Detective Jones if we did get anything.

"I can't just go into town ghost hunting," I said.

"Why not?" she asked, almost throwing a tantrum, "Your mom won't be home until after 4 pm so we have time to go right now."

"How am I supposed to get anywhere?" I asked, raising my voice a little, hoping it could break through Emily's crazy thoughts.

"I know you have a bike downstairs," she said, smirking.

"I'm not riding my bike into town," I said, "People will see me and know I'm supposed to be in school."

"What does that matter?" she asked, "They can't throw you in jail for your mom pulling you out."

"No, but they can ask my mom why they saw me out and not in school."

"That's a good point. We don't want you grounded again."

"Exactly," I said, getting comfy in bed again, "So it's settled then, it's nap time."

I tried to fluff my blanket up for more comfort. I could see from Emily's face that she did not want to drop it, but I was right. There was no way I could go out and be seen by the townspeople. Everyone here is gossiping and it will take about 30 seconds for mom to know I'm not at home.

"What about where her body was found?" Emily asked, barely above a whisper. She had to be absolutely insane if she thought I would ever go anywhere near where a dead body was.

"Not doing it," I said.

"Why not?" she asked. "I know we can help Jessica if we can just find her."

"You do realize that they'll probably have it taped off?"

"They can't tape off the whole street," she said, frustration building in her face, "We just need to get close to it."

"And do what? Hold a séance?"

"We can look for evidence. We could see if Jessica is already there. We could do all sorts of things to help her that we can't do with your lazy butt in bed."

"I don't even know how to get where she was found." I didn't recognize any part of the area that was shown on the news and with just moving here it was easy to get lost.

"I know how to get there," she said, "Get your bike and let's go."

"How do you know how to get there?" I asked.

"You do realize that you're wasting time right now," she said, throwing my words back at me.

She wasn't going to stop and I could see it. She was right, the more time we stood there arguing, the later in the day it was getting. I felt a little out of shape and wasn't sure how far I could ride a bike. Visions of the distorted horse farm from my dream flashed through my mind, causing an ache in my chest.

"Can we make it there and back before my mom gets home on my bike?" I asked, giving into her demands.

"Yeah, it actually isn't too far from here," she said, perking up. "Let's go get your bike."

"Fine, I'll go grab it but you better be outside ready for me."

As soon as the words left my mouth, she was gone. I knew she was already outside, so I needed to move quickly. I changed into dark jeans and a dark hoodie to help hide my identity in case anyone saw me out and about. I ran out the door and down the stairs to the basement.

My bike was tucked away in the back corner. I hadn't used it during the summer and once it started getting cold, I really didn't have a need for it. Getting it out, I realized the front tire was flat. I didn't remember where mom put the pump. I searched through everything before finding it tucked behind some boxes.

Vigorously pumping my arms, I realized I was probably taking longer than Emily planned to. Since I committed to her plan, I knew I needed to be quick to beat mom home. Rolling the bike out of the lobby, I was met with a blinding sun. I hadn't been expecting that since it had been cloudy all morning. The sun reflected off the snow that was already nestled on the ground.

"What took you so long," Emily asked when I eventually got to her.

"The tire was flat," I said, lifting the bike to its back wheel so the front wheel was towards her.

"Well we don't have time to waste," she said, hopping in the basket I had it the front. "Come on."

I jumped on the bike and started pedaling away. I knew how to get out of the neighborhood, but past that I would be lost. Emily pointed which way to go and told me when I needed to turn. It was like the map was in her head and she was just relaying what she was seeing to me.

My tires screeched to a halt when Emily pointed at the yellow police tape, barely hanging on to the trees it had been wrapped around. I looked around to see if there were any police patrolling the area before deciding to get closer. With the sun peeking through the bare branches, I could see nothing in sight.

I dropped the bike and moved closer to the ditch. The police had already taken the evidence off to be processed, so there wasn't much to look at other than dirt. It didn't matter if there was or wasn't evidence, we came to see if Jessica would talk to us.

"So now what do we do?" I asked, moving some branches around with my foot. I couldn't imagine we were going to solve anything here.

"I'm trying to get through to her," Emily said, walking around, touching the trees nearest the yellow tape.

"What do you mean get through to her?"

"I'm calling out to her." Emily went through the tape, to be more in the crime scene.

I stood there motionless. I was not going to cross the tape like she did. No one will ever know that she did it, but living people leave fingerprints and I did not need the police trying to pin this on me.

"How are you calling out to her?"

"Charlie, this isn't twenty questions," she said, spinning to look at me, "Please let me focus."

I zipped my lips and tossed the imaginary key in her direction. I wasn't sure she really knew what she was doing, but I didn't want a jogger to catch me talking to myself at the crime scene. I waited there patiently for Jessica to show herself.

"This is just where her body was placed." Emily knelt to the ground, running her fingers over a spot, "She was killed somewhere else."

"I mean that makes sense," I said, momentarily forgetting my vow of silence for her, "She was missing for about a month, so someone should have noticed her body if she'd been here the whole time."

"But there aren't tire tracks anywhere to indicate someone drove her here," Emily said nose to the ground looking at the different dirt patterns.

"I mean the road is just a few feet away," I said pointing back to where I dropped my bike off.

Emily moved closer to the road to investigate any potential tire marks. Unfortunately, with the road being the main one into the neighborhood and farm, there was a lot of marks in the dirt path. And sadly, Emily's investigation was going nowhere.

"Do you think the killer lives in the neighborhood?" Emily asked, walking closer to it.

"Maybe," I said, looking around. "The horse farm isn't too far from here, so it would have probably been easy."

"We should explore there, then," Emily said, heading back to my bike.

"Wait, why?" I thought we had come here to conjure Jessica and now she wanted to get me up close and personal with a killer.

"Maybe there's something of hers we can find," Emily said, "Like in trash bins or something, now that she's been found I'm sure whoever did it wants to get rid of as many links to them as possible."

"You need to stop watching so many crime shows with mom and me," I said, picturing Emily with a Sherlock Holmes hat on.

She would take her magnifying lens and look down at the ground, narrowly avoiding disaster with her Dr. Watson helping her navigate the busy streets of Twindle. Minus the Twindle aspect, it could make for a good show. We could call it *solving murders ghost style.*

"I'm not watching crime shows," she said, throwing her hands on her hips, "I'm using my brain to help me gather evidence."

"I don't want to go into the neighborhood," I said. Something about the front of it sent chills through me. The sign to the neighborhood had overgrown vines and bushes on it, making it hard to read. The sky looked darker above just the neighborhood, almost as if gloom hung directly over it. This was going way outside my comfort zone and I had not been prepared.

"We need to," Emily pleaded with me.

"We came here to talk to Jessica," I snapped back.

"She isn't appearing," Emily said, "and I think it's because she wasn't killed there, her body was just put there after some time."

"So then maybe she was killed in town since that's where you keep seeing her," I shrugged, starting to wonder when we should leave.

"No, I would have felt something if that were the case," she said definitively.

"You would have felt something?" I scoffed, "so you're a ghost psychic?"

"I am connected to your plane and my plane," she said, using her hands to demonstrate. "I can feel things in both plains and sometimes they are strong gut feelings telling me I need to do something. That is what I'm getting now and it's telling me to go into the neighborhood."

"We need to leave soon if I'm going to get back home before mom does," I said, walking towards my bike now.

"Please just let's go through the neighborhood," she begged, "Just a small ride around the main roads."

I picked up the bike and sighed. I knew she wouldn't come home with me if I didn't go through the neighborhood. Since she had directed me here, I didn't want her to strand me here in the middle of nowhere. I was going to have to give in or get grounded.

"Fine, one quick ride through," I said, hopping onto the bike seat.

Emily hopped back into the basket and I took her closer to the entrance. She said her gut was telling her to check it out but my gut was telling me to run far as hell in the opposite direction. We made our way through the street, Emily listed off different names as we passed them.

"Elm street, Walnut street, Maple street," she did this every time she would see a sign.

I could hear her under her breath repeating the streets back to herself as we made our way back through towards the front. I wasn't sure how memorizing the streets in a neighborhood was helping Jessica, but at least it kept Emily's mind busy for a little bit. Once outside the neighborhood, the weights on me were removed and I felt like my heart was coming back to a normal speed.

"Do you see Jessica?" I asked as we passed the police tape one last time.

Emily looked behind us to see if anyone was there. She looked at all the directions around us before she finally shook her head no. So the trip had been a bust with nothing to show for it. I didn't want to be harsh on Emily, but she did ruin my perfectly good nap time with her Nancy Drew behavior.

We stayed silent the rest of the bike ride home. Emily would occasionally dart her vision like she had seen Jessica, but then she would realize it was her imagination or a living person. She would just point to indicate I needed to turn. I think she assumed that I memorized the route we took when she led me here.

It hadn't taken long to get to the ditch, but the ride home felt nearly twice as long. I wasn't sure if it was because we just weren't talking to each other, or if Emily was really taking a longer route. I didn't recognize most of the ride, but also didn't know enough about Twindle to know which was true.

We got back to the apartment with barely minutes to spare. I had been walking my bike into the lobby when I saw mom's car pulling down our street. I quickly shoved the bike through the door to avoid being caught. Booking it down to the basement, I stored my bike where it had been. I couldn't get it exactly in its original spot so I moved some boxes around to make it look like it hadn't been used.

With all the strength in my legs, I pushed myself up each flight of stairs. I was able to fling the door open and run into my room. Struggling to shove my legs through my sweatpants, I heard mom's keys in the door knob. I covered myself in my comforter and tried to slow my breathing. I didn't want her to find me, red faced and out of shape, because I knew that would look suspicious to her.

Luckily, when mom came in she did her normal routine. I could hear her taking her shoes off and putting her lunch stuff away. This gave me plenty of time to make it look like I had just been napping. I laid under the covers, staring at my cracked open door, waiting. Once I heard her footsteps coming my way, I shut my eyes, trying to come across asleep. She lightly tapped at my door.

"Charlie, how are you doing?" she asked, pushing the door open.

I forced a yawn and blinked to come across as sleepy. I slowly pushed the covers down. Reaching my arms up, I sold the deal.

"I'm doing good, momma," I said, swinging my legs off the side of my bed, "I was just taking a nap."

"I just wanted to let you know that the police are having a press conference regarding your friend," mom said, avoiding saying Jessica's name. She had been avoiding saying her name since it was confirmed her body.

"I think I've dealt with the police enough for a lifetime," I said, confused as to where she was going with this.

"So you don't want to go with me?" she asked.

"Wait, why are you going?" answering her question with my own.

"Well of course I'm going," she said, moving to place her hand on her hip.

"Why?"

"I want to make sure you and my students stay safe," she started, "Whatever information the police can give, I want to hear it."

"They'll probably give the same stranger danger speech you gave me as a child," I said, rolling my shoulders.

"I think they'll give a little bit more information than that," she scoffed.

"Well, like I said, I've had enough of the police today."

"Okay, I'll get some dinner started," she said, starting to turn, "I'm not sure how long the thing will go, so I want to make sure you have something to eat."

She continued walking to the kitchen. I could hear her getting something in the fridge. If mom was going to be gone, I could actually get my nap in. I pushed myself back into the bed, getting comfortable under the blankets. As soon as I rolled over, my plans were interrupted.

"Why aren't you going to the press conference?" Emily asked.

"Why would I?"

"For the information," she said, throwing her hands at me in frustration.

"What information are they going to give us?"

"Who knows that's why we need to go," her voice raising an octave.

I almost told her to be quiet, fearing mom would hear her. She could scream at the top of her lungs and mom wouldn't hear her. I didn't need to worry.

"I already told mom that I'm not going," I said, pulling my blankets over my head, "So I'm not going."

My blanket moved down just an inch. I knew Emily had tried to pull it down. She couldn't move things often, but sometimes if she put enough of her energy into it, she could move some things an inch or two. I knew it was only when she was fully enraged could she actually throw things. I chuckled under the blanket at her failed attempt. I could hear her huff as a response.

"Actually now that I'm thinking about it," she said, "If the police are at the press conference, we could totally go to the station and steal Jessica's report."

"I am not stealing anything," I said, throwing the blanket off me. "Especially not from the police station."

"Oh come on," she said, flailing her body onto the bed, "the majority of the police will be at the press conference."

"Yeah because I'm sure they just have the files sitting out in the office," I said sarcastically.

"I know where they hide the files," she said.

"How do you know where they have them?"

She just responded with the sly smirk. Clearly she had already been to the station since Jessica's death. I guess that is a perk of being a ghost, but they will still see me so the answer was no.

"I can get you through the station," she said, confidently.

"How do you plan on doing that?" I asked.

"I can just waltz right through the door and I will signal when it's clear," she said like I was stupid.

I thought about it for a moment. I think it would be cool to help solve a murder, but I didn't have the balls to commit. I was too afraid that somehow, getting involved, would cause the police to suspect me and let the real murderer get away.

"I don't know if that's a solid plan," I replied.

"It will be dark by the time the press conference starts," she said, trying to justify her plan, "If you wear dark clothes, it'll be harder to see you."

"Why do you want to go?" I asked, crossing my arms.

"The police have nothing," she replied. "I can at least get something with their information."

"Do you really think we should be doing that?"

"Absolutely, I do."

Chapter Seventeen

Emily ran through her information that she had gotten from her different eavesdropping sessions. The more she rattled off, the more my urge to go to the police station grew. Her Nancy Drew behavior started to rub off on me. Eventually, I got up to change. Mom came into my room to say her goodbyes while I slid off my sweats.

"Are you thinking of sneaking out while I'm gone?" she asked, pointing at my get up.

"No," I chuckled, "I was getting hot."

I didn't enjoy lying to mom, but she would have never approved of Emily's plan. I had changed out of my long sleeve shirt into a black t-shirt, switching my sweats for black leggings.

"Good, I don't want you out in the dark," she said.

"Trust me, I don't want to be out in the dark either," I said.

"Okay, well I'm heading out," she said, pushing her thumb towards the door.

"Okay, please be safe," I said, moving to give her a hug.

She returned my hug, holding me tight. Her heartbeat hit me in the face faster than a boxer hitting his bag. Her anxiety must be getting the best of her. I squeezed a little tighter, hoping to crush her worries. If only she knew what I was getting ready to do.

She was more on edge recently. Her words of assurance had come back to bite her, and I could tell that worried her. She had stopped going to her weekly Pilates because it was too dark when she got out of classes. She also told me that she didn't enjoy leaving me home alone.

I could tell she didn't want to leave me alone now, but the press conference would hopefully help ease her mind a little. I heard her still in the kitchen, probably finishing a last dish before heading out. I stayed at my door, ear on it. Emily wouldn't want to waste any time.

Once mom left, Emily and I waited a few more minutes before leaving. Throwing a hoodie over my head, I went into the kitchen to grab our only flashlight. I shoved it into my hoodie pocket as we walked out the door. Luckily the police station was closer than where Jessica was found. It was only about a five-minute walk. The wind was beginning to pick up as the sun set, a small shiver running through me.

The town had a path to the police station from my apartment. I stayed on the sidewalk avoiding the broken pieces trying to grab at my feet. Emily walked ahead of me, but this wasn't a trip I needed her help navigating. Mom showed me the station when moving here. It was a big selling point when she picked our apartment.

I had never walked the path myself, but we passed the station every time we left. It was on the main road that our complex was off of. The station sat next to one of the few stop lights that was actually in Twindle. I thought it was to easily allow them to leave when there was an emergency. Minus Jessica, I couldn't really imagine them having many real emergencies to help with.

I took a deep breath as we got closer to the station. The lights illuminating the last bit of our walk. The sun was fully hidden under the horizon now, taking the heat from today with it. My body was shaking just a little. I wasn't sure if it was because of the cold or my nerves. As we inched closer, I could feel the adrenaline kicking through my veins, causing my body to shake more.

"Okay," Emily started, turning to face me, "There's a desk right when you walk in, you can hide behind it while I make sure the coast is clear."

"I can do that." My voice came out shakier than I anticipated.

"You've got this," Emily said, giving me a smile and a thumbs up.

I hunched behind some bushes near the front. I looked around the doors, expecting to see cameras pointing towards incoming people. There was nothing there though. I guessed the smaller town station wouldn't be filled with all the fancy security that the Springfield department had. Emily went straight through the doors, disappearing for a second. She came back out and confirmed that no one was currently sitting at the desk. Now was the time.

The doors slid open, a bell ringing as they did. I heard shuffling come from a room that jutted out behind the desk. I flung my body to the ground, getting as close to the desk as I could. Emily froze for a second, waiting to see what would happen. Footsteps echoed behind the wood of the desk. I tried to stay quiet, but I feared my heart would give me away.

"Hello," a woman's voice called out. The desk squealed under her weight. I watched sausage wrap around the edge of the desk, red nails barely peeking out.

It took her a few more seconds of looking before the stomped retreated back into the room. Emily gave me the thumbs up, leaving to the back of the station. Kneeling below the desk, I moved around the corner of it, getting a better view of where Emily went.

The lobby had been silent minus the sound of the buzzing lights overhead and my heart in my ears. The smell of coffee mingled in the air with disinfectant. I kept looking over my shoulder. I feared someone would walk in, seeing me hiding. It would definitely look suspicious. Emily was only gone for a few more moments before rounding the corner, running back to where I knelt.

"There's just a few deputies hiding out in the break room," she said when she returned.

I pushed my finger to my lips, trying to shush her. Once again forgetting that I was the only one who could actually hear her. She laughed at me, clearly feeling the fear that was radiating off of me.

She waved me to follow her down the hall. I peeked over the desk to confirm the lady was still hidden away in her room. I stayed low to the ground while following Emily. I kept some distance between us so if someone came out of their room, I had time to hide. The hallway to the file room felt as long as a football field.

I lightly moved on the balls of my toe, trying to keep my footsteps quiet. Emily slowed in front of me, her hand outreached to stop me while she peered around an open door. I assumed it was the break room. I let Emily pass it first, waiting for her to tell me when I can go. She peered back in the room and after a few moments she waved me on. Quickly, I went past the open door, trying my best to not make a sound.

I kept going, letting Emily get ahead of me again so she could lead me. We got to the file room, both of us holding our breath. I was half expecting the door to be locked when I pushed the handle down, but to my surprise it clicked open.

"Keep the light off," Emily said.

I pulled the light out of my hoodie pocket, knowing to come prepared. I slid through the door pushing it shut slowly. If someone was going to come in I wanted to be sure I could hear them. Realizing the door could lock, I twisted it adding an extra step in the process. The small click of the lock echoed through the dark room. Emily started moving around the cabinets, until she stopped in front of one.

"It should be in here," she said pointing to it.

"How can you be so sure?" I whispered, knowing the living could hear me.

"I watched the detectives put it back this morning," she said, trying to brush past the conversation.

"What do you mean you watched them put it back?"

"I came here this morning, before they came to the school."

I glared at her. "Did you know they were coming to my school?"

"I had my suspicions," she shrugged.

"Did you know they were going to talk to me?"

"Again, I had my suspicions," she replied, reaching to open the cabinet. Her hand went through the handle.

I could see sadness taking over her face. I pulled the handle, the file exposing what looked like a thousand reports. It started with H and ended with O. I fingered through the front until I could find the J's. It only took a few more seconds after that to find Johnson's. There were only three cases so I was able to find Jessica's report quickly.

Leaving the cabinet open, I pulled the file out and slid to the floor. I sat my back against a different cabinet and opened the file. On top was Jessica's autopsy. I didn't understand most of the medical terms but I still looked through it, gathering as much evidence as possible.

"What does it say?" Emily asked.

"Death by asphyxiation," I said, reading the report off.

"Asphyxiation," Emily repeated. "Like she was strangled?"

"Yeah, I think that's what it means," I replied, moving to the next page of the report.

I flipped through the other pages. There was a list of evidence in her file. A few photos of the scene where her body was found. I pulled the photos out and looked through each of them. There wasn't anything that stuck out to me. I flipped the photos down to show Emily.

"Do you see anything important?" I asked her.

She got down on her knees, getting a closer look at the photos in my head. She stared over them, making sure to take in all the details in each. Eventually she gave up and shook her hand.

"Nothing is sticking out to me," she finally said.

"Me either," I said, taking the photos back, "what should we even be looking for?"

"Any information that could point us in the right direction," she said, trying to look through the file.

My heart sank as three photos slid out under the crime scene photos. Blue like the sea, Jessica's lifeless body laid on a gray table. There was discoloration around her throat, her lips slightly parted like she was trying to get her last breath still. I felt like hot acid was trying to creep from my stomach to my mouth. I pushed it back, while flipping the photos of Jessica over. I didn't want my vision of her tarnished by them.

"We don't really need to be looking at those," Emily said, over my shoulder. All I could do was nod. I feared opening my mouth would unleash something I wasn't sure I was ready to unpack.

I moved the photos over, placing the crime scene ones back on top, and kept looking, hoping something would be helpful. At the very back, behind all the other forms, there was a small yellow ticket in an evidence bag. Emily's eyes got huge when she saw it. She tried to grab it, but her hand went through the file into my leg. The cold was running through me.

"This is what we needed," she practically screamed.

"How can you tell that?" I asked, examining the ticket.

"Because why would Jessica have a ticket like this on her," Emily replied, "It's clearly the murderer's."

"So we find where the ticket belongs, we find the murderer?" I asked, my voice catching in the back of my throat.

"Yes," she said, nodding her head ferociously.

"SpringFox Aple," I read the ticket, "Does that sound familiar to you?"

"No, there's nothing in Twindle called that," she said, looking. I angled the ticket towards her to make sure I read it correctly.

The ticket was old and it looked like some of the letters had been wiped off. That probably wasn't the whole thing but it was all we had to go off of at the moment. I pulled my phone out of my back pocket and slid the screen up so I could snap a picture of it. We needed to get going soon because the press conference would probably be ending if it wasn't already over by now.

"Wait," Emily said, her body bolting upright. She gleaned at me clearly piecing something together. "The Star Horse Farm gives out tickets after you rent one of their horses, maybe they have a horse named Springfox!"

"That's a little bit of a weird name for a horse," I said, scratching my head.

The handle jiggled, sending fear through my body. I quickly gathered everything back into the file, pushing myself off the ground. The paperwork jumbled into the folder, none of the pieces wanting to sit right. I was so happy that I decided to leave the cabinet open.

"Who locked this door," I could hear the person on the outside of the door say. They jingled keys and I could hear the lock twist open. I pushed the door and hid behind Jessica's cabinet as the two deputies that Emily saw came through the door. They flipped the lights on and I squeezed my eyes shut. I put my hand over my mouth, trying to control my breathing, as the fear and adrenaline mixed through my body.

The light hummed throughout as their colognes filled the room. I almost gagged on the overwhelming manly smell that engulfed my nostrils. It masked the scent of the cleaner from earlier. A clock ticked above me, counting down each second until they found me crumbled behind this cabinet.

My hands slid down the cold metal of the cabinet. The sweat rushed out of my body. I couldn't tell if my heart was pounding so bad that I was hearing it in my head or if fear was taking my control board over. My heart fluttered faster as steps approached me.

"What was the file you needed?" one asked.

"Smith, Michael," the other replied.

I heard a door open to my left. The shuffling of papers being drowned out by my heart. I sat there praying for them to find the file they needed and leave. Each shuffle of the files caused my blood to run colder through me. My body couldn't decide which temperature I was experiencing, sending signals for both through me. Hearing the cabinet and door shut, I felt my heart settle back into my chest. I sat there trying to see if I could hear their footsteps down the hall.

"You can get up, now," Emily said, tapping cold on my shoulder.

"Let's get out of here," I said, pushing myself off the ground after a second.

I opened the door as slowly as possible, peaking my head out to make sure no one was in the hall. Emily went on ahead to find the deputies. I waited there for her to come back and tell me where the deputies went off to.

"They went to the other side of the station to look through the Smith file," she said, coming back to me.

"Okay, let's get the hell out of here," I said, letting my feet carry me down the hall.

Luckily, the plump lady wasn't sitting at the desk. I took a running start and booked it out of the lobby. My feet thumped loudly on the ground. I heard movement coming from the room behind the desk, but by the time the lady had made it out of the office, I was already out the door.

My lungs were on fire, trying to keep up with my legs. It felt like something had control over the lower half of my body, pushing past the screaming that I felt throughout my body. Tears welled in my eyes as the photos of Jessica flashed through my head. I tried pushing past them, but nothing worked. I cried out into the darkness as I pushed forward.

I kept running, never taking a second to look behind me. I ran at full force until I got into my apartment complex. Once I saw the entrance sign, I collapsed on it. My sobs were coming faster now that I had stopped. I needed to catch my breath, still, my heart trying to slow itself. I hadn't needed to ever run like that and luckily my school back home stopped requiring the mile run after freshman year.

My body hung over the sign, unable to collect itself. All of my muscles shook under me, tears still pouring out of my eyes. The air was thick, causing in the back of my throat with each inhale I tried taking.

"You can't stay here," Emily said, causing my body to jump.

"I just need a moment," I replied, taking my sleeve to my nose. The cold air caused the snot to burn as it slid down my nose. Limbs still feeling heavy, I shakily pushed myself to my feet. The warmth of the lobby was a distraction from the cold of the outside world.

Mom wasn't home yet which meant the conference hadn't ended. It also meant I was safe from a grounding. I went into my room and arranged my homework to look like that was what I had been doing the entire time. I watched myself go through the movements, but it felt like someone else was puppeting me.

In the kitchen, I heated up the dinner mom had made. Running from the law had starved me, but as I watched the food rotate in the microwave, my appetite faded away. I stared at it as the beep echoed in my head.

The steam stung on my hands as I pulled it out. I let it sit on the counter, hopping the hungry cues would come back if I stayed long enough. My body was drained of energy and slowly burned my emotions out, too. My zombie-fied body went through the motion of life, waiting for mom to come back.

"Okay," Emily said, breaking my focus. "When are we gonna go to the farm?"

"Well we can't go tonight," I said, pointing at the pitch black sky, "and I don't think mom's gonna let me out tonight anyway."

"So tomorrow?" she asked, tilting her head.

"How bout the weekend?" I tried to compromise.

She didn't seem super happy with that idea, but I didn't have many other options at the moment. I knew mom wouldn't want to let me after school. It wasn't like I could just crawl out my window and sneak over to the farm. Plus, I wanted to scrub tonight from my memory. In order to do that, I needed time to erase it before jumping into another Emily scheme.

CHAPTER EIGHTEEN

Emily had not waited patiently for the weekend to come. When I opened my eyes Saturday morning, she was staring at me like she had been sitting there all night. It surprised me and definitely wasn't the sight I was expecting to see first thing in the morning.

"So when are we going to the farm?" she asked, placing her chin in her hands. Her innocence trying to shine through but failing.

"What time is it anyway?" I asked, rubbing my eyes.

The sun was barely peeking through my curtains so I knew it was still early. I rolled over onto my side to check the time. Not even nine in the morning. I plopped back into bed and covered my face with my pillow, trying to block Emily out.

"We're wasting daylight," she said exasperated.

"The sun is barely out," I groaned under the pillow.

I didn't even hear mom moving around the house, that was how early it was. Plus, I had planned on asking her to take me. I had already mentioned that some school girls wanted to go to that farm, hoping she would take the bait when I brought it up today.

"You've made me wait all week," she said, trying to move the pillow off me. I felt the cold tingle touching my face.

"Can't you wait until mom gets up?" I asked.

As if her alarm knew we were speaking, it rang through the hallway. I groaned in response, knowing Emily wouldn't let me rest now. I kicked my feet off the side, getting ready to head to the shower. I needed to get in the bathroom before I could even think about going out in public.

"Sounds like her alarms are going off, now," Emily smirked.

I ignored her as I left the room. Mom and I met in the hallway. She had already gotten her loungewear on, ready for a relaxing weekend. I nodded my hellos as I went into the bathroom. I turned the shower water on, giving it a few minutes to warm up. Mom had gone to the kitchen to make her coffee.

I went back to my bedroom to grab clothes. Emily stood in the middle of the room, arms crossed, with a scowl on her face. She was already in her spying get up. A black turtleneck with matching black leggings. I briefly peered down to look at the black hiking boots she wore, before brushing passed her. I needed to get into the closest. I could feel her following me.

"When are we leaving?" she asked impatiently.

"Can I wake up first?" I asked annoyedly, "I need to shower then we can talk."

She humpfed at that idea, but let me pass through back to the bathroom. I tried not to take too long in the shower, but it was one of the few places where Emily wouldn't bother me. So it was harder to want to leave the shower. After about fifteen minutes, I was done in the bathroom.

Assuming Emily was still sulking in my room, I went to the kitchen to see what mom was up to. She had turned on her morning news, sitting on the couch with her morning cup of Joe. I pulled out my box of cereal and made myself a bowl. I went to sit on the couch next to her.

"Got any plans today?" I asked her, shoving a spoonful into my mouth.

"Nope, not really," she said, "Do you have any plans today?"

"Well I know some girls from class are thinking about going to the horse riding farm," I started, trying to smoothly slide it in.

"Oh that sounds fun," she said, turning back to the news.

"Yeah they invited me to go," I said, practically in one syllable.

She turned the TV down a little bit and looked to face me. I could see the panic flash over her eyes a little. She was still nervous about the fact that Jessica had been killed not too long ago. I was hoping she wouldn't become a strict hover parent as a result.

"You want to go riding?" she asked, her eyebrow shooting to her hairline, "like horseback riding?"

"Yeah, why not?" I shrugged. "I only did pony rides as a kid."

"What time are they going?"

"I think eleven, but I can double check if you're saying I can go."

She nodded her head in approval, but said I needed to confirm the time before we left. I set the bowl off on the table next to us and pulled my phone out of my pocket. I scrolled through my phone for a second, pretending to look through messages.

"Yeah, it's at eleven," I said after a second.

"Well it's getting close to ten, now," she said, "I'll hop in the shower and we can leave shortly after that."

"Thank you, momma!" I said jumping to hug her.

Mom finished watching her news segment and then went back to her room. I heard the shower water start, so I went to my bedroom to tell Emily when we were leaving. I knew she'd be happy that mom was letting us go, but she would be upset to know we weren't leaving for another hour.

"Mom said we could leave around eleven," I said, pushing my door open to an empty room, "Emily?"

"Why not now?" she asked, walking out of my closet in a horse t-shirt. She must have been rummaging through there to see what I had. She had changed her pants, too. Now she wore jeans similar to the bell bottomed ones I wore for the party.

"Because she wants to shower and get ready," I said. "Impatient much."

It didn't take long for mom to finish her shower, coming into my room to let me know she was ready. After she confirmed she was ready, I went through my drawer getting socks out, the last thing I needed to leave. On the top of the dresser was Detective's Jones' card, I didn't think we'd find anything worth his time but I grabbed it just in case. I shoved the card and my phone into my little black purse, wrapping the strap around my body.

"Alright, let's go," I said, walking into the living room.

"Okay," mom said, putting her shoes on.

As we drove, we passed the ditch Emily and I explored Monday. The police tape was gone now, along with any proof that a body had been there. Staring at it, a pang went through my body as I thought of the world forgetting Jessica. I could hear Emily in my head telling me to help her.

It wasn't long after the ditch that we pulled up to the Star Horse Riding sign, eerily matching my dream even though I hadn't seen it before. There weren't many cars there, so I knew it would be hard to convince mom that I was meeting people here. I pointed to a group of girls already on the field riding.

"That's them," I lied. "Their parents must have dropped them off early."

"It's a little rude they didn't wait for you," she said with a frown taking over her face.

"I'm sure they didn't mean anything by it," I said, opening the door. I was hoping to get out of the car before mom realized why I was really here.

"What time should I pick you up?" mom asked, before I could fully get the door open.

"No later than 3pm," I said, thinking that would give us enough time to talk with the staff and see who rented Springfox.

"Please be safe," she called after me, as I left the car.

I waved her goodbye as she pulled out of the lot, waiting until her car was completely gone from view. Looking around, I tried to navigate the path to the office. I had never been to a riding farm before and wasn't fully sure where the staff or horses would be.

"Where should I start?" I whispered to Emily.

"Well the stables are over there," she said, pointing to a barn.

We headed that way, passing the girls who had been riding. There were five of them out, each horse galloping next to each other. Luckily for us the barn door was open, so we walked through, looking at each stall. Some of them had names on them, like Butterscotch or Dusty, but we didn't see Springfox.

"Do you see anything for Springfox?" I asked, peering over one of the stalls. Maybe that horse just didn't have a visible tag. Emily was doing the same thing in a different stall.

"Sadly no I don't," she huffed, lowering her toes back to the ground.

The stable wasn't very big so it didn't take long to search it. Our search was not turning anything up. I pulled up a blanket that had fallen off the door, looking to see if it had Springfox on it. It didn't so I folded it nicely and threw it back over the door.

"Um, can I help you," called a voice behind me.

I froze in fear. I hadn't been paying attention and wasn't sure who was behind me. My heart was racing and my knees were shaking. Emily continued looking through the stable. Whoever it was, wasn't seeing her, so why stop. I slowly turned to face the person who caught me. It had been Jigsaw, or well I guess Max. The fear slowly leaves my body.

"I'm looking for a horse," I said.

"Well most of them are out being ridden so you're out of luck," he said leaning against the barn door, "You're Charlotte, right? Or should I just call you scarecrow?"

He flashed a smile at me, sending all my body heat straight to my cheeks. I had made sure to leave everyday from history class since the Halloween party. I did not want to discuss our drunken night of making out. I had enough shame the day after when his paint was smeared on my face.

"You can call me Charlie," I said, voice cracking a bit.

"So Charlie, which horse are you looking for?" he asked, closing the distance between us.

"Springfox," I said confidently. Max scrunched his face in confusion.

"There isn't a horse named Springfox," he said.

"There isn't?" I asked, seeing Emily's plan crashing down in front of me, "Are you sure there isn't?"

"I've been working here for as long as I can remember, so I think I know what horses we have," he said, putting the nail in the plan.

"You work here?" That part caught me off guard.

I looked up and down at him. He didn't have a uniform or anything to indicate that he worked here. His jacket was just a regular light red with no graphics. He was in jeans with tennis shoes, not the normal get up for a rider.

"Yes, my parents own the place," he said, looking down at himself, realizing his attire was what had thrown me off.

"They do." I could feel my lids roll back, bugging my eyes.

"Yeah, mom's a veterinarian so she makes sure the horses are safe," he said, running his hands through his hair. "Dad's family has been farmers for generations, so he handles that aspect."

"Well that's pretty cool," I said.

"Yeah, it's not too bad. Plus it usually helps with the ladies," he said with a wink.

"Oh do you often bring ladies here for dates?" I asked, trying to sound uninterested.

"Most horse girls are already here for equestrian practice," he laughed, "Most of them never noticed me outside of being the stable boy."

"Is that what they're doing out there?" I asked, pointing through the open door to the field.

"Yeah, they are," he said, "Did they tell you to come find this Springfox horse?"

"No, it was a paper," I said, not realizing what I said.

Shit. He couldn't know I was playing Nancy Drew with my dead best friend. I tried to come up with a reason for why I thought Springfox was a horse. My brain couldn't move past breaking into a police station to read a murdered girl's file. It didn't seem like that would keep his interests.

"A paper?" he asked, "What kind of paper?"

"Tell him it's a scavenger hunt," Emily said walking to me.

"It's a scavenger hunt," I repeated, "I thought the clue was for a horse, but I guess I was wrong."

"What's the clue?" he asked.

"Springfox Aple," I replied.

"Well I don't know what Springfox is supposed to mean, but could Aple be a street?"

"I haven't lived in Twindle long, but I haven't seen an Aple street."

"No but there is a Maple Street in the neighborhood over there," he gestured behind me vaguely, "Maybe the M was rubbing off your clue."

"The neighborhood that guy, who found Jessica, lives in?" I asked, feeling pieces fall together. Once the question left my mouth, Emily froze, waiting to see what Max said.

"Yeah, it's called Village Park," he said.

"Thank you! Thank you so much," I said, jumping up and down, "I can still win the scavenger hunt then."

"The neighborhood is only a ten minute walk so you shouldn't have too much trouble," he said, shoving his hand into his pocket, "If I didn't have to work, I'd come help you."

"That's appreciated," I said, flashing him a smile.

I walked over to him, giving him a bear hug. When he said there wasn't a horse named Springfox, I thought this trip was another bust. He proved me wrong, now we knew Jessica's killer lived in that neighborhood. He hugged just as tight, before pulling away. I gave him a small peck on the cheek.

"Here give me your phone and I'll plug my number in," I said, reaching my hand out.

He pulled his phone out of his back pocket and slapped it into my hand. I put my number in and flashed another smile before I left the barn. Once I was sure I was far enough away, I picked up speed.

CHAPTER NINETEEN

Emily and I walked down the dirt path, the one we had been on just a few days prior. From the stables, the neighborhood sign was only a distant dot. It stayed the same size as we continued moving closer. My shoes squished in the mud, while Emily hovered over it, not leaving matching shoe prints with me.

The wind that howled between us shook my body. Emily didn't seem to notice. I caught glances of her out of the corner of my eye. She was listing things off on her fingers. Her mouth moved, but nothing came out. I didn't know if the wind was carrying her voice away from me, or if she was thinking to herself.

"So if SpringFox isn't a horse, what is it?" she finally asked.

I wasn't sure if she was talking to me or herself. She had been murmuring things to herself the entire time we had been searching the stables, gathering her own clues. I wasn't really sure what all her investigation board had on it. I waited a second to respond, seeing if she was trying to come up with the answer. Looking at me, she indicated she wanted my response.

"I honestly don't know," I said, shrugging my shoulders, "You were the one who thought it was a horse. I would have never thought of that."

I didn't really think I would be able to come up with any answer. I was bad at Clue, always missing the obvious signs. I couldn't blame her for thinking it was the stables. The killer probably did pick Jessica up from the stables, but that wasn't new information.

"But I was wrong. It isn't a horse," she said, "So what is it?"

I simply shrugged my shoulders. She tapped her chin and furrowed her brow. I tried thinking of possible options, but nothing made sense. Jessica liked horses, so linking her to the scene of the crime was easy, but we didn't know anything about the killer so my mind was blank.

"The horse guess was a good one," I said, trying to comfort her, "But I think it has something to do with the killer so it's gonna be hard to figure it out."

"What do we know about the killer?" she asked.

"I'm going to guess he's strong if he strangled her."

"That doesn't really help solve what Springfox is," she said, rolling her eyes at my answer.

"At least we know what street he probably lives on," I said, "that's got to be better than the cops have."

"Yeah but what if lover boy is wrong, too?" she asked, "I mean he did say maybe there was supposed to be an M."

"Well let's hope he's not," I said.

The neighborhood sign peaked out on the horizon. I could see the ever growing vines as the back of the sign faced us. It looked more like a plant than a sign from this angle. Street signs slowly became visible but the little white words were still too small to make out. Over the last few days, I had walked Twindle twice. My legs ache under me, ready to be resting on the couch. The cold breeze kissed my cheek, causing the ten minute walk to drag even more.

We continued trying to decipher what Springfox could mean, each theory making less sense than the one before. I was pretty sure that Emily believed Max, watching her head dart to the street signs as we got closer. I let Emily lead the way since she was paying attention to them when we rode out. Trying to remember the ones she recited as we were leaving that day, I looked around the neighborhood more.

The neighborhood was vast, rows of tiny houses filling each street. Passing the street signs, I stared at the winding roads. Passing much faster when we were biking through, Emily and I now took twice as long to get through to the back part of the neighborhood.

"This way," she said, waving me to follow her as she broke out into a full sprint.

"Wait," I said, unable to keep pace with her, "Slow down Emily."

"Keep up," she called from behind her.

"Stop, it's going to look weird," I huffed, slowly down to catch my breath.

"It's over here," she called only a few feet in front of me.

She was pointing at the Maple sign above her head. I took a deep inhale before jogging the last little bit to catch up to her. I looked down the street that was lined with houses. I felt my heart sink. I thought we were getting closer to unearthing the truth, but there was so many houses on Maple Street.

"There has to be a hundred houses here," I gasped. "How are we ever going to figure it out?"

"Don't be overly dramatic." She rolled her eyes at me. "We have Springfox to help narrow it down."

"Yeah but we still don't know what it means."

"Correct but maybe the house will have something outside," she said, taking the first step down the street, "Like maybe it's a college mascot or something."

I followed her looking at each house, hoping to find something. The first few were a bust. At least with Springfox on it. I wasn't sure if she was right about finding that outside. I figured it was a food receipt or something like that since Max confirmed it wasn't a horse, but I wasn't going to shoot her plan down.

Springfox? Springfox? What could it mean? I drew a little map of Twindle in my head. The buildings looked like blocks put together and I doubted I had all my streets in the right order. I tried to imagine Springfox on one of the building signs, trying to place it with something.

"What if it was some sort of violation ticket?" I asked when my lungs didn't feel on fire.

"Like a traffic ticket?" Emily stopped.

"Something like that," I replied. "Maybe not speeding, but like a noise complaint or something?"

Emily stared down at the ground, hands on hip and a foot tapping the ground. She tapped so aggressively, I was half expecting to hear a sound or see her footprint. I couldn't tell what was rattling in her brain, but my question must have stumped her. She started pacing into little circles, going back to her mumbles.

"I don't think it could be that," she said, stopping in her tracks after a few moments.

"Why not?" I asked.

"At least I don't think it came from the police," she replied. "It could still be some type of violation ticket, but not from the police."

"Well maybe not the Twindle Police, but highway patrol." I said.

"If the police issued the ticket, don't you think they would have known it was one of their own?" she asked, moving back down the sidewalk.

"Maybe they know," I said, following her. "But it was older so maybe they couldn't identify when it was issued."

"I guess," she said, folding her arms into each other.

As we got closer to the end, the street rounded into a cul de sac. I counted four houses sitting in a nice circle facing us. We looked at each of them. Two of the houses had empty driveways, the other one had a minivan in it. The last one had a utility van parked in the drive. Men were unloading cylinder canisters out of the back of the van. The side of the van says Springfield Oxygen in bold letters. Emily and I stared at each other.

"Springfox!" she shouted pointing at the van, "I bet it stands for Springfield Oxygen."

"Yeah, I bet you're right," I said, shooing her in the bushes, so we would be concealed to watch the men.

"So our killer needs oxygen tanks?" she asked, peering over the bush.

I shrugged, not sure what the answer was. I couldn't imagine that, but who knew for sure. We stayed there, watching, until the men finished up. They loaded into their van, pulled out of the drive and headed out of the neighborhood. Smoke from the exhaust blasted me in the face. I struggled against the cough that was trying to bubble in my throat. Once I was sure the coast was clear, I booked it to the front door.

The oxygen tanks were sitting there next to the door. Clearly whoever lived there wasn't home at the moment. One of the canisters had a yellow tag wrapped around it. The tag read Springfox. We were at the right spot. I reached into my bag to grab Detective Jones' card.

"What are you doing?" Emily asked when she saw me digging.

"I'm trying to get the detective's card out," I said, finally getting it, "he gave it to me during my interrogation, said to call if I had new information."

"Let's go inside first," she said.

"Why would we do that?" I asked.

"Because what are you going to tell him?" she replied, "that you broke into their station and realized what Springfox meant?"

She had a good point, but I didn't really want to go into the house of someone who we were pretty sure was a murderer. Even if they weren't home at the moment, it was still terrifying. I grabbed my phone, looking at the time. It was barely afternoon, so mom wasn't going to be at the stables anytime soon.

"I guess you've got a point, but we can't be in for long," I said, turning the knob. Locked.

"Not sure why you thought that would work," she laughed, walking off the porch.

"Not sure why I thought that either," I said, following her, "but how are we going to get in?"

"Hopefully an open window or an unlocked back door," she replied, walking through the closed fence.

It was a wire fence, but it was locked too. I jammed my foot into one of the low diamonds. I tried to climb over quickly, but the top had points that I feared would snag my clothes. Once I was fully over, I pushed myself off. Landing on the ground, my feet danced to stay upright. Losing the battle, I tumbled to the ground. My knee went into the soft mud, covering my jeans.

"Hey, this kitchen window is cracked," she called.

I picked myself up and brushed off the dirt on my jeans. Walking over to Emily, I realized the kitchen window was pretty high off the ground. I could barely push it completely open. Not sure I had enough upper body strength, I hesitated.

"What are you waiting for?" Emily asked.

"These guns are out of season." I let out a laugh, holding my arms up to show little muscle.

She just stared at me, her mouth in a line. Her arms crossed again as she waited for more from me, but it was all I could give right now. I was terrified to break into any house, let alone this house. I stared at the back of it. Nothing seems suspicious. No sign of a murderer inside. It looked like any normal house. I peered around the back yard, seeing a massive tree covering a large lawn.

This could be anyone's house. I imagined little kids running around the yard. Birthday parties, graduations, and more could be held here. Then turned back to the open kitchen window, pretending fresh baked pies sat there. No matter how I sliced this pie, I couldn't get over the fact that inside a murderer lived.

"I just don't think I can pull myself up," I semi-lied. I didn't think I could pull myself up, but I really didn't want to go in, potentially ending up like Emily.

"Yes you can," she said, "You just have to do it."

"Emily," my voice pleading, "I really really don't think I can do this."

"Charlie," her eyes, big, ready to plead just as hard, "I think you're the only one who can do this."

"What do you mean?"

"The police aren't close to figuring it out, but we have," she said, pointing back towards the window.

"Maybe we just make an anonymous tip," I continued, clasping my hands together.

"We're already here," she folded her arms, "Put on your big girl pants and go in."

I had a gut feeling she was right. I could try reporting this house, but I highly doubt they kept anything that would tie them to Jessica. If there was something, Detective Jones wouldn't see it in a house call to them. Jessica flashed through my mind, her bright smile taking over me. I couldn't let her just be forgotten. Not when her killer was just feet away from me.

Jessica was starting to disappear in school. The kids didn't care to continue talking about her. There hadn't been updates, so the rumor mill died down. Her memories were nothing more than a fading thought. Her smile started to fade out of my mind as I tried remembering each detail.

The vision of Jessica gave me the confidence to push out of my hidden hole, moving quickly to the window. I kept low as I ran, making sure my head wouldn't bob over the fence. I didn't want noisy neighbors calling the cops on a suspicious figure lurking in backyards. I pushed my back against the window, looking left and right to make sure no one was out.

I wrapped my fingers around the seal and pulled. My arms shook as I pulled. I didn't feel my body moving. I struggled, barely able to get one elbow through the window. I tried swinging one leg up to help push me in, but I kept missing, just barely. Finally after the third attempt. I was able to get my boot on the seal and maneuvered myself in, nearly taking a similar tumble into the kitchen. I stood still waiting inside, unsure of what to do now.

"Okay now, what should we look for?" Emily asked, examining the kitchen, "Do you think he kept anything of Jessica's?"

"How are you so sure it's a he?" I asked.

"Most killers are for one and for two this house doesn't have a woman's touch," she said pointing at the undecorated walls.

The kitchen was nearly bare. There were a few dishes in the sink and some pots on the counter, but nothing suspicious. I didn't know what I was expecting, maybe plastic wrap and blood everywhere. Moving to the fridge, I noticed the limited decor. A few magnets but only one had anything. It was a grocery list. This wasn't a crime scene, just a normal house.

A faint beep came from the other side of the house. Deciding to follow the sound, we crept through to the living room. Like the kitchen, there was hardly anything in here. A small couch was facing a TV smaller than the one in my room. The couch's couches fabrics frayed at the end, stains scattered on the seats.

The pictures on the wall were of a woman with her young son. There were a few family photos, but they were the framed ones on the back of the couch table. The boy never appeared in those ones. Some of the photos he got older, but the oldest he looked in the photo was sixteen or seventeen.

"It could be a woman," I said pointing at the photos, trying to keep my voice low. The beep a distance reminder that something else lurked in this house. It didn't sound like a beep that would come from a dying smoke detector, but I couldn't figure out what it was.

"Not likely," she said, examining the photos closer, "I bet it's the son. Does he look familiar?"

I shook my head. He definitely wasn't someone I went to school with. Staring at the photos a little closer, something about him did look familiar, but I wasn't sure why. His hair was dark like his eyes. Something about the eyes continued pulling me into the next photo. I couldn't help but stare at each of them.

"I've never seen him around school," I said.

"Well I doubt he is still this age," she said pointing to a photo where he looked the oldest.

The boy's shaggy hair fell slightly in his face. His mother had a bright smile but he just stared at the camera, no emotion behind his eyes. A chill went through my body. We continued looking around, the beeping getting louder as we got close to the stairs.

"What do you think that is?" Emily asked, staring at the long corridor that led up there.

"No idea," I said, grabbing the rail, ready to go find out.

"What are you doing?" she asked, her hand passing through mine.

"I'm gonna go find out what it is," I said, continuing to walk up.

"Do you think that's a good idea?"

"I don't think any of this is a good idea," I said, turning back to face her.

"Fair point, carry on," she said, waving her hands for me to go.

I walked up, careful not to let my footsteps sound too heavy. I was pretty sure the killer didn't use the oxygen canisters so someone else was probably in this house. I got almost all the way up to the top, when the step squeaked under my weight. The house echoed the sound throughout. I froze.

"Michael," a faint voice called from where the beeping was, "Michael, are you home already?"

"So now we know the killer's name," Emily whispered in my ear. Her hand was over her chest and it almost looked like she was breathing heavily.

I shook my head, slowly moving up the stairs. The voice didn't seem to move but I wasn't too sure how quickly the voice could move. It was a woman, so I assumed it was the mother from the photo. She hadn't looked older than about thirty in the photos, but based on the beeping I was hearing, I assumed she was. Emily was right about the photos and I wondered how old Michael really was.

I crept just outside the door where she was at. It had been cracked so I couldn't see inside, which also meant she couldn't see me. I nodded for Emily to go in there and check it out, knowing she wouldn't be seen. She understood what I meant and disappeared behind the door for a moment.

"She looks like she is on her deathbed," Emily said when she came out a few seconds later, "She's hooked up to a bunch of different machines and I have no idea what any of them are for."

The woman on the other side started coughing, making me nearly jump out of my skin. I waited a moment longer outside of the door, ready for my heart to stop racing. Since Emily confirmed she wouldn't be an issue, I was less nervous about looking around. There were three other doors on this floor. I went to the one that was open, carefully turning the

S.B. Dunn

switch on so that she wouldn't hear the click. This room was farther down the hall, so I wasn't worried about her seeing the light come on.

The overhead fluorescent hummed to life. Copper's eyes stared back at me. Fearing that I had been caught, my hand flung to my mouth trying to cover the gasp that tried to escape my lips. The eyes repeated my actions.

I stared back at myself in a mirror, realizing I was in a bathroom. Nothing was special about it, really. A small hand towel hung on the rack and the shower curtain was a generic curtain from a store. I opened the medicine cabinet to see it filled with a thousand bottles. I remembered what Emily said about the woman being hooked up to a bunch of machines.

The bottles stared back at me, trying to play a game of twenty questions. How old was the woman? Did this guy use his sick dying mother as some ploy? Why would Jessica ever trust him? I couldn't answer any of them, reaching for one of the bottles in hopes it would provide me with more information. I grabbed the one closest to me.

It was a clear orange, filled with tiny pills. I assumed they were white, but the orange hue tinted them. I turned it in my hands, the rattle of pills echoing in the silence of the bathroom. When I went to review the label, I realized I couldn't pronounce whatever the tiny pills were. Then I read the name. Mary Ann Blackford.

Blackford, that didn't make any sense?

My brain could barely process what I was reading. I had to read it over again. Making sure my eyes weren't playing some wicked trick on me. My eyes bulged when I read Blackford again. Trying to rationalize what I was reading, I flipped the bottle back in my hand. Maybe he had a brother? I didn't remember seeing any other kids in the photo, though.

Blackford wasn't necessarily a popular last name, but maybe there was another one. There had to be another one. There wasn't a way for him to be the killer. I just couldn't believe it. I turned the bottle to face Emily, her eyes nearly exploding, too.

"Like Mr. Blackford?" Emily asked, her posture stiffen.

"I can't imagine it's someone else," I said, putting that bottle back and reaching for another. I was looking for any that had his name on it.

I didn't know why but until I could see that my brain kept fighting what I was seeing. All the bottles had Blackford on them, but none where for Mr. Blackford.

I pulled the last one off the shelf, turning the bottle to read the name. Michael Blackford was transcribed across it. The reality was finally seeping into my head. We were in Mr Blackford's house. Mr. Blackford killed Jessica. Putting the bottle back on the shelf, I reached for my phone immediately going to dial Detective Jone's when I heard it.

"Michael," Mary Ann called out again.

Her voice was followed by the sound of the front door shutting. He was home.

S.B. Dunn

Chapter Twenty

The sound of the canisters being brought hid the sound of my panic. I stared at Emily, my feet glued to the floor. I listened to the clink of the metal on the floor, counting each one. I knew there were five oxygen tanks when we came in. The last clink hitting the floor. Emily gestured at the light.

"Turn it off before he comes upstairs," she said. "Hide behind the curtain."

I made sure that the click of the switch was quiet and quickly moved behind the curtain, moving the curtain slower than malaise. I was trying to keep my movements silent. I didn't want Mr. Blackford to hear me, but I wanted to make sure I could hear him clearly.

"Yeah Ma, I'm home," he called up.

I heard the deadbolt lock, sealing my fate in. The sound echoed through the house, everything else seeming completely still for just a moment. The dark only added to the uneasy feeling that took over me. I could feel my thoughts ready to run wild, but I didn't want to think about what consequences I may face if Mr. Blackford caught me.

I stood in his shower, hearing him walk up the stairs, footsteps getting louder. When he hit the step that squeaked, my heart jumped out of my chest. I had almost forgotten about the squeak until then. I tried slowing it down, placing my hand over my chest. Another squeak came from the direction of Mary Ann's room.

"How are you doing?" I heard him asking. I couldn't hear her response.

His footsteps came closer to my hiding spot. I hadn't gotten the chance to explore the other rooms, so I hoped one was his bedroom. Although,

I feared that wasn't going to be the case. His stomps came louder. I tried pushing myself flat against the shower wall, hoping my shadow would remain hidden.

The lights flipped on, sending another wave of fear from me. I held my breath, scared he'd be able to hear it. I knew I was busted. I must have left something to indicate I was in here. If he didn't know, the thumping in my ears would surely be heard by him. Any minute he was going to rip the shower curtain open, giving me the same fate as Jessica.

The sound of the toilet lid opening, followed by the sound of liquid hitting water relieved me. He had come to the bathroom to use it, not to find and murder me. It didn't take long for the toilet to flush. He stayed in the bathroom long enough to finish washing his hands. Once the light flipped off, I knew I was safe again.

"Ma, I'm running to the basement," he called, his voice slowly faded out.

I stayed in the bathroom listening to his footsteps going down the stairs. Just as I had done before, I slowly moved the curtain aside and stepped out of the shower. Light was barely peeking through the open door. I crept around, noticing the bedroom door had been left open.

I saw all the machines Emily had mentioned before. Luckily, Mary Ann had been set in a way where she wasn't able to see me. Sliding around the wall, I maneuvered down the stairs. Carefully watching each step I took, making sure I avoided the squeaky step. I peered around when I got to the bottom. We didn't explore the house enough to know where the basement was. I couldn't hear him in the house, everything was silent. I reached for the lock on the front door.

"What are you doing?" Emily asked, sending me to the ceiling.

I couldn't answer her without potentially alerting Mr. Blackford that I was in the house. I pointed to the door, making my first two fingers run away from this scene.

"We can't leave yet," she said, moving around exploring more of the house.

I mouthed why not to her. She was already dead so she didn't need to worry about the killer lurking the house. I was alive but that wouldn't be the case for long if we stayed.

"We have no proof that he did it," she said.

I threw my hands up, shrugging my shoulders to my ears. Realistically, she was right. I couldn't call Detective Jones and give him the information. He would know that I broke into the station, breaking one law, then he would know I broke into Mr. Blackford's house, breaking another law. I'd be arrested before he was. I nodded at her.

"Go find the basement door," I said barely above a whisper.

I shooed her away, immediately taking off to find any evidence. I continued to look around the living room. I wasn't sure what piece of evidence I would be able to find, but I searched. Moving around the coffee table books, flipping through pages, I was looking to see if he had any photos hidden of Jessica. Nothing fell out of the book.

"The basement door is in the kitchen," Emily said, returning, "He's down there messing with tools, but I couldn't get a good look."

"What do you think we'll need to connect him?" I whispered.

"Something of Jessica's," she replied, looking through a closed door in the living room.

She knew I couldn't open any without making noises. Anywhere I couldn't go without notifying Mr. Blackford of my presence, Emily explored for me. None of the living room closets had helpful information.

Metal clashing below me stopped my search for a second. I looked at Emily, feeling the sweat take over my palms. She nodded knowing what I needed. She disappeared, heading towards the kitchen. I glanced around me, trying to find the best spot to hide if needed.

"He dropped a hammer, but it doesn't look like he's coming back up yet," Emily said, noticing I was searching, "If you're going to hide, I suggest the dining room on the other side of the stairs."

I tiptoed around the couch to head over to the dining room. Emily was right about this being the spot to hide. Boxes of paperwork filled the room. I went to one of the closer boxes and peeked in. It was filled with lesson plans and some graded papers. I looked at the date on the top corner. 02/16/2007. It was from last year's class.

Emily went to a different box. It was filled with the same thing but was dated 06 instead. Each box overflowed with school work. Not anything helpful to connect Mr. Blackford. Another sound came from the kitchen area. I could hear Blackford's footsteps walking, getting closer and louder. I quickly tucked behind boxes that hid in a corner.

The basement door echoed through the house as Blackford opened it. Emily stood from our spot and started walking this way. I reached out to grab her arm and stop her. My hand went straight through her, nearly causing me to topple over the box. Papers started to slide, but I caught them before allowing them to crash to the floor.

I moved back behind my boxes, hearing the footsteps coming near me. The same fear I felt in the bathroom overcoming me again. I pushed my head into my knees, praying that Blackford would just go upstairs. Hearing the footsteps soften, followed by a squeak, I knew that he did just that. I peeked over, seeing Emily running back to me.

"You've got to get down to the basement, now," Emily said, her face whiter than normal, "It's all the evidence we need."

I pushed myself up and followed her to the kitchen. Peeking up the stairs to Mary Ann's room as I passed by. I could hear Blackford mumbling to her. Emily passed straight through the closed basement door, leaving me in the kitchen alone. I took a deep breath in and twisted the knob steadily, waiting until it wouldn't budge anymore. I pulled on it, allowing the door to open.

I snaked down the steps, careful to not make a sound. It was dark and I could barely see where Emily scampered off too. I could see some light peeking behind windows, but couldn't really make up much more.

"Emily," I whispered, hoping Blackford was still upstairs.

"Over here," she called, "There's a light."

I followed the sound of her voice. I felt around, trying not to knock any of the objects around me. I ran into a string dangling from the ceiling.

I reached up and pulled down until I heard the click. Lights shone around me now.

The basement looked like it was falling apart, barely anything was down there. A work bench with some tools, that's what I avoided on the way over. There were three small boxes off to the side. I didn't understand how any of this was the evidence we needed. I looked around to see if there was anything else that would help.

I noticed Emily was gone again. The basement wasn't super big so I was scared that she had abandoned me. She brought me down to a killer's dungeon and then left. There was a small wall that hid a little part of the room. Maybe that's where she went.

"Emily," I called as I rounded the corner.

She sat on the floor staring at something. I couldn't see what it was so I crouched down to get a better look. I noticed the chains she was looking at. There was a small chain hooked to the floor with a little cuff.

"How long do you think he kept her down here?" I asked, going to pick up the cuff.

"Don't touch it," Emily said, slapping my hand, but her hand just went through mine, "You'll leave fingerprints, you idiot."

"Oh good point," I said, moving it away slowly.

"This is the evidence you need," she said.

I pulled out my phone, ready to get a good photo. Detective Jone's card slid out, like an angel in disguise. I stared at the card on the floor, just inches away from the cuff.

"I wondered how long she had to stay chained to this?" I asked myself more.

"Two weeks," she said coldly.

"Do we have to keep staring at it?"

"No."

I pushed myself up from the ground, grabbing the card. I dusted the dirt off my hand and went over to the boxes, curious to know what was in them. I plopped down in front of them and grabbed the first one. Emily sat on the other side of me.

"Didn't I say no fingerprints?" she asked.

"This probably isn't evidence," I said.

It was a tiny box, black and no bigger than a computer. I couldn't imagine more tools were in here. We knew Jessica was strangled, so as long as it wasn't filled with rope, I'd be good. I inhaled deeply, still preparing myself as I pulled the lid off the box. And, I couldn't have been more wrong.

Emily gasped as Jessica's school picture stared back at us. The box was filled with items I assumed belonged to her. I started moving items around to see what else was in the box. I pulled out a bracelet that had a horse charm on it. Flashes of my nightmare played in my head. Hearing the screams echo, I couldn't look anymore. I closed the lid and pushed it away.

"Aren't you going to check the other two boxes?" she asked after watching me stare at the boxes for a minute.

"Do I need to?" I asked, "Don't you think there's enough evidence, already?

"If there's two other boxes," she started, "There's probably two other victims."

I knew she was probably right but I didn't want to look at anything else. I was sure I couldn't handle any more, but I knew Emily wasn't going to be able to get the lid off. So I took it off, a dark haired girl staring back at me. It was her school photo as well. A student at Twindle High.

"That's the other ghost I see walking around." Emily said, her voice getting fast.

"So you've seen Blackford's other victim, too?"

Emily just nodded her head. She opened her mouth but nothing came out. I skimmed through the box but since I didn't know the girl, I couldn't confirm anything was actually hers. I pushed it aside and grabbed the last box. Blackford's first victim.

I wasn't sure who I was expecting to be inside the box. I didn't know the second victim, but she was before Jessica, meaning before I moved here. The first victim was probably someone who would be my mom's age now. I worried that Mr. Blackford may have killed someone when he was just a child himself. Ready to silence my swimming thoughts, I pulled the lid off quickly.

Emily stared back at me. A photo of her in a pink floral shirt, similar to the one she wore when I first met her. I almost didn't recognize her at first. Her hair had been straightened for picture day. The necklace that she had everyday hung from her joyous neck. That was what confirmed it for me. My voice caught in my throat, unsure what to do or say.

"It's you," came out of my mouth, but it didn't sound like my voice.

Her hand went to her throat. I reached for her smiling face, pulling the photo out of the box. Her sun necklace was sitting underneath it. I quickly put the lid on the box and shoved it aside. She didn't need to look any longer. I glanced over at her, one tear rolling down her cheek.

"Emily Adren," I read at the bottom of the photo, "I thought your last name was Beckett?"

"It's all coming back to me," she said in a rush.

I looked over to her, not sure how to comprehend anything around me. I was waiting for my alarm clock to ring out, pulling us out of this nightmare. Emily sat back on her knees, staring at the box that sat near me. I thought I saw her hand reach out for it, so I pushed it closer to her.

"Beckett was my middle name, after my aunt who took me riding," she said looking over the box, she tried pulling the lid off, but her hands slid through. "I remember him taking me. Keeping me locked down here." She looked back at the cuff with a shudder.

"I'm calling Detective Jones," I said, grabbing my phone. I punched the number in and listened to the rings. It only took two before he answered.

"Detective Jones," he said matter of factly.

"Detective Jones, it's Charlie Weber. I've found out who the killer is," I said, making sure I got every word out clearly.

"You what," he said, "Wait, where are you?"

The thuds of footsteps above silenced me. I had forgotten to close the door, giving away that someone was here. I could hear Blackford trying to be quiet as he came down. He wanted to have the advantage of surprise on his side.

"One second," I whispered into the phone, placing it back in my pocket.

I tried to stand my ground, but each step down the stairs sent my knees shaking. I heard the mumble calls of Detective Jones from my back pocket. The two sounds are the only thing keeping me in the moment. After what felt like an eternity, Blackford finally made his way down the stairs. I watched his frame slowly snake around the pillars, getting closer.

I must have been concealed in the shadows, because he didn't immediately see me. I watched his head turn, scanning the area before heading towards my direction. I heard the rattle of the chain as he inspected it. Each clink sent more panic to my body.

He finally rounded to see me. I had been in clear view the whole time, but I clearly wasn't who he was expecting to be down here. Maybe he feared it was the police, but I watched his fear leave once he looked over me. Being replaced by surprise, his eyes widened as mine tried freezing him in his place.

"Charlie, what are you doing here?" he asked, looking at the open box behind me, "Oh Charlie, it isn't what it looks like." He put his hands in the air defensively.

"Then what is it?" I asked, anger bubbling in my voice. I was staring at the man who took away the closest person I had to a friend. I was staring at the man who was responsible for Emily. No he wasn't a man, he was a monster.

"Charlie," he said very slowly, closing the gap between us.

"Don't come any closer," I shouted, taking a step back, "Why did you do it, Mr. Blackford?"

I stared at him, wondering how he had taught me, taught Mallory, all year. It still didn't make any sense. Where were the signs? How did no one know? What is he truly capable of? So many thoughts began swarming my head, making it hard to focus. I needed to push passed them for now. Detective Jones should already be heading this way. Now just to stay alive long enough.

I glanced behind him, trying to form a plan. I knew how to get back to the stairs, but they had been the farthest thing from me. I needed to slow him down, get an advantage on him. I focused my attention back on him. He was nearly a foot taller than me. He probably had sixty or seventy pounds on me. If he wanted, he would easily be able to overpower me. I wasn't going to let that happen.

"I'm not sure what you mean," he said, frozen, not willing to come closer, but tired of the silence.

"You can't lie to me" I screamed, more anger coming over me. He broke through my thoughts, throwing my plans to the window. All rationale running at the sound of his voice. I was beginning to see red. I felt the heat steaming off my bottom.

"What did you see?"

"My dead best friend's picture in a box with all her stuff," I shouted, throwing my hand behind me where the boxes were.

Faint noises from upstairs caught his attention as he cocked his head to listen to that instead of me. I assumed it was probably his mother wondering what the commotion was. I wanted to make sure she knew I was here. I wanted her to know what kind of a monster her precious son was.

"I didn't realize you and Jessica were that close," he said, scoffing, dropping his facade.

Watching the mask be removed, I could finally see him. I took him in, finally realizing the teacher's look was to hide the sinister underneath. His cold gaze made it's way back to staring at me. His eyes seemed devoid of any emotions. They were dark pools into the evil in his soul.

"Not her. Emily," I said, feeling the tears roll down my cheeks.

"Emily?" he asked, like he had been hearing her name for the first time.

"Your first victim," I said, turning to grab her photo, "Emily Adren."

The twisted smile that crept over his face made me want to shiver, but I couldn't let him know he was getting under my skin. I shoved the photo out towards his face. I knew this probably sounded crazy to him, but I came for answers. Plus, I didn't care what a murderer thought about me.

"What are you doing?" Emily asked, standing behind him.

Her eyes were wide like a wild animal who had been trapped. I had almost forgotten that she was down here, too. Seeing her here, knowing this was probably the last thing she saw alive shattered my heart.

I glanced at her, causing Blackford to turn around to see what I was looking at. To him it was nothing but empty space, but to me, it was the girl who helped navigate me through my first months in this hellscape. The girl who knew she needed to help Jessica but didn't know why. Now I know why. None of them would get their closure with him still walking around, able to take more victims.

"How do you know Emily?" he asked, turning back to face me. "She was nearly ten years older than you."

"When did you kill her?" my voice was shaky, not sure if it was fear or anger.

"How do you know her?" I heard the teacher's voice coming back on with him. Maybe he hoped he could scare me into cooperating, but there was no way.

"You're a monster," I spat.

"And it sounds like you're seeing ghosts," he replied with a smirk, "Who do you think the police will believe? A respected teacher or the new girl who's crazy?"

"I'm not crazy and I have proof," I said holding up Emily's photo again.

"The proof will be gone before the police ever show up, so please don't make this hard," he said, inching towards the tools that hung on the wall.

"When did you kill her?" I asked again, wanting the answer.

"Ninety-nine," he said, leaning his back against the wall.

He had created an opening for me to be able to run upstairs, run out of the house, out of danger. So why wasn't I moving? My feet wouldn't move as I stared my escape path down. I was weighed down in the concrete, my plan still forming. Blackford was not going to have a fourth victim. He was going down today and I was going to be the one to do it. These things I knew.

"You need to get out now," Emily said coming towards me, "If you don't you won't make it out alive."

"Don't you worry, I'm making it out alive," I said, my eyes never leaving Blackford.

"Oh are you, tough girl?" he said, clearly thinking the comment was for him.

"Charlie, please don't be stupid," Emily said, her hands clasped together, "Just get out of here, you don't want to be on this side."

"I absolutely am," I said, standing my ground.

I watched as Blackford slowly reached his hand up to grab one of the tools. I knew his plan but he didn't know mine. Action ready to take over my body as I watched him leave himself vulnerable. I waited until his hand had been almost completely wrapped around one of his wrenches. His head turned slightly to make sure he had what he wanted. Now was my chance.

Once his eyes were off mine, I broke into a run. I charged directly at him, throwing my whole body into his. I worried it wouldn't be enough to throw him into the tools, but the clashing metal confirmed that my plan was starting out successful. Groans escaped his mouth as he crashed to the floor. With nothing to grab onto, I crashed down with him. I tried pushing myself up, but my arms felt like noodles, making every moment harder. Blackford had still been on the ground, flailing the hand that had the wrench in it. He was trying to make contact with me.

I pushed off of him, slightly sending him back to the floor. Detective Jones better be listening because I gathered all the evidence I could, now it was time to run as far as I could. My life depends on it. I made it to the bottom of the stairs, grabbing the rail to use as momentum to propel me up the stairs. The rust dug into my palm as I pulled.

I could hear Blackford getting his footing in the basement. I wasn't going to stop long enough to look back. He must have closed the door before he came down because I was staring at the back of the door. I raced up to grab the handle. Grab my freedom.

I had only made it about half way up the stairs, when my body flailed down. Blackford had grabbed one of my ankles, causing me to fall forward. I tried catching myself with my hands, but my fingers slipped on the step. With nothing to stop it, my head crashed into the step my hand missed. The sounds around me were deafened by the ringing that went through my ears. I felt a hot liquid running down my forehead. Blood. I turned to look down at him, as he tried to pull the ankle towards him.

His arm looked like a snake coiled around my left leg. I swore his eyes had slits in them, exposing his venomous nature. Pulling my free leg up, I jammed it down. Aiming for his face, I imagined he was nothing more than a bug I was smashing. This sent him backwards, but not nearly as far as I was hoping. I could see the anger flash over his eyes as he grabbed his head. Good, now both of our heads are ringing. He peered back up at me, ready to strike again. There was a small black scuff from where my shoe made contact.

A sense of pride came over me, but it didn't last too long as fear quickly kicked back in. Pushing off the stairs, I hopped steps to get to the top faster. I prayed that he wouldn't have been smart enough to lock the door. I didn't see another way out of the basement.

Once I made it to the door, I twisted the knob and threw my whole body into the door, nearly breaking straight through it. I toppled onto the kitchen floor, the loud crash echoing through the house as my body hit the floor again. This time I was able to brace myself, so my head avoided the tile of the kitchen.

I ran towards the front door, not sure how far behind Blackford was, but not planning on finding out. My blood rushed through my body. I felt the trickle start gushing faster. I hoped I was leaving a trail, making it harder to hide that I was here if Blackford caught me.

"Michael, what was that sound?" Mary Ann croaked from upstairs.

I let out all the air in my body in a scream. My lungs felt like they were on fire and I wasn't sure if the scream echoed through the house or if my ringing head had amplified the sound. Either way, I wanted to make sure she knew there was a girl in the house. I wanted to assume she had no part in her son's wicked behavior, but in case I was wrong, I wasn't going to find out.

A hand clasp over my mouth, silencing my scream. My feet were lifted off the ground. Blackford had me in his clutches. I flailed my arms and legs, trying to get him to drop me. I fought with every ounce of my body.

"Michael, what's going on down there?" the creaky voice called again, more worry coding it this time.

I kicked his groin and bit down on his hand. I didn't let go until liquid slid over my lips. He screamed in pain, dropping me on the floor, as he fell to his knees. He fell on top of me, keeping me trapped still. I thrashed under him until we rolled into a table. I didn't remember the glass on it, but I felt cold shards under me. A small piece dug into my arm, sending sharp sensations from my head wound to it.

Blackford showed me that I was nothing more than a little rag doll to him. He pushed himself up, my body still aching. I closed my eyes, trying to push the sting out and fight off the tears that were forming. I didn't see him reach down, but I felt his fingers interlock in my hair. I felt him begin dragging me. My eyes flung open to watch the door drift from view.

I tried fighting, reaching for his arms. Using my nails, I clawed little slices down his arm. It didn't have the effect I had hoped it would. I felt his fingers tighten in my hair. He pulled back, my head flying up to look at him.

"Knock it off you stupid girl," he spat at me.

Only the will to live kept my brain moving, I gathered as much of my saliva in my mouth before hawking it at his face. I hoped it would reach his eyes, blinding him, but it barely made it to his cheek. It slid down, hitting more of my face than his.

I knew it was a mistake as soon as the spit left my mouth, but I wasn't expecting the rage to take over his. He reared my head back further.

"Screw you, you dumb bitch," he said.

I knew my throat was exposed. I searched the ground, fearing he had already gotten what he needed. Our thoughts weren't on the same path I realized though, as he slammed my head into the corner of something. I couldn't see what it was. Lightning bolts of pain cracked through my skull, splitting my vision. I laid there as I felt his pressure release off me.

Pulling strength from somewhere within me, I reached for a shard, slicing towards Blackford, hoping to slow him down as I got to my feet. I tried to lunge towards him, but there were two of him standing over me. That didn't make any sense? I realized everything around me had a twin. I tried pulling everything back to one. I slashed through his jeans, watching red take over the color.

Frantically looking around, I knew I needed to locate the front door. Keeping the shard of glass close to me, I made myself run towards the direction I thought I had been dragged from. I was right, the cold door stared back at me. Blackford had a complicated lock on the door.

My fingers shakily turned and flipped multiple locks, just trying to get out. Each time my hands touched a new lock, the golden color was smeared with the rusty red blood that coated my fingers. I didn't know if it was all mine or if any belonged to Blackford. I turned behind to see how close Blackford was, but he wasn't. Panic went through my body, not knowing where he had gone.

Moving back to the locks, I finally got through his security system. My hand shaking as I reached for the knob. I flung the door open, seeing the world outside this nightmare. The bright light seems more like the light that you see when crossing into the other side. The world slowly came into focus. The world brighter and bolder outside, because outside was where I would live. Outside was how I survived. Inside, there was only death.

I got one foot out the door when something hard and cold smashed into the back of my head. My body crashed under the pressure, landing on the front porch. I could barely make out the bird above flying away, taking any chance of freedom with them. The bricks on the porch spun as my vision faded. The harsh light of the world faded to nothing but darkness. The cold has taken over my body.

Chapter Twenty One

Body throbbing, I slowly opened my eyes, wincing at the light that hit me. There wasn't much of it showing but it burned my eyes. I could see clouds rolling away from view. Everything seemed backwards. I laid there confused as my temple throbbed. I didn't understand where I was. I glanced around, noticing I was laying on the ground. The area did not look familiar at first. There was a rasping sound coming from my right.

I tried to lift my head to see what the sound was but pain raced through it instead. It felt like all my blood had rushed out and was replaced with drums. They banged inside my head. I lower it back to the ground, a bump hitting first. I reached my hand up, when both came to. My hands had been taped together, which is when I realized tape had been placed over my mouth.

I frantically looked around, trying to gather myself. I saw the small window I had climbed in through minutes ago. Or maybe it was hours ago now. Everything had felt like a blur. I was back in Blackford's yard. The rasping sound was still happening. I turned my head to look. My vision slightly blurred at the pain the motion caused. I could just barely make out what was happening. It was Blackford digging. The boxes are placed neatly on top of one another.

He was right, the evidence would be gone before the police arrived. Then it hit me. I would be gone before the police arrived. Pushing past the pain, I looked down at my feet, seeing they were taped together, too. I tried pulling them and my hands apart. The sticky side tore my skin as I yanked between it. No luck getting the tape separated. The tape nestled its prickles into me when I stopped fighting with it.

Each pull felt like my skin was on fire, the tape grabbing any hair it could. The sharp pain in my head was causing me to slip in and out of consciousness, the pain almost becoming unbearable. I could feel the end slipping in. I didn't have much energy left in me to fight, so I laid there, accepting my fate.

I had hoped that Detective Jones heard enough of the conversation to arrest Blackford, but I wasn't sure what he could hear. I sat there praying I would hear the sirens racing down the street. Sadly, all I could hear was the shovel crashing through the dirt and the mumbles of Blackford.

"They can't find another body outside the neighborhood," he was saying, "They're going to get suspicious of you, Michael."

He was talking himself through his master plan. Clearly, he hadn't realized I had come. He probably assumed he hit me hard enough to keep me out. Bastard did hit me pretty hard. All I could feel was the pain and anger coursing through my body. My head was still pounding from the smack on the steps and whatever Blackford used to knock me out.

"Get rid of the evidence first, then we can get rid of the girl," he mumbled to himself.

I should have assumed that would be the plan. The tape confining me should have clued me in, but my brain wasn't understanding the pieces of the puzzle as he continued on. I thought I had accepted that if I was caught in the house, I probably wouldn't make it out alive, but I realized now that the only reason I accepted that fate was because I never pictured myself here. That sense of relief I had when I flung open the door bolted from my body.

"You need to get up," Emily said, crashing me back into the situation I was in.

I hadn't realized but she had been propped up against a rock next to where Blackford had laid me. I had already tried to move and it was useless. Every time I thought about getting up, pain reminded me that was a stupid idea. I shook my head no. It was better this way my brain told me.

I closed my eyes again trying to avoid the stabbing sensation of the light. I felt woozy, my body spinning. I could feel the earth spinning, causing me to feel nauseous. If I didn't have the tape over my mouth, I would puke. If I was going to die, it wasn't going to be because I choked on my own vomit. I tried swallowing and focusing on something other than the spinning of the earth.

"Please, Charlie get up," Emily begged, crawling towards me.

She reached her hands out to shake me, but unlike every other time she had tried to touch me, her hands didn't go through my body. They rested on my arm. Once she realized she was able to touch me, she started shaking me, which didn't help the nauseous feeling. I could feel each shake she gave me, shaking the little bit of food in my stomach. I really worried I was going to get sick now. The nauseous feeling overtaking the pain briefly.

"Oh god, Charlie," she cried out, "I shouldn't be able to touch you."

I just laid there, trying to keep my eyes closed. Keeping my eyes closed kept the nauseous feeling at bay for a little bit. It was clear that I was dying. Emily wouldn't be able to touch me if it wasn't my time. It would only be a matter of minutes before Blackford buried the evidence. Once he finishes that, I knew he was going to finish me. There was no more hope. Nothing more I could do.

I'm glad that Emily was by my side, but at the same time I didn't want her to have to watch what I knew was inevitable. My chest aches at the moment, but with all the other pain in my body, I wasn't sure what was causing it. I pushed back the tears that welled in my eyes. Emily shouldn't be here, she shouldn't witness my demise.

The digging sound had stopped. I could hear Blackford patting it into the ground one last time. He had finished digging the hole for the boxes. I knew after that, he'd probably take my body to a landfill or the middle of some woods. Somewhere that would take Detective Jones forever to find me. Somewhere that wouldn't lead them back to him.

I heard the crunching sound of his shoes in the dirt. They were getting closer to my head. I kept my eyes shut, trying to convince him I was still out cold. Emily had thrown her body on top of mine, trying to prevent him from taking me. I felt the weight of her holding me to the ground, but Blackford wasn't going to struggle lifting me. She screamed out in horror. Blackford ignore it, not being able to hear anything but his mumbles. Feeling the full weight of Emily, I understood there was nothing she could do but accept my fate. It just further told me I was dying. *Why else could I feel the dead girl after months of knowing her?*

I felt his arms reach under mine. He looped his around my chest and pulled my body. My feet were dragging in the dirt. I tried to stay motionless, knowing there wasn't much more I could do. Each step he took caused a pain in my ribs, as he gripped tighter to keep me in his arms.

Our bodies sank into the ground as his movements moved us. Each step was a stabbing reminder of how bad my body was. My shins throbbed under the pressure of my heels into the ground. The backyard felt like a football field, so I pulled my lids apart to see what was happening. Where was he taking me? He continued to drag me towards the hole he had been digging. The hole wasn't for the boxes, it was for me. Panic took over my body, blocking out the physical pain while I was hoisted down into the hole.

Once my body was on a semi flat surface again, I flung my eyes wide trying to figure out how to get out. I had accepted my fate when it was just my body slowly drifting off to the other side. I wasn't ready to accept this fate. My heart raced through my chest, the panic still coursing through me.

The hole wasn't very big for a body, but if no one knew to look here, then it really didn't matter. Who was going to think to look back here for anyone? I knew that meant I was completely screwed. I was going to be buried alive, a fear I never knew I had until this moment. I tried to fling my body up, but I was hit with a pile of dirt. It sent me back into the ground. The hard dirt under me slapped into my back as I fell under the weight of the dirt. It knocked the wind out of me, my breath catching in the back of my throat, blocked from escaping by the tape.

"You can't fight it now, Charlie," Blackford said, shoveling another pile onto me, "Just lay down and accept it now."

He repeated this over to me, as if he had been in my thoughts from moments before. Maybe he knew I had been awake all along. He mixed his weird affirmation in his mumbles to himself. I wasn't sure if he was still talking to me, the dirt filling in around me.

His voice was shaky. Some of his sentences cut off in the middle. It sounded like he might have been crying. The thought disgusted me. He was taking my life and crying about it? If he was feeling so bad about it, why was he still dumping the dirt onto my body? Maybe he wasn't actually crying, but trying to toy with my mind. One last game to play before I was buried. I couldn't see his face, just the dark shadow of his figure in the light as he stood over my grave, piling more dirt onto me.

Another pile held my legs down. The weight felt like a thousand pounds. I swore my legs were seconds away from snapping. A weird pain in my shin acting as confirmation that it was going to happen. He was right. I couldn't fight anymore and I didn't want to waste my last bit of energy clawing my way out. Plus my hands were still bound together. There wasn't any hope, so I lay there.

I did what he said, laying there and accepting it. Memories with mom came flooding my mind as I tried escaping reality. I worried about how late it had gotten. Was she at the stables looking for me? How long would she think I was missing before learning the truth? My throat tightened as more thoughts flooded my mind.

What would she know?

How would dad be told?

Would mom be okay?

I worried about Emily. She was following my limp body to the hole. It was one of the few things I did see with my fleeting vision. Was she sitting at my makeshift grave now? My only visitor for eternity. Our memories merged with my parent's memories, a collage of my life projecting behind my closed eyes. A small part of me even wondered about Jessica.

Her bright smile flashed through my brain, thinking of how her laughter filled the room. I wondered if Jessica felt this in her last moments. Blackford strangled her, making sure to take her last breath, and now he was suffocating me under dirt. Trying to help her murder get solved, I ended up with a similar fate as Jessica. *What sick and twisted fate is that?*

Anger began to replace the panic that was in my body. I couldn't believe this was how he was going to get away with it. Just bury the truth in his backyard. I started my plotting on how I was going to destroy him from the afterlife, making sure he would regret this decision.

Under my rage, I still prayed for sirens. My prayers started to sound like they were being answered. I assumed that it was just the ringing in my ear from all the head trauma. I couldn't trust any of my senses at the moment, just letting my mind take over to handle what I was dealing with. A pile of dirt thrown on my face muffled the sound of the outside world.

My world had finally gone dark. No more piles being tossed down anymore. I was pretty sure dirt had covered me completely. The air around me was becoming thin. The tape over my mouth had made it hard to breathe, already, but now dirt filled my nostrils. I couldn't believe I was actually glad for the tape, knowing it was the only blockade from a mouthful of dirt. I could still hear Emily faintly crying for me to try and get out. There was no use. I took slow steady breaths, trying to make my last few second count. I didn't want to spend it in a panic.

I pushed the feeling of the dirt out of my mind, trying to convince myself I was light as a feather. Images of clouds raced through my mind, but even those visions slowly faded into darkness. Finally, there was nothing. No movement, no sounds, just nothing. This must be it. This is the last feeling before death overcomes me. I braced for what would happen next. *Would it be a bright light? Or was this empty nothingness for me?*

Maybe I didn't get the special ghost treatment that Emily had gotten. Maybe my punishment was to stay in this void of nothing. Not feeling, but not not feeling either. The moment unnerved me. I couldn't understand. All I knew was I was trapped in this nothingness.

S.B. Dunn

Chapter Twenty Two

Lids too heavy to open, I relied on my ears to tell me where I was. I tried focusing but focusing made my head throb. My ears rang, adding a layer to the confusion. I forced myself to do a mental scan of my body. I started with my chest and was shocked. I expected it to feel heavy like my eyes, but it didn't. I slowly took an inhale, letting the air expand my lungs to their full capacity.

A scorching sensation coursed through my right side as the air tried to enter, causing my breath to catch. The rest of my body started screaming in protest. The pain used my right ribs and brain like an infinity pool, swimming between the two constantly. I could feel certain muscles involuntarily jump in response to the searing aches. A wave of dizziness took over after the pain subsided.

Even with my eyes closed, I felt the room spinning. The nausea tried forcing my eyes to open and my body to hurl, but besides the shallow breaths I was taking, no movement happened. My muscles that were just shaking now felt loose and tingling, almost like they weren't there.

Panic surged through me as I tried getting a grip on what was happening. *Was I dead? Is this what dying is like?* I fought to stay as conscious as I could, but I felt it slipping away. Feeling trapped in a cocoon of agony, the stabbing pain threatened to pull me back into the unknown. I couldn't fight it off any longer. The darkness consumed me, snuffing out the warmth of my eternal candle.

Time fell silent then, the world standing still now. Coldness like I have never known engulfed me. Feeling them rattle, the cold had chilled me to the bone. I didn't know how long I was in this cold darkness, before she came to me. It felt like a fever dream. I'm still not sure it wasn't some hallucination my brain came up with, or proof that I was really crossing over.

I strained to open my eyes, a movement my pouding head barely handled. The harsh fluorescent lights blinded me at first, fully convincing me that this was the light I needed to cross into. With a few painful blinks, I realized the white continued because of the sterile hospital room. My eyes caught Emily almost instantly. Her vibrant pink blouse stood out in the sea of white we were in.

"You're awake," she said, her eyes fixated on me.

"What happened?" I asked.

"Well," she said, her hand rubbing the back of her neck. "I'm not sure where to start."

"How did I get out?" I asked, head pounding as I tried getting a better look of the hospital room. My vision was like an unfocused camera lens, though. Everything behind Emily was blurred and despite my attempts to readjust nothing was fixing it.

"Detective Jones and some officers showed up," Emily said, her body stiffening. "They said you barely had a pulse when they finally got you out of the hole."

She paused, allowing me the time to register the words she was saying. Had it been a few moments later and I may not have made it out alive. Does that mean Blackford would have gotten away with everything?

"And Mr. Blackford?" My voice was hoarse.

"Caught and locked up," she replied.

"So, I guess we figured it out," I said, trying to force myself to sit up. My arms didn't budge though. I felt like I only had control over my mouth at that moment, even my head tried fighting as I turned it to look down at the motionless body attached to me. Most of it was covered with a thin blue hospital sheet, but my arms were out. They looked battered and bruised, completely unrecognizable to me.

"You figured out a lot more than I was expecting," she gave a sad smile.

"But now it makes sense why you insisted on solving Jessica's case," I said.

There was a long pause, filling the room with a somber stillness. I waited for her to speak. The lack of words caused the air to feel thick, almost unbreathable. Her stare felt almost blank as we continued to hold eye contact. Her face had changed from her normal cheerful one, but I couldn't understand how. She looked older as she sat at the edge of the bed. That didn't make any sense, though.

"You solved my murder, Charlie," she said, sorrow filling her eyes, "I can finally cross over."

Her words hardly broke through my cloud of pain and confusion. I tried processing what she had said, but it was like the words couldn't reach my brain. Something blocked them from feeling the full impact.

"What do you mean?" I said, not ready to lose her.

"We can all cross over now," she said pointing.

My head lifted from the pillow to see my background slowly coming into focus. I looked over, trying to make out what she was pointing to. The world around was still fuzzy, but shapes started to form. After a moment, I realized what I was looking at. It was Jessica and the other victim of Blackford.

"I'm free." She let out a slight laugh, "We're all free."

I blinked, not realizing what I was seeing. Jessica and the other girl stood near a bridge. The area around the bridge is just bright, nothing else. I tried to find the white walled border that was just in my view. Instead I saw Jessica, standing and letting wind I couldn't feel blow through her hair. The wavy style danced around her face as her mouth opened wide. It looked like she was laughing at something the other girl was saying, but I didn't hear anything coming from them. This was only a small glimpse into their realm, not something meant for everyone. The warmth that grew throughout my chest felt like a sign that what I was witnessing was special.

Jessica turned to wave at us. Her smile was brighter than the harsh lights that were blinding me moments before. She seemed so at peace as she waited for the other girl. They took one final look at us before crossing through a bright light. As they crossed through, the light expanded around the bridge, almost like a fire catching on it. Now it was Emily's turn.

She was still looking at the bridge, but I couldn't stop staring at her. She pushed herself off the bed, moving to come closer to me. Her movements slowed as she got near, almost barely moving at all.

"I can't lose you," I said, voice catching in the back of my throat, "I'm not ready for you to cross over." I reached out trying to stop her, but my hand went straight through her. Tears poured from my face, blurring my vision of her.

"It's okay, Charlie. You'll never forget me," she said, "I can promise that."

She stood there smiling down on me as I tried to remember the details of her face. I knew the memories would last, but I wanted this vision of Emily to be the one with the memories. The air grew silent again, but all the words I needed to hear were flooding my brain. I felt my body sink into a cloud of comfort. My vision began filling with the most vibrant yellow I had ever seen.

Starting at her legs, Emily's body floated away, transforming into beautiful tulips. They floated into the air, leaving me alone with nothing more than just the memories we shared. I understood she was in a better place, but there was still a pang through my heart. I reached up, trying to grab the buds, wanting to hold on to the last piece of my friend. The buds slipped away. I pushed the tears off my face. Tulips took over everything I could see, until I saw nothing.

My surroundings were dark again. I could only make out faint beeps coming from my left side. My brain decided when it wanted to be present and when it didn't. Trying to remember anything after Emily felt impossible. The only way I kept time after she left was the light. From time to time, my vision would get excruciatingly bright, almost like the white light I watched the two girls walk through, but then it would fade away.

When my brain had enough energy to think, it tried to worry me about what that meant. My body couldn't care as it drifted out of consciousness again. The next time the searing light came back, I wondered if this was some type of purgatory. A weird fate in the distance constantly checking me to decide if I was finally worthy enough to get into the afterlife. When the light disappeared, I knew I didn't pass the test. I let myself float away again, waiting for the next test to be administered.

When I didn't float away again, I tried opening my eyes. My lids felt like magnets stuck together as I slowly pried them apart. I tried to get an understanding of my surroundings but the world made me feel hazy. The steady beep of the monitor registered in my ear. I strained to the left trying to see what all I was hooked on too. I could see the river's long wires that ran from my body to the machine.

My eyes fluttered trying to clear my vision of my sterile white surroundings. The ringing in my head disappeared as faint murmurs floated in. A euphoric feeling took over my body, sending me back to the feeling of afterlife. I couldn't process what was going on around me. It must be some dream, I thought to myself. My head rolled to the other side, hoping to find something to break through my fog of confusion.

A small figure crumpled itself into a chair next to me. In the dark room, I couldn't make out any of the figure's features. The lump barely moved, only a small up and down when breathing. The figure looked too tiny to be a threat, but that didn't stop the constriction that was happening in my chest. I frantically searched for something to defend myself.

Next to my right arm lay a remote covered in tiny buttons. Grabbing for it, I pressed all the buttons my fingers could. The blurry vision made it hard to know what I was hitting. First my feet rose in the air with an awful screeching sound, then my shoulder pushed forward. My body was slowly being eaten by the bed, causing tortuous sensations through my body.

One of the snake-like IVs released its bite, snapping back at the machine. In return, the machine hollered deafening tones throughout the room. I tried slamming my hands to my ears, but the folded situation I found myself in prevented me from escaping the sound. Lights flashed on as people flooded the room.

I watched the figure bolt upright. A hospital blanket falling off to reveal it had been mom sleeping. She tried to rush to my side, but too many nurses had formed a barrier between us. Helping to relinquish me from the bed's grasp, the nurses checked me over.

"Are you okay?" the tall portly one asked, shining a little light into my eye.

So he was the purgatory you were experiencing, I thought, wincing under the light.

"What happened?" a different one asked, before letting me speak.

"Where am I?"

I had answered their questions with my own. I was still trying to piece together what was and wasn't real. I assumed that my Emily visit wasn't real, but what about the other times I was conscious? I needed my answers more than I thought they needed theirs.

"What happened to me?" I asked, when they continued looking me over instead of answering my first question.

"Well we were hoping you could tell us that," a smooth voice came from the door.

The nurses parted to let Detective Jones through. They had plugged the machine back to me, the awful yelling coming to an end. Once the nurses had finished getting me back to stable, they marched out of the room. A few lingered out in the window of the room, their eyes glued to Detective Jones, mouths almost foaming.

He stood there, silently waiting, but I didn't know what for. He didn't need my permission to be here and I was hoping he'd actually enlighten me. Mom rushed to my side, wrapping her arms tightly around me. I swore I felt something pop open on my right side. Letting out a cry, she let go of me.

"I'm so sorry," she said, hands rushing up to her face. I could see the tears swelling in her eyes.

I didn't know what I looked like, but mom didn't give me hope that it was good. I tried pushing myself up again. This time, my arms worked fine and I sat up, staring between Detective Jones and my mom. I didn't know who to address first. I wanted to fall into mom's arms and let her hold me until the pieces were back together. I wanted to get whatever Detective Jones needed done and over with, ready to put the ordeal at Blackford's house behind me.

S.B. Dunn

"So how did you get from the farm to Michael's house?" he asked, hands going to hips utility belt.

"Springfox," I said, unable to come up with a better explanation.

"Springfox?" he asked, raising his brow.

"I know you had a yellow ticket that had Springfox." Twiddling my thumbs, scared I was going to get in trouble for that, "I went to the farm because I thought it might be a horse."

"You were at the station the night of the conference," he said, "They did catch you on camera, by the way. Well most of you."

"Yeah, sorry about that," I said, "When I went to the farm, one of the workers let me know there wasn't a horse by that name."

"So, the worker sent you to the house?" he asked, confused.

"No, not exactly," I said, trying to remember the conversation I had with Max. "He told me there was a street named Maple in that neighborhood."

"Aple was on the ticket," he said, "Clever girl."

"When I was looking down the street for a house, I saw a van for Springfield Oxygen."

"The ticket found in the home does match the one we have in evidence," he said, grabbing his chin.

"Once I found the home, I kind of broke into it," I admitted.

"Well we will scratch that from the statement," he said, a small grin replacing the thin line he had been wearing. "Crime doesn't really help your case, but you did catch a murderer."

"When I was in, I realized it was Mr. Blackford's house. I didn't think you would believe me if I called then so I went to see if I could find something to connect him to Jessica."

"Did you know he had two other victims?"

"Not until I found the boxes downstairs," I said, remembering the feeling of seeing Emily's school picture staring back at me, "That's when I called you."

"But he found you, I got to hear that call."

"Yes, he found me," I said, "but you saved me."

"And it's a good thing I did," he half laughed, "You were already six feet under when I found you."

"Yeah a second later and I wouldn't have made it," I returned his laugh.

"But what I don't understand is how you put everything together before we could," he said, tapping his finger to his chin.

"Well you could say I had a little help," I said, my mind flooding with tulips.

"A little help," he said, "huh."

"He's going to jail, right?" I asked.

"He has been in there for a few days, and thanks to you, he is going to stay there for a long time," Detective Jones said.

"Days?" I asked, my stomach growing heavy. "Was I in a coma?"

"A minor one," Detective Jones shrugged, "You did take quite the beating."

"But I'm going to recover?" My lip quivered trying to get the question out.

"The nurses said you should make a full recovery," mom said, rushing to my side. "They said you shouldn't have to be here much longer once you woke up."

"So what's next?" I looked between the two of them. I didn't think I was getting out of this bed tonight. The dark sky that barely crept in behind the blinds told me that it was probably the middle of the night.

"I think you should rest up some more," he replied. "When you're feeling a little better and out of here we can get an official statement from you." Detective Jones took his index finger, waving it around the room. "We'll use that at trial instead of you going."

"I like this plan," mom said, interrupting us and grabbing her blanket. "We don't need to be starting things this late at night."

"I agree with your mother," Detective Jones said. "We can continue this another time."

"One last thing," I hollered as Detective Jones started heading out the door. "Have you been waiting for me to wake up?"

"No, believe it or not, I was visiting a family member."

"In your police uniform?"

"Just got off my shift." He shrugged.

With that Detective Jones was out the door and heading down the halls. Unlike the nurses he didn't pass my window, turning the other way. I leaned my head around to see where he went, but the door frame blocked most of the view. He was already gone, probably headed towards the exit. Mom and I sat alone in the empty room. The light beeps of the machine sounded my grating alarm.

"I do really think you should try getting some rest," mom said, coming to my side. She pulled my blanket closer to me as I nestled back down on the pillow. "I think we can probably get you home tomorrow."

"Let's hope."

The hospital didn't provide me any comfort and I wanted to be in my own bed. I needed to curl up with my blankets that felt like smooth butter on my skin. Not in this lumpy bed under the scratchy blanket. My mind was ready to cave, but couldn't accept falling apart in such unfamiliar territory.

"Goodnight," mom said, leaning in to kiss my forehead. She couldn't have known, but her touch pushed into bruised skin, sending a throbbing sensation through my forehead.

"Goodnight," I replied.

There was no way I was getting back to sleep. Now that I had regained consciousness, I didn't want to risk losing it again. I couldn't risk being out for more days. The buzz of the hospital electricity kept me company as I stared out the slits in the blinds. I waited for the dark sky to change into a pink and purple hue as the sun rose.

I didn't think the nurses would be in so early but once the red clock numbers changed to six in the morning, the tall portly one came in. His movement caused my head to whip in his direction, fearful of who it might be. He was still in the navy blue scrubs from when he was in my room earlier. How long has he been here?

"Well good morning sunshine," he said, jumping back a little as he brought his hand to his chest. "How are we feeling?"

"I want to go home," I answered honestly.

"I can understand that," he said, coming to my side. "But the hospital needs to make sure you are okay before sending you home."

He pulled a small device out of his pocket. The screen was blank until he placed it on my finger. After a second, it flashed eighty two and the nurse wrote it in his little chart. He continued making his way through whatever list was in that chart. He added wraps to my arm only to squeeze them cold. The process felt like hours but the clock said barely five minutes passed.

"Is everything normal?" I asked when he was complete.

"Looks like everything is normal," he replied, flashing a toothy grin.

"So I can go home?"

"Unfortunately, I am not the one who signs off on that." His lips pressed together. "I will note it in your file, though."

I had to hope whatever it was would be enough to get me out of here. As he left the room, a drowsiness started to take over me. My eyes got heavy again, but this heaviness was different than how they felt earlier. I tried ignoring the itching feeling of the blanket rubbing against me as I settled back into bed. I knew the world would be waking up soon, but now my body had decided sleep was the correct choice.

I awoke hours later to whispers over my body. Mom and the person I could only assume to be the doctor whispered about my eagerness to leave. I could hear the agreement in mom's voice as the doctor urged another night. I couldn't imagine staying another night. I bolted upright.

"Please don't make me stay," I pleaded.

S.B. Dunn

"Oh, you're awake sweetie," mom said.

"Miss Weber," the doctor said. "We will see how you are by dinner."

"I feel fine," I said, trying to protest.

"I'm sure you do," she replied, her tone softening. "We need to confirm that though."

"It's just a few more hours," mom said.

She came to my side, running her fingers along my arm. In the light she must have realized how beat up my right side was. She continued to stay to the left side with all of her movements. She didn't realize that I had smacked my head on the left side. I didn't want to tell her that as she kissed the same spot she had when saying goodnight.

"You've got some broken bones, but nothing that won't heal in time," the doctor said, switching gears.

"Do I need a cast?" I asked, looking at my limbs.

"The bone you broke can't go into a cast," she said with almost a slight giggle to her voice.

I'm glad that my near death experience could bring some joy to her. My neck stiffened hoping that she didn't get the full rundown on how I sustained my injuries. I tried ignoring the heat that rushed through my body. Just more reason I wanted to get out of here.

I patiently waited for dinner time to come. Listening to the bustling hallways, it filled with wild characters as the day progressed. The nurses had left our station for something called a code gray. I wanted to ask what it meant, but I was too impatient. When they came back to release me, my heart fluttered with anticipation. It caused me to forget all thoughts of the previous activities.

"Let's go home," I said to mom once everything had been handled.

"You know I am never going to let you out of my sight again?" she asked, embracing me.

"I had assumed as much," I laughed, returning her embrace.

The drive back to the apartment wasn't as weird as I thought it would be. I had wondered how mom found out I was at Blackford's house instead of the stable. Was it a weird mom sense? She hadn't seen anyone riding when she went to the stables. Mom told me about finding Max at the stables.

"He was a very sweet boy," she said, "Must have recognized me from school because he came right up to talk to me."

I blushed wondering how long they had talked for, wondering if she was able to realize he was the reason my face was stained red after Jessica's party. If they did discuss that, mom didn't bring it up.

"He said you told him you were doing a scavenger hunt," she looked disappointingly at me, "which was when I knew something was wrong."

"So he sent you to the neighborhood?" I asked as we pulled into the apartment complex.

"Yes, and I remembered that neighborhood was on the news, so you can imagine how much my heart was racing."

"I promise to never do it again," I said, crossing an X over my heart.

She threw the car into park and crossed an X over hers as well. She continued with her fearful story about following the ambulance to the hospital. Apparently, the detective would only give vague descriptions. I tried pushing the feelings of guilt away. I hadn't expected the plan to go so sideways.

Once in the apartment, I went to grab clothes, ready for a shower. The hospital provided me with the same clothes I came in. They had been nice enough to wash them, but they still felt heavy with dirt.

Feeling constricted by them, I flung my bedroom door open ready to talk with Emily about everything. That's when I remembered. I felt my world caving under me. I grabbed my sweats from out of my hamper and headed to the bathroom.

I squeaked the shower head on, unleashing a wave of tears from my eyes. I climbed into the shower, letting the hot water run over all the wounds of my body. The water changed to a slight pink as I let out little sobs under the shower head. I couldn't tell where the shower stream was and where my tears began. The liquids ran into each other, drowning the other out.

S.B. Dunn

I was still processing everything that had happened and I couldn't come to terms with losing Emily yet. The hot water caused discomfort, I turned it cold, trying to remember Emily's touch. I traced over where the burn had been, it was most healed now. The last part of Emily.

Once I felt like I cried my last emotion out, I turned the water off. I immediately threw the sweats on, now the cold feeling became too much for me to bear. My body shook as I continued drying off and as I walked down the hallway. I was ready to fall into bed and forget what had happened, but I knew Detective Jones would want me down at the station soon.

I needed some time to collect myself before I was ready to give a statement. I pushed into my room, a cold still lingering over my body. The feeling brought back the sadness I felt at losing Emily. Since my vision was still a little blurry, I didn't notice it at first. I tried distracting myself with my towel. Flipping my head over, I used the towel to rub my hair dry. My tears created small puddles on the floor as I continued to stare down. When I decided to flip my head back, there it was. A small yellow tulip sat in my window.

CHAPTER TWENTY THREE

April 17th 1999.

He stared at the different girls leaving the farm. He was waiting for one girl in particular. His eyes had been on her since the first day of school when she appeared in his biology class. The caramel curls caught attention during roll call. The sky's bright eyes twinkled at him when he called out her name. She had been eager to learn, but just as eager to get on his good side. He knew she was special. He knew he had to have her.

She walked out of the stables alone. He figured that she would be. He had been watching her come to the stables for weeks. Her aunt would drop her off for a bit and ride horses, then when she was ready to leave she would walk back home. Both of them lived in the same neighborhood so it wouldn't be hard to convince her to get a ride home from him.

"Emily," he called out of his window, "It's getting cold, would you like a ride home?"

"Oh, Mr. Blackford," she was caught off guard, "what are you doing here?"

"I was giving donations to the stables," he lied, "I heard about the storm doing some damage."

She still wasn't fully convinced, but Emily didn't fear her teachers. The teachers were one of the few adults she knew she could trust. Her parents wouldn't care either way and were probably already passed out drunk for the night. After Emily thought of her dad, beer belly hanging over his sagging shorts, she preferred to walk.

"Wow, that's really nice of you," she said, staying on the curb. "It isn't really too bad out. I can manage the walk."

Michael watched his plan starting to unravel before his eyes. Heart racing, he tried thinking of a reason, but all he could think about was how the sweat from his palms was making it hard to hold the steering wheel.

"That's okay," he said, shrugging. "I was hoping to run next week's lesson plan by a student." His mouth was moving faster than his brain could really process what he was saying. "I think a movie might be a good thing right before finals," he lied.

"A movie?" Emily asked, her eyes now beaming back at Michael.

"Yeah a movie," Michael said, a grin taking over his face. "Do you have any ideas?"

"I've got so many," she said, hopping in the car, "You know where I live right?"

Her guard had fallen, allowing her to fall into his trap. She was now in his car, eagerly waiting to talk about movies. Michael remembered she wanted to be an actress or director. She would bring it up any chance she got in class.

"Yeah, just a few streets over from mine, right?" He wasn't planning on taking her home though. She naively nodded as she fastened into her seat.

They rode the short distance to the neighborhood entrance, Michael silent most of the way. Emily had been throwing out different 80's sci-fi movies that she thought could be somewhat related to a lesson that had learned throughout the school year.

Michael only nodded his head at her suggestions, focused on navigating the road. Michael watched Emily's street sign come into view, but ignored it. His eyes searched for the Maple street sign. Emily quickly realized that he wasn't planning on taking her back home.

"Hey, you passed my street," she said, turning her head back to look at her house.

"It's going to be okay." He tried soothing her, but this only sent more panic through Emily.

Her stomach churned and chest tightened. She tried to steady her breath, but she could feel it coming out fast and shaking. Fearing for her life, she tried to open the door, but it was locked. This upset Michael, so he grabbed the back of her head and bashed her head into the window, leaving a small stain of blood on his new window. He made a mental note to clean it once he was done with her.

He pulled into his driveway, the sky setting on his malicious evening. Before getting out of the car, he double checked his surroundings. He didn't want anyone to watch him carry a lifeless body inside. Luckily, everyone had turned in, closing their curtains from his misdeeds.

He carried Emily into the house, taking her to the basement before his mom could hear him. She had been getting sicker, but she could still get downstairs if she needed to. That was not something he wanted. She had always thought he was a little strange, but she didn't know the half of it.

Michael had been planning this for a few weeks, so the basement had already been prepared for her arrival. He made sure to buy the chain a few weeks after meeting Emily. He knew she would be the first girl he actually took. There had been many before her that got his attention, but something about her made him snap.

She wouldn't leave his mind from the moment he met her. Emily had been the closest to Megan. When Michael heard Emily laugh in his class, he was brought back to his summers with Megan. He remembered losing Megan, but now he could have her back.

He needed to have Emily regardless of the consequences. So he carried her down into the basement, setting her body next to the chain and cuff. She would come to in a bit, so he placed tape over her mouth. He didn't want her screaming when she realized what had happened. He made sure the cuff around her leg was tight. She wasn't going anywhere. Not like Megan did.

Megan was Michael's first love. Really it was his only love until Emily had come into the picture. She was so kind to Michael, kinder than any of the other students during high school. Michael could see Megan's kindness in Emily. He wanted to protect that kindness. This was why he had to take Emily. He needed to keep her safe.

He went upstairs ready to face his mother now. Once he got to the kitchen, he made sure the door was shut and locked. He didn't worry about his mother going down there. She could do stairs but she would never do the basement after her last fall. He continued his evening, pretending there wasn't someone down in the basement.

It only took a few days of Emily being down there before Mary Ann started to catch on to something. She had complained to Michael about the rats running rampant in the basement. He knew it wasn't rats, but he still told her that he would investigate. He brought Emily food, trying to earn her trust.

He would only bring the food at night, after Mary Ann had gone to bed. She was a heavy sleeper. He tiptoed down the steps, careful not to alarm Emily that he was coming. The chain had forced her to sit with her back to him, so he could easily bring the food to her and leave. He liked it this way because each time he would slide the food in front of her, he could catch her scent. He let the smell fill his nostrils before heading off to bed.

He would stay down with her, to make sure she ate. The first few days she had refused, but Michael would see bites taken out of the sandwiches or bread he left for her. He thought he was slowly earning her trust. He thought it wouldn't be long until he could unchain her. Michael knew if only Emily could understand why he had taken her, she would come to her senses. She wouldn't want to leave.

"See," Michael said, stroking her hair as Emily nibbled on pastry. "Megan didn't understand how dangerous the world was."

Emily had been in the basement for about a week and Michael knew he was getting through to her. She crawled to him when he came down to the basement each night. She had learned his schedule and waited for him. Michael imagined how great it would be when she didn't have to wait for him. He pictured her in a tight skirt, showing off the assets she had, waiting by the door on the couch for him. She would have a drink ready to hear about his day.

But Emily wasn't Megan. She decided to turn on Michael and he knew his Megan would have never done that to him. Megan wasn't a wolf like Emily. Michael didn't realize because of the sheep's clothes that Emily wore. It wasn't until she tried attacking Michael that he saw her true colors. He couldn't believe he had been fooled by her.

Michael came down, ready to celebrate their two month anniversary. Mary Ann had gotten sick again so Michael had the house to himself. He decorated the dining room, ready to let her out.

As he reached the basement, he could see Emily waiting patiently for him. He had let her chains loosen over the month so now she could see him as he approached. Emily lunged when he was within arm's reach. She tried clawing and scratching her way to freedom. It was a useless fight though. Michael never brought the key down with him. She scratched his eye, sending him into a rage. He flung his hand at her. The back of it made an impact, causing her to fly backwards into the wall. The clack of her head hitting a brick.

She didn't move for a moment. Michael went to check if she was still breathing, but once he got close, she lunged again. Grabbing for anything she could get her hands on. Michael held her at bay, her swings missing him by mere inches. She kicked her leg up, catching him in the groin.

He rolled over in pain, moaning. Emily pushed herself off the ground and ran, tripping once she ran out of chain. She tried catching herself but still managed to topple over. She couldn't go anywhere. She couldn't escape.

"Please, Mr. Blackford, why are you doing this?" she asked, blood filling her mouth.

"Stop fighting me," he said, crawling to her body.

"Please, just let me go, I won't tell anyone. I swear." She begged and pleaded, but it wouldn't matter.

Tears poured from her eyes, she wanted to be back home. She wanted to be annoyed by her older brother. She wanted to go back to her normal, wanted to watch TV, wanted to be out of this place. Her tears mixed with the blood on her lip, causing a pink stream to run down her chin.

"I know you won't tell anyone," Michael laughed.

This laugh sent chills through Emily. The laugh confirms what she already knew. She was never going to get out of this. Michael went to straddle her, as she continued kicking and screaming. He held her mouth closed, staring into her eyes and seeing the fear. He saw the monster in her eyes.

He didn't like what he was looking at. He wanted it to stop, so he grabbed her throat. Wrapping both hands around it, it felt like nothing more than a noodle in his hands. He squeezed and squeezed. Her eyes bulged as she tried screaming.

He didn't want to hear more sounds out of her. With his hands still around her throat, he lifted her head and smashed it back into the basement floor. The sound echoing through the nearly empty basement.

Her eyes rolled into the back of her head. Her fighting had slowed, her legs were still slightly kicking but her arms had stopped moving. Michael continued to squeeze, watching the life drain from her body. He held on for longer than he needed, seeing bruises form around her throat when he did finally let go.

Emily Beckett Adren was his first victim, but she wouldn't be his last, sadly.